About the author

Kevin Eze was born in Nigeria where he began writing and learning the piano at the age of seven. He studied Literature and Philosophy at the Jesuit Faculty in the DR Congo and Sociology at the University of Paris XII, France. A student of Theology, his stories have appeared in the anthologies *Writers Writing on Conflict and Wars in Africa* (2011), *Long Journeys* (2013), the Commonwealth Non-fiction Anthology (2016) and in *The Antigonish Review* and *Actu'elle*. Kevin lives and writes in Senegal.

The Peacekeeper's Wife

Kevin Eze

Published by Amalion Publishing 2015

Amalion Publishing
BP 5637 Dakar-Fann
Dakar CP 00004
Senegal
http://www.amalion.net

Copyright © Kevin Eze 2015

Cover designed by Anke Rosenlöcher

ISBN 978-2-35926-044-1

ISBN 978-2-35926-045-8 (ebook)

Printed in the United Kingdom by CPI Group (UK) Ltd., Croydon, CR0 4YY

All rights reserved. No part of this publication may be reproduced, transmitted, or stored in a retrieval system, in any form or by any means, without permission in writing from Amalion Publishing, nor be otherwise circulated in any form of binding, media or cover than that in which it is published.

In memory of my father,
Evaristus Okoye Eze (*Ugonnia*),
who told stories and inspired me to tell them

Prologue

Malika, the peacekeeper's wife, watched while the plane lifted her husband into the sky. She ran to the chair beneath the mango tree and sat down straight-legged, in the shade surrounded by a gentle whirl of cool breeze. As the plane flew out of sight, she considered what she would now endure as a peacekeeper's wife – how long the war would last, how long she would wait, in what shape her husband would return home. She grabbed the pack of nuts by her side, untied it and plunged her hand in. As she raised her palm to push some nuts into her mouth, a sudden pull of the wind scattered them on the floor. She jumped out of her chair and raced after the fleeing nuts. "My nuts oh," she cried. "Eh eh eh!" The cashews rolled on the ground, caked with dust, and into the gutter.

Malika glowered and signs of confusion etched themselves on her face. Her soft, black cheek creased into the furrows of a rotten pawpaw. She'd spent the evenings before her wedding listening to her mother. Of the many things her mother had said regarding how to adjust to events beyond one's control, some kept coming back to her. She must set her sails; she must make choices; she must be herself.

She felt like singing. To calm down. To sieve her stress. To strain the strain. But the words got stuck in her throat. She spat out a thick lump of saliva to release the bile in her mouth and walked over to the cement bags lying horizontally next to the gutter. She stood there, her eyes glittering in a surprised epiphany at how her life was changing.

She heard the screech of a wanderer, a passer-by, and peeked across the gate to the perambulating man. She disliked his dreadlocks and his sullen way of dressing. Taking her eyes off him, she turned to the western reach of the compound where her clothes flapped from the laundry line, helplessly dry, helplessly abandoned. It had escaped her mind to collect her clothes three nights in a row and this spawned a feeling of guilt that ran up in her guts. The wanderer's scream resounded deep in her ears; it rang like the clang of a xylophone. The wanderer's voice receded. And she remembered.

She remembered that the next day, she would set forth at dawn to Sangomar beach, and she thought of how difficult trekking along the sandy path after *Tabaski* would be. The smell of mutton, especially its roasted skin – some still on fire – acrid and strong with red maps of blood dotting the sandy streets. Malika pushed her head upwards, as she did whenever she had a choice to make. Then lowering her head, her eyes met the carving on the wall.

She looked at the carving, made by a town's boy, a self-made sculptor from their ancestral home. She admired the carving as the conscious and unconscious efforts of an artist whose work was as delightful as the sound of the instruments engraved on it when, in reality, they only came to life in music at Renaissance Square to welcome a British prime minister.

At the centre of the carving sat the drum, the king of instruments. Its strap, like the lines of the cloud when laced with a budding rainbow, curled around the other instruments, leaning tip to tip. At the top, the xylophone lounged spread-eagled across the carving. Dyed in shades of earth-clay, it stretched across the tableau as if resting after hours of praising a wrestler's victory. On the lower sides, the *udu* and the *balafon*, adorned by dark fancy squares, were joined at the hip and held the ensemble together, like a belt to a pair of trousers. Beyond them, the whooshing bells and shakers sheered downwards from one edge to another, face-down across the carving and, decreasing in size, vanished into the unseen recesses of the carving. The instruments bonded like friends. Should one not perform, Malika thought of it as robbing friends of their harmony. The *kalimba* inclined toward the... Thoughts, of her trip to Sangomar came flooding back.

"Step by step, one catches a monkey in the bush," a proverb her mother-in-law's tongue had often set free, fell from her lips. Malika said it in her polished accent, not imitating Fatimata.

She forgot the proverb, reached swiftly for a glass of water from a stool nearby and drank it to the dregs. As she put down the glass, it slipped from her fingers, the shards of glass flung across the bare concrete floor. "Thieee!" she cried. It was her husband's glass, the one that bore the Manchester United logo. As she fell to the floor to gather the glass, she started weeping. A full, body-shaking weep, one that brought back memories of their first embrace, on fine sands beneath broad skies, of the joy it brought her, a man's hands on her shoulders – protective, valiant.

"This is the work of a witch," she said. "Yes. There's a witch about; but I will fight."

PART ONE

1

Issa's departure had made her bitter-sweet. Far from home, a monstrous war devoured the vast Congo, sucked in armies from across the rivers and tainted the palms of monarchs.

Somewhere beyond her mind's eye, a place called Kivu and a land close to the borders of countries of three syllables, R-wan-da and U-gan-da, Issa, Malika's husband, was on his way to help save The Bleeding Heart of Africa.

Congo, the beautiful Congo.

If ever Issa arrives there, he will guard the UN base, witness the Second Congo War from a helicopter gunship, bar rebels from raping women their mothers' age. And in the path of explosives, he will patrol the borders of a ruined territory, once graceful, still rich.

The BBC of many tentacles named the war Africa's World War I. And each time the World News turned to the refugee camps in Kivu, it poured forth a tale of conspiracy, of steady blows, of turbulent winds, of difficulties man-made, of resources highjacked, of evil in men's hearts; a tale of dishonesty, of courage misused, of historical accident, of chance.

Africa's World War I. Malika hated the tag. "Hmm!" she boomed at the reporter. "Do you think we should be *making* war rather than love? Madam," she continued, addressing the voice from the radio, shuffling from foot to foot. "Must there be Africa's World War II? Must there be…" she then sobbed. She hoped it would stop within days; that in her stoutest expectations, all the renegade generals would face the judges-on-red-hoods, like in the Last Judgement.

Under Fatimata's eye, Malika sold fish. The fish she sold were landed from the beach by Babacar, Issa's younger brother, who loved harvesting from where he did not plough. Babacar had time to go fishing, because lecturers were on strike, again.

Malika considered selling fish a punishment. This fickle and stomach-churning work forced her to wake up before dawn every morning, often to a headache, when all she wanted was to stay in bed and enjoy the second lap of sleep. And with the arrival of Chinese trawlers, more powerful than Issa's antiquated hooks, morning fishing was *try-ya-luck*. It made her queasy.

Queasy or not, however, early in the morning, a dry wind blowing from the Sahara meaning the year was coming to an end, she and Babacar made their way to Sangomar beach. They took empty rice sacks to sit on and a half-calabash stuffed with lobworms soaked in red palm oil. They trudged along the wild grass lining the path until the banks levelled into sandy shoals. A half-moon drew an arc on the quiet beach and stars twinkled amid the moving clouds. It was the best time to land *yaboye*, a tasty fish whose ubiquity of thorns made the rich renounce it, for the benefit of the poor. The water was dim and roiling, mixed with white sand swirling up from the beach bed, and just the way sweet fish like it when they return from their nocturnal hunting sprees up Kirikou River. Malika sat down on an old dugout boat by the shore.

"Good catch," she wished Babacar as he headed to the other side of the beach. Babacar put down the rice sacks and staked his pole signal, a random collection of Coca-Cola bottlecaps as big as the eye that would jingle when the line stiffened. He spread the rice sacks on the ground and stretched out his tired joints for what he knew would be a long hunt, since tasty fish, though naïve, are still prudent and will not risk putting their heads out unless bait is beguilingly plenty and the beach charmingly calm.

On the horizon, some girls were washing clothes at their favourite place, a coveted fishing spot for the hunters of returning fish. The girls did so because a water shortage had struck the suburbs and the satellite towns that encircled the capital. Babacar thrust his head into the wind, infuriated to have lost his position to the girls. He was all the more riled by water shortages suffered by his family who lived on an extreme patch of land where the western arm of Africa reached out to the wider world, Djembe peninsula, driven forward by oceanic profusion.

Babacar's eyes flipped back to the girls. They noticed him and raised their arms in greeting. He waved back instantly. They had strong social ties, so greetings were sacred. But they could only wave at each other and not talk; they refrained from talking at the beach at dawn to avoid evoking the ire of the water spirits.

When next Babacar looked at the girls, they were ready to leave. He grabbed his pole and sprang to his feet, ready to seize the spot. Now swelling with bait, mixed with dirt and the water boiling, the spot was wholly tempting even to the shrewdest fish. "They'll dive to my hooks," he laughed, and no sooner did he reset his poles than the lines went tight and the caps began jingling.

He shook off some dance steps, swinging in a semicircle, salsa-style, for his work was done, and he wished to impress Malika. His left hand stuffed the rice bag with dry tumbleweed while the other hauled in the line yet again. Sagging from the end was another fish; its green eyes glowed with years of water wisdom; it stopped struggling, as if suddenly aware of its fate and resigned to it. Babacar cradled the fish in his palms and noted the dark blue spots dotting its silver body. He'd never seen such markings on a small fish. He thought this might be the magical fish that could bless or curse, the magical fish whose flesh, if eaten, would yield sudden madness or coveted wisdom. Fatimata had warned him: "Refrain from bringing home such nonsense." And now that he had caught one, he would be bringing bad luck to the family. But then he thought about Malika, how wildly he desired her, how breathy his excitement was…

He held open the sack and dropped in the fish. "In life," he muttered, "you may have to buoy yourself into trusting that something will pull you through." For one long moment, he recalled the most recent TV report on peacekeepers, how scratched their blue helmets were, how smeared their hands, how hyphenated their moustaches, how rough their faces and what about the dark scars at the corner of their ears. Babacar mumbled, "Malika will be mine," winked at the fish and at the quiet river, and hauled in the line once more. Four more fish dared his hooks and ended up just like the others. With the morning broken and fish unlikely to lurch any longer towards the shores, Babacar gleefully rejoined Malika and they prepared to return home.

Sacks on their heads and their feet in sandals, they picked up their fishing paraphernalia and started back the way they had come. Sand lorries drove past them. Then they met two women coming back from a nightclub, arguing fiercely. They observed the women. One had a wound on her left calf. Blood from it oozed visibly through her torn trousers. The women walked at a fast pace and seemed to accuse each other. They held their sandals and walked barefoot. With the pounce of their feet slapping against the still damp tar, they sounded like rivals. Babacar held Malika by the hand, as if to protect her. From what they could gather from the women's backbiting, the one with injuries had been thrown across a table covered in glass bottles. The women entered the lane leading to the market stalls and, just then, Malika and Babacar turned in the opposite direction. Facing them was land sloping downwards into a narrow, pebbly flank off the tarred road, arid and horribly dry. They followed the byway to the spot where the bumpy path expired into a compound occupied by three houses enclosed by walls. At the entry stood a thickened baobab, surrounded by bricks in shades of yellow and brown. That was their compound and they entered it.

Malika's father-in-law, Salif, an old and wizened cloth-weaver, was saying his prayers. He did so daily at the crack of dawn, on a raffia mat, his eyes fixed towards Mecca. Malika unloaded the fish. Salif whispered his last prayer, stood up, took his seat and crawled towards his booth, an aluminium boutique that stood flank to flank with his sheep pen that opened into the streets. Salif, bent like sugar-cane, dragged his stool over. Ever since his childhood, for seventy-two years, Salif had lived in this compound, plausibly contented and reasonably strong.

Malika washed her hands and entered the House of Youssou, the head house, where Issa – or "Isso," as she tenderly called him – had first brought her.

She entered their apartment and arranged Issa's suits, shoes and acoustic guitar. She acted out of love. She was quiet. It just *felt* different. In a while, she came out and stood in the corridor, grinning at some writing on the wall: "You cannot direct the winds, but you can set the sails". She took no notice of Fatimata who was bustling from the kitchen to the sitting room and back again. What to make of that writing? "Heh." Lizards and geckos were warming the desolate walls of their apartment. Who could have foretold it? She stared at the writing on the wall, like a poet. The words were like the bricks-and-mortar engine that must drive the boat of her life.

"What are you hunting?" Babacar asked Malika. She turned in the direction of the House of Dudu, the auxiliary house, where she stayed with Ami Colle, Salif's second wife, and Ami Colle's daughter, Dieynaba.

"What?" Malika replied, shrugging. She hiked up her skirt, revealing her thick calves, studied her legs and let her skirt fall. Babacar ran his eyes over those substantial calves, but immediately Malika adjusted her skirt, since a married woman from her tribe should not expose her legs.

She scrunched her eyes tight shut and whispered, "Madman." She wanted to try more, but was afraid that Fatimata, who did not like to see her whiling away her time early in the morning, would thrust her head out the open window. Malika had so much to do in the mornings. She was the product of their past. In Segol, the family is large; it has been so since the time of the ancestors, since the days of the first griots, from the itinerant times when their forebears slept outdoors, watching their cattle through closed eyes. And when the ancestors sold their cows and became landlords, they built houses side by side, forming an array of buildings; a testimony of a familiar story; a story of a bond; the bond that tied Malika to Salif.

The proposal was that the earth ate, but did not know what it ate.

Death had stolen the former head of the House of Youssou, leaving a wife and a daughter. The elders had given Youssou's widow in marriage to Salif, his brother. According to ancient wisdom, a widow should not be thrown out after the husband's demise, lest the spirit of her spouse seeks revenge.

A tale was told of two brothers. When the elder brother died, the younger one drove his brother's widow and children into the streets. In revenge, the elder brother resolved to trouble his younger one from the netherworld. As friends and well-wishers gathered for the Eighth Day supper, the spirit of the elder brother appeared and tortured the younger brother while he sat among friends. He slapped him, gripped him by the neck and, disgruntled, squeezed his nose so hard he screamed like a man bewitched. Among the guests was a marabout who rushed to the rescue of the younger brother, suspecting this was a ghostly torment. The marabout tied amulets around the younger brother's wrists, put magic charms over his legs, placed jangles above his waist and spread ghost-repelling leaves across his chest. As calm seemed to settle, the guests returned to their teacups. Suddenly, the spirit of the elder brother broke the discussion with sounds of rattling chains and challenged the marabout's charms, giving the younger brother a chin-tearing slap that whisked him to the ground.

Some of the guests took to their heels; the marabout drew back, recited more verses and the spirit appeared to listen; he bade it to speak. There was a pause. Then in raucous sounds, the spirit of the elder brother vowed, "As long as my wife and children are living worse than pigs, I will drive you crazy."

In clattering chains, the spirit left the compound before anything more could be said. Yet he returned immediately to continue tormenting the younger brother. Several guests hurried to the slummy warehouse where the elder brother's wife and children had been sent to pack rubbish and brought them back. Of all the stories Malika had heard, there was none about which she felt quite such a deep and unchangeable fright.

2

Because the tale of the two brothers had survived in its telling, Malika assumed she wouldn't be kicked out. Salif was a real man and had a feather to his cap for it. As soon as Ami Colle was weaned from her mourning cloth, Salif proposed to marry her and the House of Dudu sprouted. Approved as an autonomous household, it had its own fittings: cooking pots and mortars, a barn for cassava, charcoal and chickens and a small recess that served as a nursery for planting okra seeds. Although each household cooked its own soup and swept its corridor, they were a family.

The enchantment was real; the joy was real. On those dusky evenings, they sat round sharing lemon juice to relieve their throats, sore from the changing weather. As they were sitting together like that one evening, news came that Issa, by fate or by misfortune, was enlisted in the MONUC, the pet name for the UN peacekeeping mission in the Congo, as of immediate effect.

Issa bowed before the force of the winds and convinced Malika it was for their good and for the good of the children they would one day have. A navy blue jacket over his khaki uniform and his feet in combat boots, he kissed Malika goodbye. That Tuesday morning, Malika smiled as Issa left the house for the airport, bound for Kinshasa.

The plane made the steep, tactical descent to Kinshasa International Airport. It was a pleasant flight, aside from the layover in Johannesburg. Issa descended from the aircraft, from inside the velvety and lustrous plane, grabbed his luggage and headed towards the arrival terminal. He slung off his hand luggage, pulled out his documents and joined the queue that wove erratically through the sizzling lounge behind the counter marked "foreigners". Security was tight; the lounge was flooded with officers and plain-clothes security, roaming around strangely.

Each check lasted several minutes. If you let go of your luggage, it would be taken. If you got distracted, you would be robbed. If you conversed or let something grab your attention, someone would pick your pocket. Issa's turn came to be checked. The officer behind the counter was drinking Coca-Cola and smoking Marlboro. Issa handed over his passport. The officer looked at it and yelled, "Yo men! Yo men!" He directed Issa and the queue behind him to the officer on his left, a no-neck linebacker with teeth-like corn kernels and hands like T-bone steaks.

'T. Boyoma', according to his name tag, examined their IDs suspiciously and, raising an eyebrow separated from the other by a gummy black scar, said to Issa, "Remember me when you spend the dollars." He swore he was being sincere, before adding, "Hurt those who hurt our country, and if you must go down, go down as Patrice did."

Issa was in Kinshasa, Mazabongo's Zaïre, Pepe Goodie's Democratized Republic, a high, emerald country at the foothills of the Congo River. His college geography teacher, Mr Faye, had said the land was destined to become an African supergiant along with Nigeria, South Africa and Egypt; that it had all the makings of an uplifting tale; that it was two-thirds the size of Western Europe; that the land beneath it was so rich, a pilot had once called it a geological scandal.

Issa looked at the Congo and thought of a shattered jar. He crossed the checkpoint and, amid the whirlpool of touts and thieves, spotted a man in uniform holding a placard that read "UN

Peacekeepers". The man led him and his friends to a forty-four-seater air-conditioned bus marked "United Nations" on either side. They headed straight off for Goma Base.

Goma Base was a collection of one-storey, fancy-block buildings interspersed with verandas and bright green lawns, standing on a sixty-acre base in the hills just outside of the eastern city of Goma. As he lifted down his luggage from the bus, Issa heard the mooing of cows, the bleating of sheep and the war song of the 7th Battalion, 34th Squadron. He sighted other UN cops and could tell from the wave of their hair they were non-Africans. Just about all of them had been deployed as the New Liberators of the Congo and in six months, they hoped they would purge it of rebels, set fire to all the AK-47s and restore the national army. The driver wished him Godspeed and the gates of the base drew closed behind him.

Issa picked up his luggage and walked to a notice board. There, he read the list of contributing nations in forces and found Segol after Russia, just before Uruguay. At the call of the Force Commander, he turned and followed the man upstairs.

The stairs creaked and groaned, making the noise that old school stairs make when students have gone up and down them for centuries. He hoped they would not collapse under him. He trusted that with time he would know which step squeaked and which peeped and where to tread, should he wish to walk unnoticed. Upstairs all the fluorescent lamps were on and all the doors stood open. Issa entered the door bearing his name and put down his luggage. The room was warm and neat. Almost immediately, he came out, closed the door and strolled along the wide, desolate veranda overlooking a terrifying forest. He retreated to the furthest end, at which he caught an aerial view of the refugee camp in North Kivu. He had seen it on TV. Then he said a prayer. Drained from the long trip from Segol to Johannesburg to Kinshasa, he returned to his room at a snail's pace, showered and got ready to sleep. Although his bed was as narrow and constricted as the squeaky stairs, Issa enjoyed a quiet night.

Despite wanting to sleep longer, he awoke to the cracking sounds of military helicopters roving the sky above the roofs of the base. He climbed onto a chair and peered up at a score of green helicopters. The roofs looked broader and hesitant and the horizon seemed diminished. He looked at everything around him. The action was so close, it was as if soon his head would be chopped off. The helicopters moved further away, circling the palm-studded forest from which vociferous sporadic shooting ensued. The floor shook. It shook as if everything would sink into the earth. There was a din, a clamour, a noise, added to shooting, and shooting and shooting.

Before long, scores of government forces emerged from the bush, their faces darkened from the scorching sun, their biceps trembling from fatigue, their palms smelling of rifle smear. They rushed into the base's canteen, scrambling for whatever they could find to eat and drink. These forces, a jumble of troops from Angola, Namibia and Zimbabwe, with labels that sounded like AFDL and FDLR and UNITA, did push-ups in the lawn, referred to seven o'clock as "nineteen hundred hours" and would high-five, shouting "To finish the enemy!" Some had blood splattered on their foreheads or streaking down their temples from their helmets. After a while, all the soldiers activated, they climbed into a grey van and pressed their arms to their loaded rifles. They gave the Goma Base the bravest, most confident smiles you could imagine and were shipped off for the Kivu battlefield, from where Issa heard the prolonged sounds of random shooting.

While he made every effort to write home, Issa's letters were few and far between.

Salif's doorbell rang, and it was Usman, the postmaster, in horseriding boots and a zombie hat, carrying a pack of letters.

"Take," he said, pulling out an envelope. "From the Congo."

Babacar held his breath. "I don't want to be the one to announce his death," he whispered.

"Don't be silly! C'mon…"

Babacar glanced at his father. Then opened the letter and read it out aloud, nervously:

Beloved,

Habari. That's Swahili for "greetings". Don't raise your drinking glasses to say chin-chin yet; the people want our skin. They stone us for not halting the war, for not saving them from the rebels. Ubiquitous rebels! Rebels that made a pact with the devil. Rebels that reduce children to skulls. I cling to my prayer beads every day. A UN official, one that has been to so many wars, told me I would feel better if I write my feelings down. "If this war bothers you and you can't make sense out of it," he says, "jot something down." I miss home deeply. I think of everyone, especially of you, my darling wife, Malika. You occupy my thoughts, and I know you're worried about me too. Death is part of the mission, regretfully. Yesterday, I came across a grave with the inscription, Homage to a Fallen Peacekeeper. I thought of you. May Allah keep us from it.

Issa

There was a graveyard silence. Salif knew his son. He could tell Issa could not come any closer to admitting he was in trouble. He was a man in love, yet starved of it.

Malika raised her eyebrows. "You said?" she asked, listening. Her hands were clasped at her chest, her heartbeat as tremulous as a squirrel's. She imagined Issa out there, with his blue helmet, his sleeves rolled up; she imagined the rebels' shooting mixed with the late-afternoon sun and sudden, sharp shards of light suggesting their reckless disregard for life. Malika's face lowered, she changed her position and pulled her wrapper tight. She stood with her back to the wooden window, where the wind dried her tears and she closed her eyes. Her stomach fluttered as she swallowed her saliva repeatedly.

The battering sound of Ami Colle's mortar resounded from the auxiliary house. She was pounding millet in a giant wooden mortar while chatting to Dieynaba. The noise of the mortar made Malika think of work. Work infused her with meaning, chewed up the days and kept her mind out of time. It made her think less of Issa. She laboured from dawn to dusk, selling smoked fish on a low stool, before the endless crowd that milled around the Thursday Market.

She was busier than soldier ants. Even when her hands hurt badly from scaling fish and roasting them on the fire, on she whacked. Given that her fish was well spiced and smoked, customers bought it, and never did anyone have to queue up at the health centre from having eaten dirt in her fish. Malika's fish bore the aroma of onions and, despite the headache of removing the bones entwined in the flesh, its sweetness was so pleasing to family, neighbours and friends.

Cooking too occupied her and she was indomitable in experimenting with local recipes. She mastered her cooking pots as Dewel, Youssou's sensational dancer, mastered her dancing steps. She liked cooking so much that even after listening to Issa's letter, she still ladled out a delicious fish soup for dinner, followed by the main course, a special meal, *boulette*, because she cooked the fish – a fleshed-out sweetened one – inside a hooded garment. The whole family crept over to the House of Dudu in anticipation. She laid a mat for them in front of the kitchen and served them a plateful each, which they ate with a ravenous appetite. Providence, to make things tolerable, had put Ami Colle by her side – with her eyes and nose so watchful and thorough.

Babacar thought Malika was far prettier. Babacar liked Malika and she liked him too. Gradually, their closeness blossomed day after day. Babacar threw out his second-hand coats. He called her "Maalii", and she called him "Smallie", a name implying just the opposite. It belied his physique, as he was muscular and beefy with a head that weighed against his shoulder and a stout chest.

Fatimata noticed their marked affection for each other, but judged it as customary. Besides, she was most interested in the smooth running of the two houses. She bought French bread – Segol-style – from the grocery store for breakfast, and dropped milk and sardines in a basket on the kitchen dining table of each house. Broken rice, salt and groundnut oil went in the deep drawers below the stock shed. With tufts of hair fringing her ears, she sped off into the streets in search of table oil. She would not forget to set millet behind the house to ferment.

Babacar helped his mother as a donkey helps a load-pusher. After returning from the river, he chopped wood and burnt it into charcoal, in case the cooking gas ran out. He set on his shoulders all those tasks the girls avoided to keep their nails attractive. He would then beckon Dieynaba to help deliver. With her witty gestures, Dieynaba captured Fatimata's attention and drew her sullen spirits away from thoughts of her son in Goma. Babacar was amazed at Dieynaba's creativity. She electrified the house with her jokes and made Fatimata turn sweet, erasing the creases and folds on her face. When Dieynaba showed her fallen-out tooth, Fatimata raised her hand to her white hair and, amused, beamed at Dieynaba, "You'll scatter my lungs, oh… scatter my lungs, oh."

Not so with Salif. Quite the opposite of Fatimata, Salif wanted something else from the girl. Uninterested in comedy, he lifted his tiny chest in something like a shrug in reaction to Dieynaba's entertainment. As far as he was concerned, she should be revising her Maths. His eyes followed her, serving a stern or warning look, especially when none of his debtors showed up at the door. Fatimata would mediate, shifting closer to her husband, placing a roughened hand on Salif's belly, shaped like a comma. Salif would then roll out his anecdotes; anecdotes within anecdotes, jokes, perfectly recorded stories, snippets of the folklore of the Segolians, and barred Dieynaba's comments with the wave of a hand.

Since none of his debtors showed up, Salif sent Babacar to see Mansu who owed him the equivalent value of a horse. When Babacar returned and pushed open the gate, he found Ami Colle and Malika engaged in worried discussion. Ami Colle's hair was scattered and in disarray, in twists and tatters. Babacar hissed and leaned forward to eavesdrop on the conversation, unbeknown to Ami Colle.

"It's dead?" said Ami Colle.

"Yes."

"Something that used to lie in front of the kitchen waggling its tail has now fallen for the worms to enjoy?"

"I wouldn't say that," Malika said. "I would say it's only having a momentary death."

"A *mulatto-lamb*? Malika, this lamb is dead."

"I saw the ewe going into the barn," Malika said. "It was after lunch and this one, the fattest one, was by her side, as usual. I assure you, Ami Colle, this is the mulatto-lamb which comes, goes, comes again, and goes in a sort of ceaseless cycle. One life in many. There'll be trouble if it refuses to return to the afterlife."

"But, Bab'…" Ami Colle said. She was slow to remember people's names when something had hooked her mind.

"You mean Babacar," Malika said, pointing him out to Ami Colle.

"Yes, Babacar," Ami Colle nodded, but not looking at him. "The water bowl looks dried up. It ought not to be so. The lamb surely died of dehydration."

"Ah, I don't know," Malika said. "It looked strong, did not fuss and digested its food well, almost as well as the ewe. That is not the answer."

They were perplexed. Ami Colle could not believe it. She had been so careful with the lamb, even allowing it to suckle with the ewe more than usual. She had been as attached to it as if it were a beautiful daughter. Everyone in the family was puzzled by such an outpouring of attention when, ordinarily, Ami Colle would have left all the tending of the sheep to Babacar. After all, Ami Colle and Babacar had originally agreed that he would cater for the sheep and, after they were sold, share the proceeds evenly.

The morning sun beamed down on them. The other sheep were milling around each other in a somewhat bemused way, the lambs hopping on each other's backs, as if to share the joy of their budding tails.

"In the name of Allah, may my lamb awake!" Ami Colle prayed loudly. She had always prided herself on having the prettiest lamb in town. In fact, she had not been planning to sell the lamb at all. Rather, she had thought in time to kill her as a sacrifice, as an offering on behalf of Dieynaba, so that she might marry a wealthy white man.

"It'll return once it arrives there," Malika replied, with unflagging optimism. "It's a pity it didn't give us a sign before leaving." "Yes," Ami Colle agreed, in a voice that captured the spirit of *Why put off its waking till tomorrow, when I want it today?* "This smoke is not without fire."

"You mean someone has a hand in it?"

"There's a great marabout in Camberene," Ami Colle said. "I'd like to see him about this. He's well-versed in magic charms."

"Perhaps, but... it's not such a big deal, really," Malika said. "It's just a trifle."

"What? A problem is a problem," Ami Colle affirmed. "Only the bereaved can know the pain of their loss."

"Marabouts are making a lot of money," warned Malika. "They're only interested in receiving presidential aspirants. Just read the newspapers."

"You don't understand. I'm talking about Serigne Darkanke."

"Oh, Darkanke!" cried Malika. "I've heard about him. He is the great marabout of Abass-Abasshe who just funded the founding of a new political party."

"Aminata, his daughter, is my sister's friend," Ami Colle said. "I can meet him without going through red tape."

"Hmm... but why bother, Ami Colle? Won't his house be filled with *caftan people*, I mean presidential aspirants?" Malika sneered. "Your lamb was strange in character. Lambs are usually warm, you know, gregarious. But yours stayed alone all the time. It was weird."

Ami Colle became quiet and bent her head. Though she knew Babacar was nearby, she wouldn't look at him. She seemed to be shoring up all her energy to utter a single word. She was wearing a print dress, dark blue and loose, its print detailing shades of cassava leaves. It hung freely and the harmattan wind blew it about furiously. She tried to hold her dress together with one hand, but each time the wind kept whipping it about.

"So? Bury it." Malika said, reaching to the poor thing lying on the floor, swathed in a tiny assortment of leaves, forage and hay. The wool along its back, lifting in the wind, almost seemed to rise of its own accord.

"You don't seem to grasp what's about to happen," said Ami Colle.

"Like what? Apart from the lamb being dead?"

"Yes, the lamb is dead, but this is not a natural death. A death in this land is never natural. It couldn't have waggled its ears just a few hours earlier and then passed away *naturally* in the night. The more I look at it, the more convinced I am that something shady is lurking behind this and I must act quickly."

"We live like friends," Malika comforted her.

"I know," said Ami Colle. "But I'm not a schoolgirl. When a thing like this happens to me, I must open my eyes."

"But everybody likes you," Malika said. "Don't they call you Amy Cherie?"

"Forget all that," Ami Colle said. "The same people that 'needle' you are the same to lead a dancing troop to your funeral."

There was a pause.

"It's terrible, isn't it?" Malika shook her head, as if struck by the phrase "needle you", yet paralyzed and unable to absorb its meaning.

"Terrible. Yes," Ami Colle agreed, pointing at her dead lamb.

"I think you're making a gulley out of an ant hole."

They looked each other in the eye.

"I've lived here for forty years!" Ami said persuasively, as if that was enough to convince Malika. "So – "

"So?" interrupted Malika.

"I know what our people are capable of doing."

"Like what?"

"Are you forcing the words out of my mouth, Malika?"

"If you're not accusing anybody in particular."

"All save that."

Ami Colle moved round Malika, her dress still flapping in wind, more furiously than the leaves on the tree and her scarf, shaped like a butterfly, twisted as the wind. She motioned in the void repeatedly and her gestures became confusing and erratic.

"Ami Colle, spit it out of your mouth," urged Malika.

"You think it's blocked in my mouth?"

"So talk, then."

"I've seen many things in this land which I did not understand."

"Those cock-and-bull stories that people invent?" Malika said.

"Do I look amused?" Ami Colle said.

"No," Malika replied, instantly. "I know you too well for that."

"You know Aisha, the woman who sits close to us at the market?" Ami Colle said.

"Aisha Ndiaye?"

"No," Ami Colle said, after a heavy pause. "Aisha Mbo."

"I see, the woman that sells salted fish?"

"Yes," replied Ami Colle, her voice growing increasingly perplexed. "Yes, the woman that sells salted fish, four tables to our left, in the lane of the butchers' stand."

"I see."

"When she complained that black cats were crawling past her window, people laughed it off as a yarn. Weeks later, she had a miscarriage."

"You don't mean it!" Malika exclaimed. "With all the progress of medicine, even in our remotest villages, such an event is rare nowadays."

"Listen to me," Ami Colle said, clearing her throat. "The truth is, Aisha went for regular checkups and even the doctor, a white man, assured her she would deliver her baby without a hitch."

"Yet she had a miscarriage?"

"Yet they ate her baby," Ami Colle said emphatically.

"That's weird and – "

"Listen to me again," she cut in, then clearing her throat repeatedly, as if choking and unable to speak.

"Take it easy," Malika said. "Again?"

"Two months later, her husband fell from a mango tree and broke his ankle," Ami Colle added.

"Chooo! Was it not an accident, or was it…? You know… try as we might, unexpected events still come our way."

"Listen, Aisha's husband has climbed all sorts of trees, even Serigne Darkanke's coconut tree. That is the tallest tree in the district, the slightly curved one, and it is feared for having mystical attributes. This earned him a reputation as a master climber. Now, do you really think he could have defecated in his trousers falling from that stunted mango tree, a tree that any child in this village could climb?"

"It could be his share of the little haps and mishaps of life," Malika said.

"Stop dreaming, my dear. We're in Djembe."

"Djembe, island of peace; Djembe, land of unity; Djembe, that sang the old griots," Malika recited.

"That was then," Ami Colle said.

"And now?"

"There are seeds of evil. We live in fear of one another."

"You exaggerate, Ami Colle," Malika said, in a not very friendly manner. "I agree, some people are wicked and even harmful in nature or power. But is that a sufficient reason to declare every mishap, every stroke of bad luck, the design of witches?"

"When Aida's husband's ankle refused to heal, he travelled to the cave of Nidia, where marabouts told him a strange hand was eating into his bowl," Ami Colle answered, as if to have the final word.

Babacar stood nearby, listening in, his baggy trousers, his shaggy hair, the invoices of the transactions he had carried out for Salif all sagging loosely on him. Ami Colle and Malika shifted reluctantly, cheerless.

"Is the broken ankle now healed?" asked Malika.

Ami Colle sighed. Malika looked at her, waiting for the answer. "Is the ankle of Aida's husband now healed?" Malika repeated.

"Why don't you ask her when you see her next? She'll be at the market tomorrow. Single-handedly, she's raising five children. The eldest is fifteen and the youngest, a six-year-old girl, accompanies her to the market every day. Just ask her. Ask her."

"Eh, Ami Colle. You began the story, so tell it to the end," Malika said.

Ami Colle did not speak again. She turned back in a semicircle and looked at her lamb, lying stiff on the ground. She did not agree with Malika that it had died a natural death. She gazed at it, paralyzed, unable to fully grasp the incident. She had been involved in a heated argument the previous day with a townswoman who told her she would "needle" her.

Tears fell slowly from her eyes and rolled down, over her jutting chin. Then with sudden abandonment, she threw herself into Malika's arms. Ami Colle's tears now increasing, Malika led her into the House of Dudu. Ami Colle would not talk nor shift. A long, rough bench stood on a cement slab behind the house, facing their kitchen. There, Malika quietly helped her lay down. Ami Colle was undone by her loss that distressed her body and disturbed her soul.

3

"Vote for change! PPC is for change! Vote for the Pee-Pee-Cee!" boomed a voice through the microphone.

"Caftan people!" Malika screamed, running off and lifting herself up to the gate like a monkey to watch the electoral convoy. "I have the steam kettle on the fire," she said to Dieynaba. "Be careful. When the water boils, call me."

She had done all she could – washed the fish, knives, plates, basins and vegetables in the bowl under the table. She had even cleaned the kitchen. She had left enough sugar on the table so Babacar would not think she had hidden it. Then she threw on a shawl and lifted herself to the top of the gate at the rise of the politician's voice, leaving the front door closing behind her.

It was Usman Diallo, the presidential candidate for the People's Party for Change. He struck a pose, his head and hands raised from the car's open roof, indicating that he had stolen more money than any of his opponents had. His cap was at a rakish angle, as if it would fly away. The street, the entire neighbourhood, was unnaturally wound up by him appearing. Whether his supporters were mounted or on foot, they were not exactly gregarious, but they weren't shy either. And they were so young. Many were the age of Issa. A supporter dismounted, approached the cast-iron gate, and approached Malika. Standing at the foot of the wall, he greeted her and said she should have nothing to fear. "Usman Diallo will transform Segol into Dubai," he said.

As he walked on, he presented the same sentiments to whomever he met on the street and at each house, he left behind a postcard of Dubai. Stationed up by the gate, Malika smiled at him, pressing her thumb against the postcard. She nodded and glanced back toward the kitchen to check if Dieynaba was there.

By the time she turned back and looked out again, the street was thronging with supporters. DJs kept the beat, but the thugs walked in a carefree manner, chatting and laughing, looking anything but dangerous. A deep misgiving arose in Malika. She saw much of Issa's figure on one particular thug in the passing crowd, nobly assigned to a limousine, and she fixed her eyes on him.

There were so many of these young men that they overflowed in the street like a river widening its banks. Expensive, black Pajero jeeps appeared, driven by teams of inexperienced drivers with their sleeves rolled up who beeped their horns. Behind them came yet more thugs, the cars' gleaming windows catching the early-morning sun, shining new and bright. Malika tied her scarf tightly, stood with her back to the house and closed her eyes. She could hear the singing of deep voices amid the crack of balloons bursting. This was not a campaign, it was a mega-meeting.

She voted only out of duty, yet she thought of voting seriously. Whom should she vote for? What should she vote for? It was more of a practical hope than a diversion to see the caftan people riding up on luxurious jeeps, waving their hats with a broad smile on their faces, telling people like her about mountains and marvels.

"They began like this in the Congo." That was why Issa said he was going to fight tyranny. Those were his last words to her as he kissed her goodbye. He'd looked so gallant and cocksure in his uniform: the emblem of the turmoil, the strife, the commotion.

Now, what she saw were men not in their last hours of campaign, but in their conquering movement. They looked as if they would melt from disappointment if they were not elected. A trumpet sounded at a distance. She heard rousing voices, as of the supporters at a wrestling match. She could not help herself and looked out over the gate again. Everywhere, they were setting out like soldier ants, on the streets, in the filling station at the end of the street. And now, someone pounded at the gate. She jumped down. Dieynaba had come out of the kitchen and fear shone in her eyes.

"The water dried up," she gasped.

"What! What is happening?" Malika called nervously.

"Danger, Malika, danger!" cried Dieynaba.

Rushing to her in the kitchen fearfully, Malika asked, "Did Mama see it?"

She knocked the kettle down deftly and stepped back as a swarm of black smoke shouldered past her and headed skywards.

That night, Malika could not sleep. She and Dieynaba now shared one bedroom, as a consequence of Issa's departure. She lay curled on the bed. The man she loved was away. Up near the ceiling, she heard a mosquito buzzing in the chilly night. She supposed she was fortunate that their wedding had been organized before Issa left.

All through the night, Malika heard strange music and a coming and going. A cricket shrieked by the end table beside her. There was traffic down at the outbuildings and occasionally, tobacco smoke drifted into the room.

How those people enjoyed tyranny really unnerved her. She realized this was similar to madness – a dislike for reason, just animalistic, all the more offensive because they were so conscious of what they were doing. They let the desire to govern dominate them. She had felt this way even when, as a young girl, she read the story of Mazabongo. Even Mazabongo, dear Mazabongo, would somehow lose the pedal. He took up more room than he should have. His appetites were prominent, all of his appetites. Being with him was like living with a jungle creature, the animal look in his eyes as he professed he would not die. That was why he had said yes to the war. A man who had properly sucked at his mother's breasts would never go galloping off, waving guns and screaming about infinity and eternity.

Malika refused to believe the Congo war would destroy her love for Issa or would consign her to infinite waiting. Suddenly, she rose from the bed. It was as if something had tickled her. It was perhaps two or three in the morning. Although the cool breeze was back, there was no movement. Only moonlight lit the chilled room. She went to Dieynaba's bedside. Dieynaba lay quiet on her back, her jaw had dropped open and her hands were clenched in fists above her bedspread. Malika touched her cheek which was dry and cold to the touch.

"Dieynaba, Dieynaba," she whispered urgently, not wanting to disturb Ami Colle who was sleeping on the floor at the foot of the bed. Malika shook her. "Wake up, wake up!" There was no response.

Alone, Malika ran from the room and out of the house into a city she did not recognize. Posters in every yard, on every wall, were like a banana plantation that had sprung up from the earth. The embers of burning tyres cast their red glow into the moonlight. Sheep were tethered to lampposts. She heard a strange music and arriving at the Renaissance Square, saw dancing taking place by torchlight. There was a band of political supporters, their party shirts torn, supplying the merry tune from a clarinet, a tuba and a flute and their women and bodyguards were holding hands and dancing in a circle. A PPC flag was flying from the top of the square. Bank documents blew about in swirls and scuttled along the ground like dry leaves. Flyers were flying out the windows of the square down to the thugs below, who caught them. She heard the screams of a girl coming from the darkness towards the end of a street.

The Renaissance Square was dark. She rattled a doorknob and peered in at the windows. She ran to the back of the square. The reception room was empty. The fountain was gone. There were no more statues. She could not understand what had happened. She ran on into the night. She saw a dim light and ran toward it. Behind one of the party houses, the yard was lit with torches. A line of black limousines stood there, Pajero jeeps in their hundreds. She heard groaning and slipped between two cars to the rear. The thugs lifted out a supporter on a pallet who raised himself on one elbow and grinned at her. His party shirt was soaked in red wine.

On the ground, outside the tarred area, lay something from which she could not avert her eyes in time. She didn't want to believe what she was looking at: a collection of whisky, beer bottles and packs of tobacco. The light inside was so faint, like that of a lantern running out of kerosene. Beside a table, stood the party governing council, surrounded by their team of reporters. One at the back turned to look at Malika, frowned, and muttered something. He was the man that so much resembled Issa. At this fearful moment, Issa's image appeared, indelible, in her mind. The man was a short, neatly put-together man who seemed inviolate amidst the extravaganza around him. He wore a rubber apron over his tunic. A tarnished rod rested in his hand. He had thick eyebrows, and the eyes that had peered from under them were red. It seemed to Malika that his eyes were filled with an uncertainty that reflected her own.

One of the thugs ran toward her. "You shouldn't be here, Madam," he said, pushing her towards a door.

"I was deprived of my sleep," Malika said. "My husband is a soldier and I can smell that something is wrong."

Saying this, she gasped. What was wrong, she realized, was that Mazabongo had begun like this in the Congo.

A car drove in.

"Usman Diallo is our man," Malika heard someone say. They laughed gorgeously. "PPC is powerful. PPC can kill and revive." Malika was transported by those words, by the spray of wealth. At the same time, it confirmed her belief about what failure could lead to. When a driver was sent to summon the party speaker, Malika was almost too stunned to speak. "The chief's house had been vandalized," she reported. "They tore out the rugs for their campfires. They befouled his parlour."

"Do they who did this call themselves Segolians?" the woman asked. At this, Malika, felt bereft and, pensively, she walked home.

By morning, the voters were on the march, moving through the town in an endless procession. Car tyres had been set alight. Muffled explosions came from the city centre. Usman Diallo's house was devastated – the windows broken, the gardens stomped on and the bar stripped of its bottles.

Malika went into the apartment she had shared with Issa and removed the bedding in their room. She opened the windows to the cold sun and swept, dusted, and packed away Issa's scattered magazines in a box. Only when she had put his slippers and caftan in his closet, together with his beret, cutaways and cowboy hat, did she begin to shake. She felt like ice as she swept up the dirt and tobacco ash and general mess: Issa's signature. Malika worked with a servant's possessiveness, yet she worked with love. When she turned around, the apartment was as it should have been, but for the absence of the man.

She removed the brown curtains at the windows. With her hair loose and falling about her face, she sat dry-eyed in the family kitchen, staring vacantly, while Dieynaba brewed tea. When Malika became aware of Dieynaba standing beside her, dressed for school, holding an exercise book in her hand, the tea was standing cold in its cup, forgotten. Malika studied the girl's black face, as if she had never seen it before. Its dark eyes were familiar, and their slightly Arab corners. But they stared back at her. The broad rounded forehead, the firm mouth and high cheekbones suggested a girl growing into a beautiful woman. Dieynaba finished drinking the cold tea.

"I'm off to school, Auntie," she said. The two of them had been sleeping in the same room for two weeks.

"What will you have to eat at break time?" Malika asked.

"Nothing," Dieynaba said.

Malika thought a while, silently. Dieynaba set off to leave. Just then, Malika felt as if the scales had fallen from her eyes. She opened her eyes wide, wiped them repeatedly with her handkerchief and yawned. She looked at Dieynaba, now at a distance. Malika jumped and ran after Dieynaba.

"Wait, wait!" she called. "Dieynaba, please wait." Malika raced back into the bedroom to where some of her belongings were. She took out the Gucci bag she had hidden and, after withdrawing a few coins, she wrapped up the bag and hid it again. She ran out, after Dieynaba.

"Please take this."

Dieynaba shook her head.

"Take it," Malika insisted. "For uncle Issa's good, take it!"

4

Malika began to feel the weight of separation, so like grief, like death. It created a crater in the centre of her body. She regretted having conceded to Issa's persuasion, to marrying a soldier. She gazed at every plane arriving, wondering if Issa was in it and she hooked her eyes to the TV, whenever a correspondent in Goma filed a report, hoping to spot a familiar face in the background. She walked along the flowerbeds that flanked the inner walls of their compound. She mused over the romantic promenades of their first days together. Her walking increased her inner solitude. Her marriage meant nothing without the sheltering arm of he who had brought her there. She flooded the flowers with her tears. She stood still, lost in myriad thoughts. Only when Fatimata cried out to her, giving her a new list of rules, did she regain her bearings:

"Sweep the compound once the sun reddens in the east. Don't leave the refuse unpacked. The brooms belong in the tool shed, before and after. No haphazard work! Some litter is hiding around the water pots. Move the pots when you sweep. The sanitation van comes around nine o'clock. Pull out the bin at the sound of the van's horn. You can visit with friends on occasion, but don't go off without telling me. The neighbourhood is crammed with gossip. Mind your business, there's a lot to do. Just, you know it, make yourself useful. The way you behave shows how you'll look after my grandchildren. Oh sure, if someone spits on your feet, clean off the mess, but don't be the first to spit on someone else's. As always, strive to maintain peace among us."

"Yes ma."

Malika rose before the imam's voice went off at half past five, rolled up the mat she had slept on, washed her face and chewed a piece of chewing stick to clean her teeth. She fetched water in a bowl from the kitchen and walked down the compound to the gate, where she poured the water in three splashes across the gate.

"Away evil spirits," she said with each splash. She adjusted her wrapper and held her long black braid behind her neck. Then she brought out the barbecue grill and filled the container with charcoal. She made sure the market basins were clean, then took the broom from the tool shed and began to sweep the compound. She moved up and down, her breasts pointing towards the ground, her broom drawing layers of semi-circles on the sand. When she had swept the whole compound, she lit the charcoal for smoking fish and checked for coins in her purse. Change was a worry with customers. Fresh for the day, she sat and reflected on this, the blueprint of her mornings.

Knowing she was married made Malika stay. She was scared of wasting away like an old woman, of being without a man who would *die* for her, who would really do his best to figure her out. Into each of the basins she folded a cement bag that she used to wrap fish and slid in a kitchen knife as well. They were gleaming under her meticulous touch. Then she returned to her room. The chewing stick still at her lips, she brought out her wedding album and paged through it, examining each photograph, one by one. When she got to the one where she was dancing with Issa after the ritual of champagne, she held it close to her heart. She remained in that position until Babacar brought out the fish to be smoked to sell.

Babacar had heard his mother's voice instructing Malika the other day and he trusted her, as a friend, to meander through the labyrinth of taboos and trivia that abounded in the house. He trusted that she was mature enough to show forbearance in the face of the mentality of an elderly mother-in-law. Malika's own mother was a local nurse and working with her in the waiting rooms of life had taught Malika patience. "Malika would hop into a hospital bed to console a terminally-sick patient, not caring at all about contagious illness," Babacar remembered Malika's mother saying. And it was that beauty within her that had evoked Issa's tears.

Their love cart had ridden off on a warm December day. While Christmas fever bloomed over the shops and shoppers, Issa boarded a bus from the 4th Battalion, heading home for Christmas holidays and then he lost his wallet. Marooned, Issa had complained to the conductor of his missing wallet, but his complaint fell on deaf ears. Issa suspected someone in the bus must have picked his pocket. Stranded at the terminus, he could neither travel onwards nor go back. Malika had been standing at the bus stop when Issa alighted there. He looked confused. Malika approached him to ask why he looked so depressed in December.

Issa opened his heart.

"I was sitting on the third row of that white bus," he answered. "We departed from the cantonment in Saint Denis. I placed my wallet, with all my money and documents, in the side pocket of my trousers. It was a three-folder case. And, yes, I was dreaming of happy holidays. My mind was racing with the pictorial countryside and my eyes were admiring the harmony of birds migrating south from Europe when those professional pickpockets scooped my wallet."

"What a pity!" Malika said politely, trying to make a good impression on him. "What next for you, if I may ask?"

"I don't know, trek home," he answered.

"Where do you live?" Malika asked.

"Djembe."

"Impossible! You'll collapse on the way. I know Djembe. I've been there several times. It's a long way off."

"I don't have a choice," he said.

"Nor is trekking the solution."

Malika paused, bit her tongue and thought a while. "Come with me to the house and I'll ask my parents to help you. They're nice people," she said.

"And where is your house?" Issa asked.

"Here in Tekui," she answered, pointing towards the horizon. He could see nothing but palm trees, although he searched for signs of human habitation. "There's my village."

"Well, thank you for your concern, but I don't see myself walking into your house with a begging bowl in my hand, being neither blind nor disabled," he replied.

"Don't worry about that. I'll talk to my parents. They will help. After all you're not a vagrant, you only ran into trouble."

Although Issa admired her, he remained reluctant to follow her home, for he was afraid of humiliation. He couldn't imagine a man his age walking into an unknown household in the middle of the day to beg for his fare. First, Malika requested that they walk together down the road to buy black pepper, but Issa was still undecided as to whether to accept her invitation. Soon they reached a junction.

"Let's go on," Malika said. Issa wavered, shrugging his shoulders.

"Nice of you," he said. "I will trek slowly home rather, even if it takes me a week."

"No you can't!" she replied firmly. "You're a vagabond? If you do so, you may faint. And if you faint, you may die, and a careless death is an offence against Allah."

"I should be the one to offer you something and not the other way round."

"It doesn't matter."

"It does," he protested. "We all need help at one point or another. It's human. Be it man or woman, everybody. When we can't do otherwise, we need someone to help us."

"Who else is in your house apart from your parents?" he asked.

"My siblings."

"Eeh!" he yelled. "Begging in front of children… Don't bother, I'll find my way. I will wave down passing cars. Who knows, one might be kind enough to help."

She sighed, "Ngh-hunnh… Generosity has been stamped out of drivers' dictionary. 'No credit, be warned' is what you read in buses these days. And, you know, waving down passing buses in that manner is unsafe. You're looking for trouble. A man did it the other day and ran into thieves. A problem like yours calls for a wise solution."

"What would you tell your parents?" he asked, ill at ease.

"That we met at the bus stop, that your wallet was stolen in the bus leaving you with nothing to get home."

"Pssst, not like that," he said. Then he dug up another excuse. "Yes, I remember, now. I bought a few Christmas gifts for my nieces at home. I'll try to resell some and use the money for my fare."

"No."

"Yes."

"Christmas is a time special for children," she said. "You had your time. Don't deprive your nieces of those small gestures that go a long way. Think of all the respect afforded an uncle who returns home with gifts."

"You! I've never met a girl like you. You know, Malika," he said, using her name. "I hate to be a burden. I like to be independent. I am loath to be in debt, even a moral one."

"Come on," she said. "You're not begging me, are you? I noticed you were in trouble, then I offered to be of assistance. So where's the problem?"

"Okay," he said, having spent his last bastion of excuses. "I'll come with you."

Malika offered to carry a piece of his luggage and he did not object. She carried it on her head and led him off in the direction of the route where she had pointed out her village earlier on. Issa followed her, glowing with marvel at her: that she was so gentle; that she was so open; that she walked correctly, showing who she was; and smelled of something like citrus or bergamot. He could not make out the aroma entirely, but knew it was just right for her. They walked on, each carrying a piece of a luggage, toward Malika's village.

After a half-hour walk, they arrived. She dropped the luggage she was carrying by the door.

"Sit here and wait for me," she said pointing to a bench. "I'll be back in a moment."

With his elbows on his knees and his hands loosely clasped, Issa sat and stared down at the floor. He breathed uncomfortably, his mind clouded with doubts as she disappeared into the porch of their house built of stones, surely stones from Dialaw. There was silence.

Her village had been in the news when it was devastated by locusts, but the locusts were overcome and green leaves were visible once more. As if a fleeting reminder of the plague, dead locusts were scattered all over and wilted crops lay in a trench plastered with red hue. The mud buildings with their raffia thatch were timeless. The sun was glistening and nowhere was there sign of a returning farmer. Issa sat on the bench at the end of the porch. He no longer knew what he thought and was uncertain of what lay in store for him.

That was the position in which Malika found him when, minutes later, she returned through the dim corridor, amid the echoing of voices. In front of her walked an elderly man who, from a distance, could be heard asking if Issa was the one. Malika said yes.

The elderly man had a long white scarf wrapped around his neck. They bent their necks and approached silently. The man led the way and Issa could tell from the shape of his nose, as well as from the manner in which Malika followed him, that he was her father.

As the elderly man approached, Malika slipped back, barely visible. Issa stood up naively and greeted him, "Peace be with you."

Malika's father answered, "And to you peace." Issa stood still like a schoolboy, respectfully.

The man continued, "I'm Faye. Sorry about what happened to you. Here's something to get you home. Be careful. Many thieves are operating at the approach of festivities."

"You're welcome to share our lunch," Malika chipped in enthusiastically.

Faye turned around and walked back up the corridor. Malika hesitated to follow her father. So intently, yet timidly was she watching Issa that she did not look ahead and almost hit her head on the door post. She nodded, insisting that he accept her invitation. At that moment, they connected and felt that somewhere from within their smouldering flames, a love story would arise.

Issa tried to pick up his luggage, but Malika ordered him to put it in the corridor. He followed her to the parlour, where a large traditional mat was spread on the floor, at the centre of which stood a tray of broken rice.

In Segol, the gate of Africa, a land of elegance and colours, eating, like cooking, is an art. A meal seduces the eyes before it sugars the tongue. Indeed, Malika's rice and fish displayed their fine colours. A heap of broken rice filled the tray. To the side was a stock of tiny aromatic grains that, according to admirers of things flavoursome, is a love song. The rice and fish exhibited a mix of the best gifts from the earth: red for pepper, white for cassava, green for cabbage, orange for carrot, purple for eggplant and other wondrous gifts.

"Let the fastest win!" cried Malika. This was a traditional saying to urge them to eat well, especially the fastest and the luckiest. They sat around the tray and began to eat, the women dishing out the fish for the men.

Issa ate to his satisfaction and praised the food. "Never ate rice like this."

"You're welcome," Malika replied.

"Anything good is a blessing," her mother added. "It was a good thing she met you. You may spend the night and travel tomorrow."

Issa greeted them again and stood up to leave. At this, Faye asked Malika to assist him with his luggage. Issa smiled and chuckled as he looked at her, the woman who had turned his sorrow into dance. Together, they headed down the road and when they got to a stone outcrop, they sat down. Issa began to talk. He spoke of how his soul had wandered in search of love. His voice was shaking, his hands were wet, tears filled his eyes and stars shone through his soul. Malika listened to his words, noticing the stress on his face and the tears in his eyes. Rolling her eyes, she took his hand.

"I love you," Issa said suddenly.

"Hé hé hé…" she laughed, but did not reply. She had resolved never to give away those words gratuitously. Instead, she kept her distance, assailed by doubts, unsure whether she was crossing the right bridge in discerning if he was Mr Right.

"But you're Muslim and am Christian," she said.

"You'll always be free to go to church."

"Hmm… are you sure?" she asked, winking. Issa liked this about her, that she could voice her feelings so simply, so openly. "I-s-s-a," she called, shaking her shoulder-length braid. Her smile was infectious.

"Here we are," he said, looking into her eyes, "alone, isolated from the world."

He looked steadily at her, concentrating on her eyes, and remembered what he had said after eating her rice and fish. She talked. He held still. Love blossomed between them and when the bus arrived, they were in that mood.

She waved him goodbye, "Okay, next time."

Issa climbed the elevated step of the bus's back door, took a seat at the rear and the bus departed. They gazed at each other until they vanished from view.

Christmas came. Issa was tingling with excitement and his whole family wondered why. No one knew he was at the beginning of a love story. He had no thoughts other than of Malika and how to live with her and be with her alone, for the rest of his life.

He spent a week instead of two with his family, upon which he said he was returning to the barracks. On the way back, he stopped to visit Malika and gave her gifts of bridal value: forget-me-not jewellery and apparel. The jewellery was personalized and bore the engraving: "Two things I seek in life – a rose and my Malika. A rose for a day and my Malika for life."

Malika was thrilled. She jumped up, hugged him, and ran into her mother's bedroom. She wanted to serve Issa some food, but could not do so without her mother's consent. She came out through the kitchen carrying a bowl of well-reddened okra soup. Issa drank it with a spoon, spots of it splashing onto his shirt.

They ambled around the village square, Issa holding her hand, like a settled-in-husband. Issa spoke of making a home and living happily together. He spoke passionately, trying to appear intelligent, to show he was in control. At the mention of each new idea, his lucky lady chuckled, as if she had hit a goldmine.

Later, to his father's question, "You've made your choice on a wife?" Issa replied, "Of course."

Salif was not expecting such a sudden affirmation. After that, Issa renovated the uninhabited old structure of the Dialaw stones close behind the House of Dudu, sealed it with corrugated iron sheets and his parents fixed a date to assemble their relatives. The relatives met, discussed the matter and reached an agreement. They informed Malika's parents who also met with their kith and kin to decide. They approved of the marriage and a day and time were fixed for the two families to meet.

Salif delegated the most reputable elders of his family to ask for Malika's hand, conveying Issa's presents of money, wrappers, cows, and sheep and all the goods that Issa had decided to give. Malika's family received the gifts and gave their approval. They drank palm wine, danced to traditional music, and ate jollof rice. Issa posed like a happy conqueror. He seemed set to decide, negotiate and love.

They married the next December and the entire village shook up the dust for the occasion. Malika appeared at the nuptial night dressed in a colourful, beaded cloak, holding the beaded staff typical of a Segolian queen. She received gifts from the entire village. The newly-weds were rocking the eight-day wedding party, according to custom, when a phone call came from the brigade commander informing Issa of his enlistment to the MONUC.

She had a beautiful heart: was serene, soft-spoken and humane. Malika spoke like a queen, sang like an angel – oh, singer manqué – and walked with a glamorous step. She could make you cry out, "Creature of loveliness!"

On principle, she refrained from gossiping. When provoked, she applied silence as means of control, except on one occasion. When Thursday Market let out, Malika and Anta slung off their wrappers beside the bush and got ready to fight. On the grass, in the jumble of wild flowers and dirt, they tested their strength. Malika stormed in, overturned Anta's basin, and aimed her fist at her rival's chest. The two fell over the wild flowers, crushing several and flattening others. It went on for three full minutes. Malika's eyes brimmed with terror while Anta's face turned into a mixture of brown, black and pink. Malika left the ring. Anta hurled a blow and missed. Neither yelled, neither wept, only the cracking of their joints were to be heard. A scissor-like punch from Malika made Anta's chin swell up with a slight cut, her lips bruising around the edges. A passer-by separated them, yet they continued at each other verbally.

"You're lucky," said Anta.

"You mad woman," Malika told her. "You think I'm a fowl. I'm still going to break your jaw."

"Witch!"

Malika was back. "Say that again!"

"I said you're a witch!" Anta's eyes shone from above her bruised lips. She held out her lower lip to look at her injuries and was caught by Malika while doing so.

"That is just a tip of the iceberg," said Malika. "I'm Madame Ndiaye. Mind the way you talk to me."

"I say, you're a witch. Go to..." She stopped and began again, with fresh insults. "You sucked my blood."

"And where were you when I sucked it?" asked Malika.
"Instead of showing your strength, you suck blood."
"No! Where were you when I sucked your blood?"
"Do I know? Does anyone know?"
"Who is this 'anyone'? A mad person, like you?" Malika asked.
"You have got a mouth like margarine."
"You've got feet like ketchup."
"Lady Misfortune!"
"Old bag!"
"Mosquito!"
"Not just old bag. You're a father-marry-me."
"I'd rather be that than like you, ruining a man," spat Anta.
"Which man could you possible ruin? Do any men ever look at you?"

"Many, many of them. So many," retorted Anta. She wanted Malika to hear her reasons for being single. But, come now, her explanations appeared off target.

"Five boyfriends, no *visa*," Malika said.
"Heh! All of them proposed to me."
"Old bag. No one proposed to you."
"You are marriage-crazy!" cried Anta.
"Are you jealous?"
"Of what?"
"Of Madame Ndiaye."
"And where is Monsieur Ndiaye?"

"Stop it now, you mad woman, stop it now. I can stomach whatever you say about me, but don't you utter my husband's name. Or else–"

Like air escaping from an overheated machine, the sound of "or else" came at Anta from all around.

"Or else what?" Anta said.

"I will knock you unconscious."

Anta's heart thumped as she rejoined, "And I will make you deaf."

"May the gods strike…" Malika swallowed the rest of her words as she realized she was at the gate of their compound. She opened the gate, swelling as she walked through the courtyard, silent and fuming. Anta's voice, raining insult upon insult, could be heard from afar.

The next morning, before the chicks had woken from their sleep, Binetou, the next-door neighbour, was at the front window knocking. Fatimata turned a deaf ear to her. She considered it too early, not to mention foolish to knock on windows when doors were provided for it. Binetou persisted, so Fatimata opened the door, grimacing wearily and gesturing her in, reluctantly.

"What is this news am I hearing?" Binetou began, scrubbing her teeth with a long chewing stick.

"Such as?" asked Fatimata, arranging her head tie in the mirror, hurriedly searching for a suitable arrangement. She had to carry vegetables to the early morning market and she was behind time.

"Yes. I heard that Malika was fighting with a girl in the district and made her nose bleed." Binetou continued brushing her teeth, waiting for an answer. She pushed the chewing stick farther back into her mouth and it made a noise.

"Eh m…" Fatimata hesitated. "My daughter-in-law is the quiet type. If she did that, if at all, then that girl must have poured hot water on her."

"But the gossip has gone round the city," Binetou said.

"Oh, that's our stock-in-trade," Fatimata replied, reaching for her basin and stepping out of the house.

On her way home after selling vegetables, Yaya, a woman from the other side of Djembe, greeted Fatimata: "What scatterbrain of a daughter-in-law are you living with? She's been here barely six months and she's already pulling out our hair. No modesty, eh, no respect? Just like mad Sambou."

Fatimata looked at her quizzically through the dusty wind. "Good. I'm glad. I'm so glad she's a shocker," she replied. "Malika is someone that speaks her mind, and does not paint over the truth."

"So you encourage her to punch–"

"Quote me right, Yaya, quote me right. I encourage her to be herself. And I prefer her like that, I prefer her to those girls who smile at your face and spit when you turn. We like to paint words, but she does not. And since you were talking about misconduct, go and tackle those young women of ours who pretend to be immaculate when, in reality, they are spoilt coconuts. Proper outside, putrefying inside."

"Excuse me Fatimata," said Yaya. "I did not intend to insult you. I was just expressing my anxiety, for I see your chin is swollen."

"It's no problem," Fatimata said, sniffing. "Let the songbird sing!" At that, she retired quickly from Yaya and pursued her way home.

5

Babacar was stunned that his mother sprung to Malika's defence. Fatimata was so cool and chic to have grasped the fancy of a free daughter-in-law. Despite having given her consent to the marriage – she had her preferences – she had not been excited about the wedding. In fact, she considered Malika unsuitable for Issa and had nearly boycotted the wedding reception. She found fault with the men in Malika's families, called them lazy for waiting on their wives to provide their daily bread. Even when Fatimata agreed to attend the reception, she turned down everything she was served, screamed at a server, and refused the "Mother and Son Dance", causing tears to ripple down Malika's cheek.

"Every good marriage begins in tears," Issa consoled her.

From then on, Malika felt strained, as if she were jumping one hurdle after another, struggling to win Fatimata's smile. One night during the first days, she shared a joke hoping to please Fatimata, but her response was simply, "Not funny."

Malika's face froze, however she was resolute to fight on. Perhaps something might change the heart of stone that Fatimata was serving her. When the following evening fell and it being Wednesday, Malika dusted the furniture. She murmured to herself about Fatimata, "Mystery. Poison snake. Unpredictable. Unity of opposites."

Just about the time she finished her work, the atmosphere released searing hot air through the thin walls of the house, forcing Dieynaba and Malika out into the courtyard. They waited there for the return of the cool breeze. Unexpectedly, Fatimata joined them and told them this story:

"'Work, work, work your fingers thin. Work is the magic charm,' Alassane told his children when his death was near. 'Give up,' he said, 'from destroying the tradition our ancestors left us: a providential coin lies beneath work. Its exact location I cannot tell, but with an ounce of courage you'll find it. Early, my children, early! Plough, peruse, clear, leave no grass standing that the hand can pull.' Alassane later died and his sons lived by his words. They harvested abundantly – yam, cassava, beans and groundnuts. They cried out joyfully, 'We owe this to Papa,' and they built a statue in homage to their father who had taught them that work is the true magic charm."

Malika and Dieynaba applauded and whistled as Fatimata came to the end of the story. With the sea breeze back, they began to shiver. They pulled in the benches and entered the house, retiring earlier than usual.

At about midnight, Malika began to yell, "My husband! My husband!" The moon was out; there was no movement, no traffic. Only the moon lit the chilly air, so yellow-black, so black-yellow, Malika's voice echoed beyond time, in the silent night.

Malika got up, dashed into Ami Colle's bedroom and lay down clumsily beside her. Ami Colle's jaw was slumped and her hands were clenched in fists above her pyjamas, as she lay sleeping. She rolled over, bumped into her and woke up. Frightened, she jumped out of the bed.

"I'm here. It's me," Malika said. Ami Colle lit the room, peered at Malika and touched her feet. "Ami Colle, Ami Colle," Malika said again.

Ami Colle went over to check on her daughter in their room. "I said I'm here!" Ami Colle answered. She found Dieynaba sleeping at the edge of the bed. They called her "rabbit" because she slept free from care, rolling over only rarely, keeping her eyes firmly shut. Ami Colle stretched out her hand.

"My husband! My husband!" Ami Colle heard from her room. It was Malika screaming again and Ami Colle rushed back to her.

"What is it, Malika?" asked Ami Colle. Malika screamed again, in her sleepwalking. Ami Colle ran out in the direction of the House of Youssou to call her co-wife.

Ding-a-ling, ding-a-ling, ding-a-ling. Ami Colle rang the bell at the front door and Babacar, who was watching a late-night movie, opened it.

"What's wrong?" he asked.

"Malika. Malika. She... she... she crept onto my bed, screaming like she's possessed."

"Why go crazy about that?" Babacar said, and scratched his beard, unsure whether to reveal what he already knew. Malika had told him she was deeply troubled and he was close enough to her to know it was more than that.

Babacar left the door ajar and rushed into the House of Dudu. Seeing him, Malika woke up and asked him if he had seen the rebels.

"The rebels? Which rebels?" Babacar asked. Malika said she had seen rebels pressing forward to Labaambashii.

"Where is Labaambashii?" he asked.

"Labaambashii! Labaambashii!" Malika cried.

"You mean Lubumbashi?" said Babacar. "Lubum, *not* Labaam!"

Her face flushed black, her lower lip trembled and her eyes, both red and green, beamed at Babacar in a dry, unblinking way. Three times in a row, twelve times a minute, she screamed, her voice climbing progressively, as if addressing an unseen person.

Ami Colle then succeeded in waking Fatimata who gripped her wrapper and shuffled into the House of Dudu. She approached the bed, leaned over it and whispered, "Nightmares, hum, bad dreams." She looked at Malika's mouth, half-open, her breathe heaving in and out. Fatimata jumped away from the bed, reached for the fire pot, lit the charcoal and dropped morsels of *thiouraye* on it. She raised the pot and took it round the walls of the rooms and then placed it centrally, so the burning incense could spread across the room.

Usually, Fatimata used incense as perfume, but now she was using it to ward off evil, to appease Malika's spirit. Then she sat next to Malika and assured her Issa would come back, soon. She told her to dispel all her negative thoughts. She told her not to doubt. When the smoke from the incense faded, Fatimata extinguished the charcoal and helped Malika back to bed, next to Dieynaba. But as she could not sleep, Fatimata stood by and served her some fruit and vegetables left over from dinner. Malika ate the fruit and her eyes moved about in the manner of a fly that flits from a ripe mango to a morsel of breadfruit.

The next day, Malika was the first to get up, her face shining, as if nothing had happened. Around her neck there hung a small transistor radio. She was listening to her favourite programme: a drama series based on the book of an English author, lauding the qualities of a man who cooked better than his wife did.

"That man your star?" Babacar teased her. "Always listening to that thing."

"More than a star."

"Oh, you disappoint me."

"It's the other way round. If all men were like him, there would be no heart of darkness, no Everest for war reporters, no refugee camps to make me cry."

"I'm not so sure."

"Just cook. Cook. Do the dishes. Clean the tables. Wash the babies. You would be more sensitive to human suffering and predicament."

"I don't agree," Babacar said. "It makes no difference. You know, Malika, Mazabongo was a great cook, still he called rains upon the Congo. From his dining table, he predicted the deluge and hastened it to come about."

"They all loved the culinary art, no doubt they loved it. Yet they set fire to the Congo, making it burn from genocide to a continental war. Could there be any better laboratory for the crisis of contemporary Africa?" Malika looked at him, admiring his sense of intrigue. She wiped the crust that had settled around her eyes from her crying.

She winked twice and smiled at him, "Nose like Pepe Goodie."

Despite Malika's humiliation about sleepwalking, so deep, her beauty and personality endured. Her love for children remained. The child next door cut his finger and she leaped over the wall to assist him. Nobody arrived as promptly as she did. Dare-to-be-different summarized her.

"Praised be Allah," Fatimata said to her, while washing vegetables. "You married into a respected family, a decent family, a large family. You're lucky."

"What do you mean, Ma?" Malika said.

"Ha, but you should know what I mean. Has any member of this family been sent to the prison at Wiland? Or detained for corruption? Or for illegal transactions? Or far above the ground because of weeds? Hm, my daughter, you're lucky, eh."

"Thank you, Ma."

"And you'll fully settle when you have your own children. Yes, my daughter, children are the joys of a mother. And if Allah fills your basket with food to give them and your pot with water to quench their thirst, then you'll be proud of our good name. What good is money without a good name?"

"A good name is number one."

"Good you know, so good that you know."

In the evening following this conversation, Malika went to get her hair plaited. For a few hours, Salif and Fatimata appeared haunted by Malika's behaviour. At times, it was the fate of her husband that bothered them, at times her follies and at times both. Something about their daughter-in-law made their tongues sour.

"Everything gets her tingling with excitement," Fatimata said. And, indeed, Malika could burst into laughter, with the ecstasy of a lottery winner. Ami Colle brought the news that hundreds of their compatriots had drowned at sea, trying to reach Europe.

"Hey, what's up?" Malika responded and she began to hug everybody, seeking comfort. Also, she spoke to herself, gesticulating with her hands and nodding her head.

She wore sparkly eyeliner, a pair of low-waist jeans and a belly button ring, in the rainy season.

"Would you change out of that nonsense!" cried Fatimata, slapping her. "Don't you leave this house with that thing showing." Tongues had begun to wag in the neighbourhood about her manner of dressing. She would not tie her wrappers when going to see friends, but decked out in her low-waist jeans that made her look like an ice cream cone.

In the end, Salif swallowed it all with his problem-free philosophy. "You were all like that once upon a time," he said, pointing at his wives. "I lived to see your youthful adrenalin shrink."

Babacar was part of the problem. "I love you in those tight jeans," he whispered to Malika when she returned. "Your calves give me a thrill."

Babacar brought out the ludo game. Midway, he handed Malika a package. "Take it," he said.

"For me?" Malika said, kissing him. He was joyful at how she cherished his gifts to her.

To look at Malika was to forget the day's work. She was slim and tall, with thick hair framing her delicate face. When she smiled, like the antelope, her teeth, a little big for her mouth, beamed like a full moon over Segol River. Her shoulder-length, kinky twists tossed around elegantly such that the men of Djembe stroked their beards and clicked their tongues. Her feet were outstandingly long, her nose sharp, her teeth flawless; her neck firm on her shoulders; her waist in harmony with her thighs and the rest of her body, balancing her hips; her palms felt firm to the touch; her forehead glittered; and her lips glowed. Malika was a jewel of the coastal villages with her black eyes that talked, her round ears that smiled.

She could not miss putting on her best the day her guests were to come. At five minutes to six, she was ready and had prepared chicken salad sandwiches. She was wearing that white button-down gown of hers, the one she kept in the front closet. When Thierno, the first guest to arrive, rang the bell, she walked to the door slowly, her hair dangling long and her eyes wide. Thierno was so funny, he noticed nothing until he sat down and looked up. Spotting Babacar across the table, he tried to act cool, greeting him casually, "Salut, boy."

Their jaws exploded with laughter, Babacar, Malika and Thierno too. When Malika asked Thierno what he would like to drink, Babacar observed that Thierno was admiring her with a two-of-us look. Unable to get the smile off his face, Thierno stared down at his plate. Only then did Babacar's nimble brain figure out that something was afoot: Thierno had fallen in love.

After that, Thierno did not say another word.

All the guests arrived. Malika sat in her room, absent-minded. She came out later to greet them, wearing a sleeveless blouse over the white gown from Des Moines, fanning herself with a copy of *Women's Magazine*.

She dove into the discussion, knowing just how to, however Babacar was not impressed with her speaking to other men. He tried, unsuccessfully, to interrupt her by signalling that something was burning. He joined in her conversation and pointed her insistently towards the kitchen. Malika stopped mid-sentence, stood up, and followed his finger into the kitchen. The Segolians say that if you throw a frog into a pot of boiling water, it will jump out of the pot, but if you put it into a pot of cool water and slowly bring the water to the boil, it will boil to its death.

Malika collected the plates used for the starter and in preparation for the main course, turned to take them to the kitchen. Just then, Thierno touched her knee and slipped a note into the bend in her elbow. "Let's meet on Friday," it read. Malika showed the note to Babacar, who had followed her into the kitchen.

Babacar waited until Thierno was preparing to leave, then trailed behind him and said, "You know her husband?" Pretending not to have heard, Thierno rushed to his car and slammed the door closed. This was not his first attempt – he had special names for Malika, had called the UN office in Goma (asking about Issa, his friends and colleagues), had given Malika Valentine's Day gifts, had followed her on the freeway, bought all her fish, paid her transport fare, and even pretended once to be her husband to a stranger who asked if he knew her.

"If you invite my wife, you'll see me with her," Babacar said, standing to attention like an aide de camp.

"How can one visit a married woman without asking after the husband?" Babacar asked himself over and over. For Thierno had a wife. They were both cloth stylists. Their workshop was known for its tangles of scabby pieces of cloth, as if they practised cut-and-patch. Thierno had shared the space with his wife for ten years, but they had been separated for months and he was trying to be no longer in need of her. They were successful together, people had always said. The trouble had begun because young women were phoning Thierno after midnight and he was spending his father's money on them.

Despite the incident, Babacar and Malika held on to each other. Early on Saturday morning, as Malika gathered and sorted laundry, Babacar stood by her side. Malika retrieved papers and other objects from the trouser pockets. She even took out cigarettes, matchboxes and spent phone cards and was surprised to find that men no longer forgot money in their pockets as they once did. She felt disappointed that she had been looking for matches to light the stove the previous night, and had walked down the street to buy some, meanwhile there were full boxes sitting in the pockets of some trousers, just for cigarettes.

"All men are the same," she sighed.

"Why do you say so?"

She gave no reply. Babacar lifted the bucket full of clothes high on his head. If anything disturbed him about the beach that afternoon, it was the muggings and the crowds. To steer clear of annoyances, they took the West Boardwalk as if they were going towards the suburbs. Diouf's football pitch sat right in the middle of the sprawling suburb, only a block from the new bridge, and the road was lined with caterpillars, bulldozers and other construction machinery. They walked past the bridge and advanced toward the highway, beyond the game park and Julius Berger's residential buildings alongside it. Babacar wondered what it would be like to live along highways and to hear horns and sirens and screeching and bleating day in and out, almost knocking down on you, deafening you.

Djembe, like all the satellite towns anchored on the waist of Cap Vert Peninsula, was not what Malika had dreamed of as a small girl. She had dreamed of a better life, yes, healthier than the one she led in her village, but not of this struggle of so many for so little.

They reached the sandy shores that opened up on the beach and passed through the stores lining the shores. In front of the stores sat men who looked through at them across the slanted electric poles. Babacar suggested they ignore them. The men whispered to each other, chuckled and kept watching them. Malika closed her face sternly. The men whistled. One of them got up and pursued them, dreadlocks dangling past his elbows in variegated shades of brown. He wore a pair of blue jeans, a white shirt splattered with primary colours, and some sort of leather sandals, through which his toenails pointed. His face was as white as alkali. He walked up to Malika, greeted her, walking alongside her and put his hand on her shoulders. Malika pushed it away and increased her pace. The man insisted on trying to hold her hand, but she shoved it away. He tried to help Malika carry the small bucket she was clenching tightly. His eyes fixed upon her buttocks and in a shaking voice, he asked, "Don't you need it?"

Malika shook her head at him. "You worthless rat."

"Ah. Your man is better? Okay."

"I don't blame you. I just don't blame you."

"You blame him then."

"Blame who?" she asked.

"Your chevalier."

"Stupid sheep!" She turned to Babacar, "You see why I'm so cheesed off by Issa's persuasion. If he were home, would this rat of a man talk to me?"

The man could hear her. "Exactly. And now that he's not around, you're talking to a rat."

"Imbecile!" Malika snapped, her face hardening. She fell into a rage and clenched her fists. She wished the man did not exist. She glared derisively at him, sighing fiercely. Her stomach growled. When she coughed, something flew out of her mouth and her coughing was so loud that one could hear an unpleasant grunting deep in her throat. Her feet twitched and rubbed as if calm could never come to her. She looked as if she would cry. Behind her, Babacar was frozen, waiting for her to speak. When her silence persisted, the man gave up.

Gradually, sand lorries began to leave the beach. She dropped her bucket in the sand, put on her blue apron and began to wash the clothes. Her face was tightly locked and she was tight-lipped. When she handed the clothes to Babacar to rinse, she did so wordlessly. Despite the tears falling from her eyes, she continued washing the clothes.

Once the laundry was done, she sat down on the wet white sand. Malika tapped a quick finger on her thigh, closed her eyes, and moved her head slowly to the clicking of her earrings.

Suddenly, her eyes opened to the majesty of the setting sun. It confirmed her plea, a plea for Issa's return, a prayer to the Maker to be spared of the water's tempest, of the trial of her soul. It confirmed her goal, her aim to be cleansed and not carried away. It reminded her that troubles come in life, but the same shoulders that bear them live to enjoy their solutions.

The sun shone on Malika's face and she seemed to forget her earlier row. Her forehead dazzled in splendour and she pulled out her tongue. In her eyes were tears of assurance, of accession, tears for the sign that humans receive from the sun, from its rising and its setting.

"*Salimata, Saa-lii-mata*," Malika sang, smiling radiantly. "I just remembered the song that made my days as a small girl."

"You're still thinking about that guy. I almost fought him." She paused, her eyes following the retreating sun. She raised her middle finger as her grandmother would when tasting her soup.

"I must direct my sails," she whispered and the radiance returned to her face.

Babacar stood up to pack up the clothes, soap and other items they had brought to the beach. Malika sped off. In a flicker, she was at the table of the women selling *mad*.

Babacar could hear her laughter echoing through the wind. A vulture flew across and landed where Malika had been sitting. When the women roared in laughter, it stretched its wings and flew to settle in a nearby tree. Babacar could not tell why Malika was laughing so loudly. Perhaps it was finding other women to chat with; perhaps sucking the seeds of mad; perhaps because of the beauty of the setting sun over water; or perhaps the beach at evening reminded her of boat cruises she had taken with Issa. He hated thinking of Issa.

"I'm in charge now," he said again and again. He was not gifted with a deep male voice, but he attempted to make it sound imposing. Malika looked at him, picked another fruit of mad and ran back to him. They fixed each other with their eyes.

Malika offered Babacar the fruit. She put her small finger into the coat of the mad and pulled up a seed, laying it delicately on her tongue. The water was raging turbulently. She looked at Babacar who was licking his seeds noisily and even eating the outer layers.

"Hmm, sweet, juicy," he said.

"Mama will kill me today," she said, getting up to leave. She lifted the bucket up on her head. Babacar objected, took it from her and carried it instead. A strong, breezy wind tossed Malika's apron round. She picked up whatever was left to be carried and ran after Babacar whose mind, at this time, was occupied with thoughts of the vulture.

6

Vultures don't perch for nothing. Vultures and omens have been linked in the fables of Segol since the earliest times. And each tale, dreadful or delightful, ends with a stroke of good fortune or just the reverse. Babacar mused over this, but could not realise how close his own fortune lay. He swore that he'd rather die than see something bad happen to Malika. His feelings for her had become those of a lover. The springs of his heart flowed into hers. This was not an obsession and it faded when Malika was out of sight, but once she was visible, it ran briskly, vigorously. Babacar enjoyed the emotional flowering within him. It gladdened his heart. Going to the market was the only reason Malika was ever out of his sight for long.

He drifted after her. In the morning, he sat by the flower pot, a little way from where she passed while leaving for the market. At twilight, he sat at the kitchen stool and watched her preparing dinner. He had seen her a million times, but that meant nothing. Every time was like the first. She made him feel unique. He hunted for news on the Congo. Although listening to news was not a habit of his, he did it to please her and to appear to care.

Relating the latest news from the Congo provided an opportunity to be alone with her and hook into her emotions. The frequency of their proximity weakened her. The news no longer had the same place in her life as before. Something must be burning. If Angola had not sent troops to support Pepe Goodie, Zimbabwe would sustain his enemies; if South Africa had not sent weapons and cash, Pepe Goodie would accuse Rwanda and America of having a hand in the rebellion. Babacar commented on a war he would never fight in. It surprised him how busy the world powers were in the Congo. "Did they forget their snuff-bottle there that they keep going back to the Congo?" he joked.

Collecting forage was another opportunity for Babacar to be alone with his sister-in-law. She liked to feed the sheep. He could not say why, she simply did. Whenever the sheep bleated plaintively, Babacar and Malika went out with ropes and cutlasses to hunt for forage. Babacar would not let her do the foraging alone, however. She listened to him as if there was nowhere else she would rather be.

On one trip toward the end of October, she complained about the cost of recharging her phone card, so Babacar stopped by a shop to buy her one. His trouser pockets were full and it never crossed his mind that the money he gave her was almost falling – just the way one would fall when soaring. His turn came to make his purchase and he stepped forward. An old man was behind him in the queue. A discussion was being held in Malinke, a language rarely spoken in Djembe. None of the men seemed in a hurry. It was a ghostly topic. Mansu, who still owed Salif the equivalent value of a horse, tapped Babacar on the shoulder and drew his attention to the coins slipping from his pockets. Mansu, who led the conversation, his smoking pipe resting in his hand, was talking about the rebel forces in North Kivu that fought not only with the force of guns, but with black magic, *mai-mai*. He whispered, as if he did not want the mai-mai to hear him speaking.

Mansu was yet to finish when another man, leaning on the doorframe, smoking what seemed at first to be a stick of Marlboro, cut in suddenly. He clarified that the deity was placed at the centre of the Basin Forest: a giant wooden bottle holding water in a large, black cavity, bearing a snake slithering up to its cap. The bottle was adorned with ornaments and jewels and any woman who saw it would be blinded.

Mansu took it up again, his smoking pipe now in his hand. He demonstrated how, before marching into battle, the priests of the deity anoint the rebels with protective liquid nostrums, give them water to drink, spray them with water mixed with powder made from human ashes, tie red and white bands and you know what – things sacrificed to the idol – to their arms. The rebels danced the "dance of followers" until they would fall into trance, a mystical dance. The rebels attributed their victory to it. If they pushed off the rag-tag Congolese army, it was the power of mai-mai. If they captured a new village, mai-mai, if they fended off peacekeepers, mai-mai, if they sieged a city, prompted the flight of refugees, or massacres, it was always thanks to the mai-mai.

Babacar ran out of the shop his hands on his head, frightened by what evil could lurk in the hearts of men. Malika was waiting for him.

"What is wrong?" she asked.

He told her the story about the mai-mai.

"Nonsense!" said Malika, with certainty. "They use modern weaponry. I see it on TV all the time."

"Maybe, but they believe modern weaponry is enhanced by mai-mai, that's the thing." He put his hands around Malika's neck, his eyes on her pert breasts.

"Listen to me," she said. She told him of what had filtered into her ears when she went to plait Kristen's hair. Kristen's landlord, Modou, and his three visitors had been arguing about the Congo war and its link with cannibalism. That day, they reported the rebels had cut up the body of a slain pygmy, dug out his heart and eaten it, to possess its strength. It was a witchcraft ritual.

The rebels ate the vital organs of the pygmy to obtain supernatural strength in battle. "It is the ritual of simbas," Modou had insisted before his visitors, "that is, the ritual of lions, *simba* meaning 'lion' in Swahili," he had explained. Modou believed that it was the hottest news out of Africa that day. He was ready to bet that African wars were not only military struggles, but mystical warfare too.

Babacar asked her to sit down. He collected the forage, bundled it up and carried it. They did not talk on their way home. Approaching the house, the sheep heard their footsteps and began to bleat uncontrollably. Babacar dropped the forage, served each sheep a portion for the night and stored the rest in the conservation bank. Meanwhile, Malika picked up the water basin, washed it and refilled it.

Later that same week, they lay together out on the terrace to look at the lights across Independence Park. Babacar put his leg over Malika's and held her face in his cold, damp hands. He smelled of mouthwash and perfume. He was on the verge of kissing her face.

"Do you think Issa will ever return?" he said, suddenly. "Last time at the beach, a vulture came and sat down where you had been sitting."

"I reject that witch."

"It doesn't matter, I'm here."

"I like you by my side, but I still love Issa. He and I are still married."

"Oh...Oh, dear. Don't you believe in fate?"

She stared out into the dark. "I'm just sure of one thing: we're still married."

"Yes. Yes. But what happens if he doesn't come back, when and how we'll live, what comes about, the changes, that's fate. Right?"

"That's your brain," she said, stroking the tip of his ear.

They remained quiet, watching the lights and the followers of Serigne Douta singing under the Baobab tree.

Babacar spoke again, "If Issa had not been transferred to the 4th Battalion, if Commandant Thiam had not been named the Artillery Commander, the chances are that he wouldn't have been sent to the Congo. His transfer there led to his fate."

"You mean his paths through life were mapped out? That anything other than, well, what have not been planned – things like random events, as you said, make no sense?"

"Exactly."

She stretched her feet out and sighed.

"Belief in fate and circumstances," she said. "It has killed more people than the warlords of Chad and Liberia combined, and it has now ruined the chances of a happy life for the rest of us."

"Listen to me," he said.

"What should I listen to?"

"There is something like fate, something like a ruling principle."

Malika held his ear again, looked into it and shouted, "Your ear canal's so dirty! It smells like a rotten orange!" She got up, ran into the house and came out with a damp, soapy washcloth. She asked him to sit. Kneeling, she bent over his ear and began to clean the outer portion. She worked so quickly, he became worried about his eardrum. However she assured him she was mindful of it. She recited an adage her mother had taught her, "Put nothing in your ear smaller than your elbow."

Babacar felt like she had poured him a Scotch. "Continue," he said. He wanted it to last. And it went on; he closed his eyes, entranced, luxuriating in the pleasure that came with it. "Huu, you're wonderful," he said. He bent his head at every turn upon her request and his imagination was boundless. He wished that dawn would never return.

Malika went over the area she'd cleaned with another side of the cloth, pushing the cloth to the perimeter of the ear canal, removing the earwax gently and resting her hand along his hairline, and he sat there, taking great pleasure in it. He could not believe her hands were so soft.

Soon his neck and upper arm were covered with goose bumps. She noticed them along the little lines where she had scratched his neck with her nails.

"Tell me," she said. "Is it your fate that I am doing this? That the songs of Serigne Douta resonate in the air while I do it, that it be a Friday night that I...?"

"Exactly."

"Hoopla!" she cried, smiling. "Chance happening."

"Chance what? Not at all. We have no real choice as to what happens in this life. Neither of the past, nor of the future."

"I thought at first that you were so proper, with your tidy haircut and everything. And... how appearances deceive us humans, you know. I always admired how you looked. I admired you. And... I'm beginning to find you more attractive. You're no longer that innocent, natural Smallie. You call me Maa-lii. And I like it when you call do. Life is a gift. A joy despite pain, but I am not convinced there is such a thing as fate."

"There is, Maa-lii," he said. "You said it yourself."

"Said what? I make choices and decisions."

"Mm hmm," Babacar turned his head pointing his left ear toward her. "Everything that happens to us connects to the past: where and how we are born, the name we are called, the environment, the activities... If you look back in time, the forces are the same."

This bemused her. She changed the position of her knee slightly. "Please talk like a university student."

"That's what I'm doing. No fate is no date. Yet we live by dates, and, you'd say, expire by dates also. Maybe it's the way I say it. Maybe discussions like this don't go well with a local drink."

"I'm glad, you know. I'm only afraid that soon you may be seeing animals in the stars, and Serigne Douta in a piece of bread."

Babacar laughed and looked at her with tenderness. "You're funny, Maa-lii, funnier than Fara Jial Jial."

"Nooo. Fara Jial Jial is indomitable." A moment later, she added, "The tip of your ear is clogged with dirt, so I need to get a fresh swab."

"No."

"Why no?"

"Just use what you have rather than going into the house again." He said this not because he didn't want to inconvenience her, but because he did not want her hands to leave his head.

"One moment," she said as she hopped down into the bathroom at the House of Dudu. Babacar stretched his legs, put his Jamaica-style wrist trinkets back on, then lay straightened out on the mat, looking out through the vast vacuum into the dark clouds. The singing in the background built up. A dog sent a three-note protest into the chilly air.

In the bathroom, Malika cut a piece of cotton swab and then walked through the passage to the kitchen. "He may like some local juice to drink," she said to herself.

"Never at night. You've forgotten?" Babacar objected when she offered him the drink.

"I drink juice all the time, day or night."

She began again administering to his ear, holding a cup of juice in her right hand and cotton swab in her left. "Now begins the most delicate part."

"You don't want to share your juice with me?" he asked.

"Thought you said juice is your night-time demon, Smallie."

She held out her cup for him to sip from. He drank only half, so she shrugged. "Get away," she said pushing his arm back. Babacar's teeth knocked at the rim of the cup.

"You want the butter and the money for the butter."

"It's special when you serve it."

"Come on, juice is juice."

He looked at her sipping the juice. "You know, Maa-lii, it tastes special when you mix it."

"Leave me out of it," she said. "Hmm, everything about me is special, according to you."

She dropped her cup, and pulled her leg across him, reaching for his right ear. He closed his eyes, and threw his head backward. He could never have imagined they could spend this much time together without Fatimata yelling out for Malika. His heart was thudding against her the touch of her fingers. He was in ecstasy. He suddenly experienced a kind of chilling sensation that he was on a road at the end of which lurked an explosion – there was something ominous about his emotions. He could not tell if it was something that came on its own or if he was being manipulated by a marabout. He did not believe he had done wrong. After all he had only been helpful and supportive to Issa, Malika, their parents, their relatives, the extended family, to everyone who cared about news from the Congo. He gasped and stared at her with his mouth open, as if he was dissolving before her eyes.

She held open his ear, in an upward position, and gently inserted a cotton swab. He shifted into her laps, where her wrapper lay folded in. His back touched a vein on her calves that he loved to tease her about and, turning to see it, his head brushed against her breasts. They burst into laughter. He rubbed his finger over the vein, saying it was an earthworm's line and she laughed.

"You're funny," Malika added, rolling the cotton swab slowly. Babacar read somewhere that women look out for various things in men; that their attraction tends to be far more nuanced; that they're affected by men's olfactory cues, by the personality of their partner, especially his sense of humor and confidence; his social status; what other women think of him, as well as many other factors, in addition to the visual cues – men's faces, bodies and voices.

He asked her if it was true.

"Smart. I love that, very good. You missed your calling. You should have majored in psychology, think so?"

None of them spoke again, none made a sound. The only sound was her hand moving against his ear.

"Maa-lii."

"Y-e-e-s," she answered gracefully, cautiously moving the cotton to a spot in his ear that produced a particularly fizzy sensation. "Sweet, oh, so sweet. Sweet thing."

"Be quiet," she said sharply. Babacar felt his back being scratched as she moved to blow something off his neck. He sensed the thrill. "I'm done."

"Oh, let's continue, dear. Let it continue," he appealed into the void of her laps.

"I'm tired," she said. "Go have a shower."

He wanted to get under her wrapper. After delaying, he reluctantly got up and moved in the direction of the bathroom. While showering, his mind wandered to her hands around her neck, his head leaning on her laps, his back fingers stroking her vein. The sensation seized him, and he hummed aloud. Anyone could hear him and tell that he was happy.

Malika went to fetch a bottleful of juice for both of them. She thought filling the cups and stirring the local juice with a long spoon and showing him how it worked at night without causing a stomach-ache would provide an enjoyable distraction. He had never believed it was possible to drink local juice at night and still sleep comfortably. "Juice," she smiled. "Natural juice."

Now, drying off on the mat, Babacar saw mental pictures of Issa and of Issa's letter – unwanted reminders. He brushed them off, just as he was rubbing himself with the towel. He put on his traditional trousers and went back to be with Malika. They sat there, enchanted by the serenity of the cool night breeze sweeping through them as they sipped the purple juice.

Malika finished hers in one gulp and perched on his knee. "Good night," she kissed him on the cheek.

"Good what?" he exclaimed. "You want to leave me?"

She heard her name, as he kissed her, and unclasped her suddenly. He held her by the arms.

"Don't answer."

"I should."

They waited. The voice rang again, fading. Finally she detached herself from him and ran off to see who it was. It would be unfair to turn a deaf ear to a call from the household. It was Ami Colle, calling to tell her she was about to lock the door.

"Oh, Ami Colle," Malika said.

"You're not coming to bed tonight?" she asked. "You must be deaf. I have been yelling and yelling. My voice is almost quenched."

"I was with Babacar, helping him unblock his ear."

"Did something fall into it?"

"Yes."

Ami Colle took a deep breath. "Malika, what is it?"

"A piece of match fell into it," she lied.

Ami Colle slowly breathed in and out. "I'm locking the door now. You'll open with your key."

"I'm ready to come to bed; I'm done with Babacar."

"No, help him."

"Is he my husband?" Malika laughed.

"Who knows?"

"Hmm, Ami, you too..."

Ami Colle closed the door behind her and switched off the florescent light. Since the government had announced an eight percent increase in the price of electricity, she had been meticulous about turning off the lights.

"Oh," Babacar said when she returned to kiss him good night. "We've got the whole night."

"Babacar in wonderland, it's quarter to midnight."

"Does it matter?"

Malika rolled up the mat. She moved down into the kitchen, to the sink, where she washed the cups. The moonlight peered in through the wooden window, casting a white light on the room. A quiet presence enfolded her and she paused at the thought. She had only stayed out for so long with Issa, alone in his arms, her hair draped across his chest. At these thoughts, tears streaked down her face.

Babacar slipped out later to get drunk. But before he went out, he stood by the tool shed and watched her retiring from there. He went to some stores on Morocco Avenue, where he felt like he was a boy of eleven again. He bought her four pairs of pants, two pairs of dress socks, three shirts and a red petticoat. It was as though he had a new wife. It was the first time he understood the number of times they had had together. Ninety-nine. He hoped the next time would make it a hundred.

He never thought about the fact that Issa had not been declared dead. He believed there'd be time. But it all went so quickly. The night he came to her with all the questions and thoughts he'd been saving up, her anxiety rose to the roof such that she wished he could take her to a dinner. He taught her the poem by Mr William Wordsworth that he had learned at school and she said, head pressed into her pillow, that it was unbearably beautiful. She knew that she was sick from something, and in bed, but she thought she was young and in bed with flu. And she asked him on one of those days if he could make sure her shoes were dry, because she'd washed them the night before. He took them into the shed, and when they were dry, he brought them to show her.

At this point, Babacar closed his eyes. "You know, I said everything I wanted to say to her and she appreciated it. But I never cooked for her while she was in bed. That will make her agree to marry me." Outside the gate, he declared, "I'm like Ousseynou, the wrestler," and smiled stupidly. "She's so adorable."

He entered his room. It was a standard school room, a sunken space decorated with a nice wooden armchair and couch that must have come from Salif's early life. He passed out in his clothes for an hour or two. Then he slept with them off. At around four in the morning, he woke up sweating and startled from a nightmare. Malika wasn't in this one, however. In his dream, Ousseynou was thrown by Diatta and Ousseynou was sorting through his charms and he was showing his marabout to journalists. He asked them each, "Have you seen the man who fights against the gods?" It took some effort to determine that Salif was snoring in his bed a block away, and his relief at this understanding was so overwhelming that he wept. The next morning, Babacar was curious to awake and find himself in the parlour and not in his room. He heard car horns and a loud speaker announcing the arrival of Ousseynou's fans in the city. He felt tired still, but in a different way to the usual fatigue in the morning, as though he'd been drugged.

He noticed then what was missing from the fight. The drumming. He stumbled over to the clock on the drum in the parlour. Twenty-four minutes to eleven.

7

Wrestling Day. The atmosphere was festive, the streets heaved with traffic, the media spun with the ceaseless refrain: "Ousseynou versus Diatta, the fight of the millennium." The radio stations aired predictions about the new king of the ring. Was it to be Ousseynou, the lion of Djembe, or Diatta, the dragon of Lokuta? A famous griot sang that traditional wrestling had been practised since time immemorial in Segol and had been admired by the first Europeans; that it was the national sport, a symbol of the enduring past; that it upheld the belief that men ought to be strong, not shaky; and that the first name a child learned was that of a wrestler and not of a king.

Every mouth sang the names of Ousseynou and Diatta, every neck wagged at the sum of money they both would scoop. Each wrestler's fans trooped from the far reaches of the countryside to the national stadium and crowds swarmed before the television screens at outside restaurants.

Babacar was a fan of Ousseynou. "Would you like to go with me?" he asked Malika. "It will help you take your mind off the troubles."

Malika could not resist. She had said she that had she been a man, she would have been a wrestler. She knew all the tactics on how to fall an opponent. "Mama said I can go with you," she said.

They hurried over a lunch of rice mixed in peanut puree and served with fish, and rushed to the bus stop at Azikiwe Street. A commuter bus pointed its nose towards them. They waved it down, hopped into the already crammed bus and were driven to the stadium. Winding through the hordes of fans, they squeezed through to the local stands to where Madiagne, Djembe's most famous living griot, amid drumming and screeches, was singing. He danced and directed the crowd to chorus "Yeah" at the end of each line:

"If the harvest is good,
yeah!
Young men measure their strength,
yeah!
And young women watch to see,
yeah!
Who they want to marry,
yeaaaaaah!"

Ousseynou entered the ring gilded with amulets, gems and cowry shells and danced along the VIP stand. Before long, Diatta, in a loincloth, was brought in on a platform carried by four men amidst clapping and shouting. He jumped down and danced cheerfully toward the wrestling ring, his steps gyrating to the drumbeat, drumbeat after drumbeat, the noise of his fans shouting to the steps of his dance covering every sound in a staccato. Overlooking it was a fight. Madiagne's troop beat the rhythms of heroism and valour in praise of the wrestlers, waving their handkerchiefs. The wrestlers wore only a loincloth around their waists.

There was a pause for effect.

Diatta took a drum and placed it in the middle of the ring. Ousseynou, biting the bone of a goat, a magic charm, leaped toward the drum and overturned it. Both pawed at each other in charged aggression. Silence enfolded the arena as the wrestlers gripped each other's shoulders, at the first attempt. Dust rose and their lips trembled. Diatta tried to unsettle Ousseynou's balance, but failed. The crowds replied with a deafening roar. Reporters and cameras followed the wrestlers every step and outside the ring, marabouts intensified the concoctions they were brewing for their clients.

In a swift, intense move, Ousseynou gripped Diatta's thigh, pulled it up, served a fatal nose-punch, and a *sukubi*, a sudden kick from the outside left foot. Diatta lost his balance and staggered to regain it. Blindfolded, he rotated twice, struggling to regain his balance. Ousseynou delivered another well-measured punch to Diatta's forehead. Diatta fell face forward, eating a bite of sand. "Weeeeeeh!" the spectators screamed.

The umpire ran to the wrestlers and raised Ousseynou's hand to stamp his victory. His fans leapt for joy, and poured into the ring, clad in colours of fire and earth, knocking over security barriers in their hustle to greet Ousseynou, the new king of the ring. Babacar jumped up, dancing in the same manner as Ousseynou. Just then his cell phone rang. The screen indicated it was Ami Colle calling. He was unable to make out her voice due to the clamour. "Your father…" was all Babacar heard and the line went dead.

"Who's that?" Malika asked.

"The old man," he answered.

"Something wrong?"

"He's calling me."

"I'm staying on here," said Malika, dancing to the music, her shoulders hunched down, her breasts bouncing up and down.

"Be careful," Babacar said. He fought his way through the ecstatic fans blocking every bit of space towards the stadium gate. At last, he reached the exit where several taxis lay waiting. He approached the first driver in the queue and negotiated with him until they agreed on a fare. Getting out of the spot was a headache. They endured the worst traffic jam out of Central Terminal, from Djembe's widest thoroughfare, to the opening on the eastern side of the Trade Fair Centre. Even with the construction of flyovers on the city's main routes, there was wrestling traffic congestion and crowds trooping out from every corner. In between the hold-ups, the driver admired the "Ousseynou, Lion of the Ring" T-shirt Babacar was wearing. Babacar's cell phone rang again.

"Papa," he said, before Salif could speak, "I'm on my way."

Babacar pulled out some money from his pocket and gave them to the driver. He watched the taxi driver searching cautiously, earnestly, for change. His friendly conversation with the taxi driver soon twisted into a row. "You should have told me you were holding a boss's note before entering," brawled the driver. They lurched from one trader to another searching, arguing as they did. The driver had just what was needed for Babacar's change, but would not hand it over. "I work with my coins, I work with my coins," he repeated.

Salif rang Babacar again. In the frenzy, Babacar opened the car door, jumped out and slammed it. He handed a note to the driver with an injunction to bring his change to the house later. The taxi driver nodded with a humming noise. Babacar dove into their compound and ran to the backyard from where Salif's voice rose and fell like Madiagne's talking drum.

"Papa," Babacar said.

"So you've brought back your putrefying self?" Salif was ticked off. "Your brother's life is in danger and you have time to go watch people serving punches to each other."

"Put on the TV," he ordered, handing the remote control to Babacar. "France 24," he said in a grave voice. Babacar wondered why he was interested in France 24 when everybody else was watching the fight on the local station. "Yes, sit down and watch," he added, looking skywards, closing his eyes. Fatimata, Ami Colle and Dieynaba were watching as Babacar sat down. Salif has made it a tradition to have Babacar watch reports of the war in the Congo by his side. The women quickly dragged their stools forward to join them.

Babacar's mind still resonated with Ousseynou's dance, he increased the volume with the remote control at Salif's command, his hands shaking slightly. He took a deep breath, lifted his eyes at the screen.

The shootings.

Rebels, gun carriers, destroyers marshalled all along the horizon in Goma, under siege. How many rebels were there? One thousand, two thousand, three thousand maybe, stretching out for miles; dark clouds gathered over the refugee camps; blood smears on the walls; large pools of blood on the floor; rebels lying beside the artillery, with mortar as a pillow, a machine gun as a mattress; the jarring, discordant gun shots; the remains of children littered the fields, denied of burial; the rains of September, that keep the mangroves green falling on them, washing off their skins like an oblation.

"The war will be long," a deep voice said as the reporter's camera turned to scan a collection of human skulls.

"Oh, Issa!" Ami Colle shouted at that last image, struggling with her fleeing scarf. "May Allah protect him," she said raising her hands toward the ashy skies. She looked straight at Salif in that typical way of hers. Salif stood up suddenly, shook himself, and walked up and down, grumbling, "Why can't the white people stop those rebels? What's the point of the European Union? Does Belgium exist only on paper?" He stopped to tighten the drawstring of his trousers, snapped his index and third finger together twice and pulled out his prayer beads from his caftan.

"It will be alright Papa," Ami Colle said looking at him, trying to take his hand.

"Stop that nonsense!" Salif rebuffed. "It will be alright in the grave."

"I mean it. I do," she mumbled, confused. Salif ignored her and she withdrew.

"Has the UN become a cloth-weavers' association?" Salif shrugged, "tepid, influenced, toothless. Trouble in any land profits the chiefs... those killing machines cannot be masquerading in the Congo. Great Allah, the big Congo, without drummers hiding in the bush... pshuuuu." He sighed in disapproval, exposing all the septuagenarian wrinkles on his face.

The imam's voice ascended and Salif spread his mat to pray. "Peace to all," he said. He then dropped his prayer beads and asked Fatimata to bring him a bitter cola. Salif took to his head-of-the-family seat. When Fatimata brought the bitter cola, he scrubbed off the outer tanned cover with his fingers, put it on the side plate on the stool close by, and pushed the peeled cover neatly aside. Ami Colle herself couldn't help staring. Everybody was staring, even Dieynaba from the other side of Fatimata's seat, as if Salif was performing a ritual. Only Ami Colle hastened to bring the washing bowl over to him and to hold the dangling sleeves of his caftan so he could wash his hands.

"Issa is a soldier, so he's prepared for the bullets," Babacar chipped in softly, turning down the volume of the TV. Salif pushed a stool aside and engaged him strangely.

"You're wicked," said Salif. "What on earth prevented you from replying to your brother's two-year-old letter? You're not of my blood! You're the descendant of a vulture!"

Since he had returned from the Traditional Cloth Weavers' Union, Salif's curses all ended with "of a vulture". He took on sayings of this sort when something affected him deeply. When he saw *Zambula* at the National Theatre, he sang that the fall of a dancer is a vulture's somersault. Then when his tooth fell out while eating

Mansu's coconut, he buzzed that a man should eat coconut while he has teeth, lest his lost tooth be carried away by a vulture.

So Babacar bent his head, waiting for his father to decide on how to reach Issa. Babacar waited for Salif to accuse him of selfishness, of having a dog's love, of living a chameleon's life and now that he waited, Salif had accused him of carrying a vulture's gene.

Fatimata saw the chagrin on Babacar's face, but signaled that he say not even a scrap of word. Salif was not the sort to be challenged. If Babacar stood up to him, the situation would worsen. So Babacar simply remained stock-still. He was clueless as to whether to return to the local channel or to stay with France 24. He held the remote control in his sweating hands and his mind roved back to the letter his father had mentioned. "Never mind that Issa did not address that letter to me. Never mind that he did not mention my name, nor ever send me a pinch of his peacekeeping dollars," he thought.

Salif's head began to ache. He leaned on Fatimata, picked up his bitter cola and threw the rugby ball-shaped seed into the bowl of his mouth. As he chewed it, it made a crackling noise. He chewed the cola until a quarter of it was ground to a powder in his mouth. He used it as cure for hypertension. As a fan of traditional medicine, he never took modern drugs. Instead, he chewed bitter cola when he had a cough or sore throat, drank hot liquid from the leaves of lemon grass to relieve stomach-ache, ate rice with sauce made from bitter leaves to fight malaria and sniffed the leaves of *asofeyeje* to regulate diabetes.

His father, Hadji, a herbalist, was even more devoted to traditional medicine. "It's a secret from our ancestors," Salif said often, quoting Hadji. But he would never comment on the side effects of modern medicine on herbal concoctions, like the convulsions that struck Khadim, Mansu's son, after his impotence was treated with *imbiza*.

Salif swallowed every particle of the bitter cola, except a morsel that lingered on the prominent mole above his lip. He kept chewing. There wasn't the slightest chance that he would not finish it. Just a crumb lingered along a stretch of white foam around his mouth. They all looked on as he chewed. There was only the sound of him swallowing cola, adding to noise from the fans of Ousseynou in the neighborhoods.

Babacar drew nearer to his father's hand and, while keeping a distance, rendered the remote control. Salif snatched it back as if Babacar was returning stolen property. In an attempt to steer clear of further quarrels, Babacar veered from the backyard to the bedroom. He attributed his father's behaviour to his age.

Babacar praised himself. He had burnt night candles to gain admission into the university. When lecturers went on strike, he took to fishing as a kind of lecture, the lecture of life. Fishing involved ritual gestures, the twisting and picking and hoping, each set of the rod an attempt to realize a dream, to see his reflection in the surface of the sea, and wish a fish would come. They were rewarding efforts, satisfied in a minute or in hours, answered with the arrival of a fish or a shrimp. He saw a river, made of water and time, then saw another.

"Now let's see. Let him reply to me if he's still alive." He picked a pen and a sheet of paper and wrote:

Hey Issa,

Just an SOS to request that you send me a chunk of your peacekeeping dollars. I need the money to buy the latest in cell phone technology. All my friends are going high-tech. I don't want to be left behind. I'm sorry about the war. Malika is in good hands.

Babacar

He giggled at his allusion to Malika. He was happy to have gotten straight to the point. In his letter, he was neither striving for literary culture, nor searching for inspiration from Victor Hugo. He folded the letter into his pocket and set off to buy an envelope. Ameth's shop was closed, as he too had gone to the wrestling. At another shop on the corner, he was lucky to find a Fulani apprentice. The lad spoke neither French nor Wolof, the local language, so Babacar used gestures. After several guesses, the boy touched an envelope and Babacar indicated his agreement.

Babacar took the envelope, slid the letter into it, sealed it with saliva and continued on to Commandant Thiam's house. There something unusual: there was no guard at the entry. Thiam's gate was not even locked. Babacar rang the doorbell, waited, rang again, waited, and in the absence of response, tiptoed in. Commandant Thiam was lounging in a sofa in his parlour, copies of the *International Herald Tribune* folded on his laps, a drink in his hand, his eyes glued to a flat-screen TV. He was watching Ousseynou's triumphal acrobatics and displays, to the two-two-three rhythm of the drums.

Babacar greeted him, "Peace be with you, Sir."

Commandant Thiam replied, "And also–" the rest of the phrase was trapped under his tongue as Ousseynou delivered a triple acrobatic galore.

Babacar said, "Letter for Sergeant Issa. Goma Base."

"From?" he asked in a high-pitched voice.

"From his family, Sir."

"Okay. Drop it there," Commandant Thiam said distractedly, pointing at the centre table, his eyes on the TV. Commandant Thiam knew the letter would not move any further than there.

"Thank you, Sir!" Babacar greeted and slipped out.

Several hours after he left Commandant Thiam's house, Babacar ran into a group of four men in animated discussion about the day's wrestling, their dream profession.

The tallest of them was the first to address Babacar. "Wow man! Did you see that fight?"

"Ousseynou is a hammer. Think of how he contrived Diatta as if he was going to strike; Diatta dodged him, slightly lifting his feet; Ousseynou grabbed the flying feet, pinched his nose, shook the other foot, another punch and Diatta was finished," Babacar demonstrated.

"It's a mental thing. Ousseynou won psychologically before he won physically," the shortest said.

"Right. Ousseynou watched Diatta and sized him up. He detected his weaknesses. Diatta was good at hurling blows, but bad at technique. But why weren't you at the stadium?" the tallest asked Babacar.

"He's afraid of all the mystical conjurers," the fattest said.

"That reminds me," the shortest said, addressing Babacar. "Does the victory go to the strongest wrestler or to the one with the deadliest marabout?"

"Magic charms are part of it, for sure."

"But how?"

"Each wrestler sees a marabout for several months of mystical bathing. They enter the fight swathed in talismans, as you can see. The marabouts follow their clients even to the ring. Didn't you see a squad of marabouts behind each wrestler, manipulating amulets in favour of their client? Some recite verses, some work with plants, some mark the grasses with chalk, others hold onto bones or keep threads in their teeth."

"At what cost?" asked the thinnest.

"Ask the marabouts! But top wrestlers pay for powerful magic, meaning the marabouts receive a lion share of the wrestler's cash."

"Who did Ousseynou marry?" asked the shortest.

"I didn't listen to his interview. I left the stadium right after Ousseynou threw Diatta. And he already has four wives. His fourth wife is tallish and supple. She was dancing with the fans' club. When her husband won, she ran into the ring, removed her outer wrapper and threw it around her husband's neck."

"So you were watching her?" asked the tallest.

"I was," said Babacar. "Weren't you?"

"Watch out. Beware of your nose," said the fattest.

"At some point, I was even attracted by her breasts," Babacar said.

"Thieee!" yelled the thinnest.

Babacar laughed excitedly. "I only said I was watching."

"Were they big?" asked the shortest.

"Ah, man, I went to watch the wrestling, not the breasts of Ousseynou's wife," Babacar answered. "But they were bumped up, you know."

A busload of Ousseynou supporters passed them, singing, clapping, blowing whistles and waving an American flag.

"Why was Ousseynou dressed in the colours of the American flag?" the shortest asked.

"He trains in America," answered the fattest.

They trekked along the North Boardwalk, leading to the Fire Service. Babacar and the tallest followed from behind, talking about brandishing an American flag in Segolian wrestling.

"You think Ousseynou won by magic?" the tallest asked.

"He won, that's all," Babacar said. "In Segol, a wrestler's strength is measured by the strength of his marabout. Again–"

"But when will our wrestling become a real fight?" the tallest interrupted.

Babacar was about to answer when an old woman passing by stopped, facing them. She was bent and over a walking stick and the wind ruffled her clothes. She gripped them tightly, coughed and gesticulating with her head asked, "Did you see a boy wearing a cap?"

"No, I didn't."

"Nor did I."

The shortest and the tallest wagged their fingers to say the same.

"Are you dumb?" the old woman asked Babacar.

"What is wrong, old woman?" he said.

"Did you see a boy?" she repeated. Babacar raised his face to the skies as a response. "Who are your parents?" the old woman asked.

"Why do you ask?" The rest began to laugh, leaving Babacar behind with her. The old woman shook her head and spat. Babacar chuckled.

"You're from Kappa?" she asked.

"I'm Segolian."

"You behave like a cow. Let your mother know."

8

Toward the end of the serialized TV drama, *Marina*, while Babacar was in a fit of anger about the taxi driver not bringing him his change, Malika came in through the door. She arrived just as an advertisement for Maggi was being broadcast. Her cloth and body had the same colour as the Maggi stew: her hair was covered in red dust; her face wrapped with fatigue; her white blouse tainted with brown spots; her feet plastered with mud; her hands soiled with sweat; her armpits moist; her sandals torn; and her makeup worn.

The word *Angel* printed on her blouse read *Ange*, as the *L* had been torn off in the after-match stampede. The door hinges squeaked and there she stood, returning from what was yet her longest leisure time out. She crawled in not like a tortoise, but in an unusually quiet manner, which beckoned the surprise of her in-laws.

If there were any signs of excitement that she had gone to the wrestling, they were no longer evident. Though shabby, her makeup of red and purple stripes was still noticeable. Seen through the silhouette of the slanting door, her eyes sparkled in her face. She put a hand on her breast to adjust her bra, and then proceeded to where Salif was reclining against a cushion. She cleared her throat, as if to seek his pardon for returning late and said gently, "Peace to you, Papa."

"And peace to you," Salif replied. "We thought you had followed Ousseynou home."

Dieynaba burst into laughter.

"No Papa. Coming back was a tug-of-war."

"Tug-of-war," Salif repeated. "You never heard the saying that after wrestling, spectators wrestle their way home?"

Malika began explaining how she had escaped Ousseynou's fans by diving into a commuter bus. She was demonstrating her escape when the evening news began. Right away the newscaster cast a spotlight on Goma.

"What?!" cried Malika, as she steered herself to a corner, eyes fixed on the screen as the correspondent's camera delivered the rebels' march towards Goma. The north and south wings of General Kpanpa's rebels had converged on a village outside Goma. Rebels searching for those who had fled the capital had moved through it and kept going. Endless files of them and caissons holding ammunition, commissary wagon trains, refugees and herds of goats. Children lay dead on the ground. Many people had died of hunger and disease. The streets were lined with trees through which rebel forces and wagons were making detours, while pioneers with two-man saws were felling the trees. Some men stripped off the branches and still others loaded trunks and limbs aboard carts being pulled by teams of six and eight men wearing masks. They looked unperturbed. It was a matter seemingly of only a few moments to crush the city. Malika was struck dumb a full twenty minutes, her shoulders stiffened and she blinked, over and over. She had made the resolution not to watch the evening news anymore, but this edition had caught her unawares. Her heartbeat grew faster as her thoughts roamed and her skin was covered with goose bumps. She clutched her chin anxiously. The rebels seemed to be celebrating the massacre.

When finally she spoke, her voice quivered "So where is God in all this?" She had spoken to Father Du Buit and given her tithe to the church so Issa might be recalled. She took hope in what Father

Du Buit had told her and had recited aloud her prayers, striving for an angelic tone, even as the rebels marched on.

Malika brought out her pocket Bible to pray after the news. She slowed down towards the end of the prayers. She halted at the line "Why do nations rage?" She lowered her head and tears flowed down her chin. She wept at what the war had done to her life, at the tragically absent obituaries for the dead children. Her cell phone fell from her hand and she reached for her handkerchief. She decided not to wait anymore for the reappearance of the rebel leader with the sullied manners and his strange name, Kpanpa. Not since she began with Issa had she known such emotional torment.

She looked to Babacar, but he was silent. Malika could have known all along that her husband might have died, he thought. "Is he there?" Malika asked. He did not answer, did not care to answer, but got up, took her by the hand and led her to the House of Dudu to take her bath and change her clothes.

Later, when Salif heard she would not eat any of the soaked millet that Ami Colle had prepared for dinner, he switched off the TV, strode over to the House of Dudu, beating his chest, "It's either you eat that food or I take you back to your parents!" Salif knew she has lost her appetite from grief, but was angry that Malika had not confided in him. He slammed the door and returned to his parlour, arms swinging like a marshal.

Malika sat on a stool and stretched her legs around the plate of millet. She pulled the cup of water closer to her, sloppy in her movements, and swallowed a few spoonfuls of the millet soaked in milk. She ate with her fingers. She tried three times, then stopped. Something was stuck in her throat. "Ghaaaagh!" she coughed, "Ghaaaaagh!" and she began to vomit.

"Malika," Ami Colle called, jumping over to her. Ami Colle plunged her hand into Malika's mouth. She bent Malika's neck backwards, steadied her, then while raising her neck, she thrust a second finger deeper into her throat and pulled out a bulb of saliva. Ami Colle was surprised as there was no fish in the millet. Malika nodded twice, her eyes glowing like a runaway protester. Her fingers trembled, her pulse surged and she coughed.

Perplexed, Ami Colle sat beside her. "Allah forbid it," she repeated, drawing a circle with her hands over Malika's head and pushing them in the wind. Malika licked her fingers, leaned her elbows on her knees and inclined her head.

"What is wrong with you?" Fatimata asked her, walking in from the parlour. "Are you the only woman whose husband has travelled afar? Are you the only wife whose spouse is there? No. You are not alone here. That war is a biting sore on us all, a deep cavity in everybody's teeth. We bear it as you do. We bear the sight of seeing that mass of cadavers; we also worry about the safety of our own there. And Issa wrote home and wrote to you. Console yourself with that. If you must lament, keep it within you."

Malika shut her eyes. She recalled Issa's last letter and what he had written about her. But her melancholic, obstinate silence seemed to retort: "He's a soldier and I'm not. It's all too easy to write a letter, but so difficult to bear." She did not voice her thoughts, however.

Ami Colle offered her a glass of water which she declined. So far she had played the good wife, but now it was enough. Anyone who so wished could call her a "bad woman", as far as she was concerned.

"Concentrate on his love, Malika, concentrate on his love. Let go of excessive worry. It will eat you up," advised Ami Colle said. Malika kept silent. "Do you hear me?" Ami Colle asked.

"I married Issa to live a normal family life with him, not to sit a thousand miles away waiting." She wiped tears from her eyes with the handkerchief. "I'd prefer it if he ran back home from the base."

"What?"

"If he came home."

Ami Colle turned to her. "I don't understand. To run away is a big offence. And he just got a promotion in rank: another stripe, a rare promotion."

Malika squirmed. "He's got a wife as well and needs a child to call him father."

Ami Colle fixed her eyes on her and then broke into nervous laughter. "You're a dead-pan comedian." Malika stamped her feet. "Want some drink? Hibiscus flavour?" she continued.

"Coke would be fine, thanks."

Ami Colle went to the refrigerator below the minibar, took out a bottle of Coke and handed it to Malika. It was cold. "I really think it's admirable, you going out to watch the wrestling."

"I don't think of it that way, really," Malika said, talking of her situation. "I was told I'd be here like this for one or two months. Now, I've completed two years, with no end in sight. This is too much suffering. I mean it. This is too much."

Ami Colle feared Salif would find fault with Malika for not confiding in him, so she returned to her task, crocheting a strip of wool. She worked the needle meticulously, her fingers nicking and furling. She paused to look at Malika. Then she sang, "I'm knitting a hat for Malika's baby – a perfect match for a bouncing baby boy."

Malika folded her arms and nodded, letting her know with a pointed stare just what those words had struck within. Malika believed that some day, in a way yet unknown, she would lift her child in the air and press him to her slightly fallen breasts. She sipped her Coke and slowly moved closer to Ami Colle. She pulled off her bracelet, allowing it skid along the ground as she scrutinized the baby's hat. A few centimetres before the tip, lay an opening in the knitting. What looked like a stain appeared on its head and its border was dirty. It revealed the flaws of a learner.

Ami Colle's finger was not spared: the plaster band at the head of the second finger was laced tightly around, showing where the razor she used in cutting the wool had nicked her. Malika sneezed and sneezed again. The breeze had suddenly become chilly. Pushing back to where she had been eating to retrieve her handkerchief, Ami Colle warned her, "Eat some more; then fast with us for Ramadan in a few days, if you like."

Though a Christian, Malika sometimes participated in Ramadan, with the rest of the family. "To accompany them," she liked to say. The thirty-day fast of Ramadan was Malika's poison. She had adjusted to the fasting schedule of her Muslim in-laws and had been worn down by hunger and thirst. She had conformed to the religious observances, facing the traffic jam after the market when people went to the mosque, their chaotic timetable and endless prayers. She noticed signs of the imminent fast when shepherds pitched their tents across the street, sleeping alongside their thick-haired white sheep. They sheltered under the tree, knees up, head flat, a red strip of cloth tied around their necks.

She was lost in thought when Salif emerged at the porch, his broad black chest puffed out and his head dangling in regret. He sighed. "Did you hear the reporter?" he asked.

"What?" Ami Colle said, setting her work suddenly down on the ground. Salif walked round the house and then stopped, shuffling one foot on the slab. He gently lifted one hand and placed it on his head. "Dig my grave beside my brother's and don't invite a griot," he said, his eyebrow split as wide as a chewing stick.

"Ah Papa, what sort of saying is that?" asked Ami Colle.

"Did you hear the radio?"

"Which radio?"

"Pepe Goodie of Co-co-co-congo is dead," he stammered. "The rebels killed a pea…keeper whose name sounds like Issa's," Salif spoke in a dialect, so that Malika would not understand.

"Fatimata! Fatimata!" Ami Colle screamed. Fatimata answered in a faint voice and came out.

"Did you hear what Papa is saying?"

Fatimata looked at Salif, observing the position in which he was bent. Having heard his earlier exclamations when the headlines were read, she suspected something was wrong, but strove to divert Malika's attention from it.

"Help me get things ready for the fast," Fatimata said to Malika, wanting to distract her, "lest we get into trouble." They gathered oil and tomatoes, onions and potatoes, goods that had become rare at the market since the approach of the Ramadan fast. They opened a bag of Thai rice, omnipresent in Segol's cooking pots, and served out portions in an energetic pour-and-carry manner. They turned then to the fruits, mangoes, bananas and pawpaws. They peeled them, chopped the flesh into tiny pieces and mixed them, adding orange juice to turn out a home-made fruit salad.

Salif remained immobile, refusing to heed Ami Colle's plea that he lie down. At last, he did so, stretching his legs across the passageway and resting his head on a half-filled bag of rice. He held his cell phone in one hand and the TV remote control in the other. "I can't reach Commandant Thiam," he groaned. "I tried his number and a foolish voice told me the number I was dialling was not correct."

"Where did you call from?" Ami said. "The western side of the compound gets no reception in the evenings." Salif squirmed and asked for a glass of water. Ami Colle brought him a bottle from which he drank from at once. When Ami tried to return the bottle to the kitchen, he scolded her, "Couldn't you have asked me if I wanted more?"

"I'm sorry Papa," she pleaded. He complained of a pain in the chest and disclosed, in a few sentences, the names of his debtors should anything grave happen to him that night.

Fatimata winked, and turned to see if Malika sensed what was going on. She told Malika how much she admired her smooth face, new hairstyle and artificial nails, though really she disliked them. Fatimata switched to stories of hearts – not directly, but openly. Of all topics, Fatimata never discussed premarital love adventures.

"Were other men interested in you before Issa?" she asked Malika.

"Of course. As usual."

"As usual? You seem very sure of yourself. I hear your generation of women do the proposing."

Malika fell over on a sofa laughing.

"Who and who was after you? Who were they?"

"They're too many to be listed," replied Malika.

"No white man by any chance?"

"By any chance?"

"Yes."

"Why?"

"Segol is not Fraace."

Malika giggled at the way Fatimata pronounced France.

"But they come here," Malika said.

"Old ones."

"Even young ones."

Malika nodded twice.

"But my father never wanted me to marry a white man."

"Why?"

"He was afraid I'd be gone forever. He ruled that a Segolian man was the best for me."

Although Ami Colle was attracted by the conversation, she refrained from joining in because of Salif. She had enough worries, foremost of which was what would happen to her and to Dieynaba should Salif die. She looked at him lying face-down on the mat. It was after ten in the evening. He had never before spoken of death. He simply sensed things. He had that gift.

Fatimata avoided Ami Colle, focusing instead on Malika. She held her hands and shared the story of the man who could have married her. The way Fatimata told the story, it hadn't been a special day in any way except that she, as a young girl, had accepted to meet with a man called Latir. She was coming back from the stream and was alone on the deserted road. She was uncomfortable, as the patch on her water pot had grown worn and had begun to leak, so she sweated from village to village, her shoulders wet with water. She thought about turning back, not because there was no flesh on Latir's bones, and not because he drank too much alcohol, but because there was not a drop of water at home and she was too late to put lunch on the fire.

"I thought about how unprepared I was for marriage," Fatimata said. "That was fifty-six years ago, even though I didn't know what being prepared would mean at the age of thirteen." The timing was wrong because she had a wonderful mother who would not allow her to get married at that age. She was just not ready to subdue herself to a husband and to relate to co-wives. She leaned in and whispered to Malika, "And when things go badly – and I assure you, my daughter, they do – I was not one to queue up at the marabout's to ask for a talisman in order to control my co-wives."

Fatimata continued her story. She didn't cancel her meeting with Latir. She tied her wrapper at chest-level and had not an ounce of fat on her arms. The path to the place where they would meet seemed longer than before, though it was the same old road, and soon, Fatimata arrived at their meeting point. She stopped under the shade of the trees, a line of trees that were once believed to house the spirits of twins. She looked at the trunks which were strange, as if a ghost had been living in them. "I was there before time and before Latir," Fatimata laughed.

"Then what happened?" Malika enquired, eager to know more.

Fatimata described how she put down her water pot after she arrived, dusted off the stump of a severed log and sat down, uncomfortably, trying to repair her leaking pot. She waited for him, anxious about what her parents would think of how long it was taking her to get home, longer than usual. The leaking pot was a good excuse and repairing it appeased her anxiety for about fifteen minutes. She later discovered that Latir was tired and nervous and had thought of cancelling too. He was afraid of his first wife. Fatimata placed her elbows at the rim of her water pot and clasped it close to her chest, her face pointing to the floor.

"I was in that position when Latir suddenly appeared from the left, bent over and kissed me on the cheek," she said. "He did it happily, and gave me something, I've forgotten what, a little gift. We looked at each other for a moment and knew somewhere within, in the deeper layer of our skin, it would be once and for all."

Salif rolled over when Fatimata finished telling her story. He asked Ami Colle to help him back into the parlour. She held his hand as he scrambled to his feet, and the two of them walked the corridor to the parlour, Fatimata alternately humming and slapping at mosquitoes, her black knobbly eyebrows rising and falling to monitor her husband.

Salif stretched back in his traditional sofa and asked Ami Colle for some cold water to dampen his body and bring down his blood pressure. She stepped into the bathroom where she found a small, damp washcloth. Then she shut the door, picked up her cell phone, and in a soft voice, called her nephew in the army to speak to him.

Fatimata was distracting Malika, entertaining her with childhood tales.

"What's wrong with Papa?" Malika asked, unexpectedly. "He doesn't look in good shape."

"Thing is," Fatimata said, "he doesn't admit he's over seventy. He lives like a twenty-five year old."

"Has he started smoking again?"

Fatimata did not reply.

"Does Mansu still owe him for that festive cloth?" asked Malika.

"I don't know."

"His behaviour is unusual?"

"Just..." Fatimata patted her shoulders to calm her.

A few hours later, the phone in the parlour rang. Mansu too had heard from the radio that Pepe Goodie had been shot in his office, and a Segolian UN peacekeeper had been killed in Goma. Despite the debt that lay between them, Mansu and Salif were close friends. They were often to be spotted in a corner booth at Thiof Restaurant, their mouths oily, hands busy, foreheads almost touching, and their voices too low to be heard. Now and then, they could be seen sporting berets bearing the photo of the presidential candidate of the Cloth Weavers' Union they were supporting, as if they had graduated from Paris or Lyon. "You're in Africa's westernmost country, for heaven's sake, fish and groundnut exporting country. Where do you think you are?" a graduate of Lyon, now a madman, had once told them.

Ami Colle took the phone when it rang and Mansu asked to speak to Salif. All he whispered to his friend was, "May your enemies not hit your chest."

"*Amin. Amin,*" Salif uttered, adjusting his sprawling overalls.

Malika pushed forward the bench she was sitting on. Her favourite English pop song, *It's Good to See You* was playing on the radio. She scooted backward, crossed her legs, adjusted her gown and rested her elbows on the table. "Oh, I like that song."

"You're tuned to the Radio France International," suddenly said a radio voice. Fatimata rushed to the parlour and Malika followed.

"Shuuu," Salif ordered. He turned his attention to the radio and turned up the volume. The radio dated back to the time when he worked for a Spanish employer. "Shuuu," he hushed the women again, "I said I'm listening!"

"The Congolese conflict has taken a new turn," began the newscaster. "Pepe Goodie was assassinated in the presidential office in a failed coup attempt. A Segolian UN peacekeeper was shot in the head. His name is Issaitou–"

"Not my son!" Salif interrupted, pressing the off button on the radio.

Fatimata shook her head. "Has it gone to killing foreigners?"

"Who was killed?" Malika asked.

"Issaitou, one of Issa's—"

"Shut up your mouth!" Salif hollered, interrupting Ami Colle.

"One of Issa's what?" Malika asked. When no one spoke to her, she assumed the rest. Immediately she pulled off her hair clip, a gesture of grieving, ran to Ami Colle and embraced her with abandonment. "What happened to Issa?" she began to cry. "Oh, what happened to Issa? When he was leaving," Malika said in-between sobs, "they told me not to worry. Now, tro… tro… trouble."

Ami Colle pulled out her wrapper and wiped her face. "Sorry," she said. "It's not Issa. It's Issaitou. So stop crying."

"What is she saying?" Salif asked in a guttural voice.

Ami Colle stroked Malika's head. "Her head is aching," she said.

Ami Colle led her to the veranda for her to get some fresh air. "You're pretty, stop crying now. Everything shall be well." But her words blew like wind across Malika's ear. Between Issa's departure and now, Malika has lost weight and Ami Colle could not find a more fitting time to tell her so. "You need to refrain from whatever is making you lose weight."

Malika ignored her.

"Oh Malika's head is pounding," Ami Colle said, rubbing her head.

Malika sat on the staircase. She rested her head on Ami Colle's shoulder and gazed at the top of the baobab tree. The signs of rain were strong in the air. In the next compound, a group of boys were sitting together chatting. Music from a party outside the neighbourhood could be heard dimly, and countless insects chirruped from dark corners. Malika rested her head on Ami Colle's thigh. There, she remained motionless, except when saliva rose in her throat and stirred her, just as a puppy that hunger has driven to sleep continues to dream of food. From her slightly parted lips came the question, "What next? I know not what next?" She stared vacantly, mumbling the words, shrouded in an air of anguish. Her pulse beat faster and her legs began to shake. "Sorry, sorry, sorry," Ami Colle repeated, soothing her.

Malika stood up an hour later. She took a long bath, pulled her hair together with a ribbon Issa had given her for her birthday and donned a purple nightgown. At quarter to one in the morning, with Salif snoring on the couch, Malika went back to the House of Ndiaye. Fatimata was inspecting the kitchen, arranging her cooking utensils as Malika entered and Ami Colle was tending to Salif's feet, rubbing in a gel to ward off mosquitoes. They were awake so late in the hope of hearing more news.

"Goodnight," said Malika almost in a sultry voice, holding her hair before her chest.

"Have a peaceful night," Fatimata and Ami Colle chorused.

On the second day of the month after the thirty-day fast, Issaitou's body was returned to Segol. It was received by a massive crowd that turned out at the airport, young men and women, old men and children. They dressed mostly in black and white and lined the way leading to the arrivals lounge. Government officials arrived in convoy led by the motorcades of the gendarmerie. Commandant Thiam stepped out from his car and was welcomed with a sergeant's salute. He led senior officials through the VIP lounge. Many sympathizers stood outside, holding their prayer beads and moving their lips in prayer. Some men in uniform raised their cell phone, pacing up and down. They spoke in listless tones and gestured with their hands. The military band, dressed in full regalia, filed in to face the crowd. Directing the band was a conductor said to possess mystical powers. His acrobatic displays were acclaimed throughout Segol and beyond.

His voice rang "Seven Rolls Band Start!" and the silence gave way to the boisterous sound of the official music of the Armed Forces. The side and base drums, the brass, the flute, the tambourine, the French horn and the trumpet all blended in splendid harmony. The commander directed the flow of the rhythm and the transition from tempo to tempo, his arms widespread, his hands in dazzling white gloves. Cadets, with ropes and whistles, barred the crowd from pushing toward the band.

The band conductor geared up his acrobatics, now that all eyes were on him. He swung his baton from hand to waist to ankle and slid back and forth like the king of pop. He dropped it to the ground and embarked on a series of acrobatic gestures to pick it, neither with his hands nor feet, nor elbows nor teeth. He bent over backward and somehow, curiously, the baton rolled down his abdomen and stopped at his waist. He pulled it up beneath his arms, pushed it through his legs over to his head, sprang up, and rolled it swiftly and repeatedly around his wrists. A band conductor normally would not perform such acrobatics at the returning of a war hero, a very solemn occasion. If he did here, it was because Issaitou was a band conductor, long before his departure for the Congo war. Emotion rose. The fascinated crowd celebrated the young conductor's prowess as if he had scored a winning soccer goal. They seemed to have forgotten it was a memorial.

"The arrival," the announcer said. "In five minutes."

Issaitou's body was borne in a UN aircraft. It was midday on the dot. His remains were carried toward the lounge and welcomed with a twenty-four gun salute. His coffin was draped at the head with the national flag, and at the foot, with the UN flag. Officials rallied around it, silently, before it was rolled out before the crowd, now sober.

Tears rolled down people's cheeks. The smell of residue from the gunshots and musty cartridges filled the air. Malika spotted Melissa, Issaitou's fiancée and a member of the Young Soldiers' Wives Association. She was standing at the head of the line, surrounded by members of Issaitou's family. Even if there had been a million women there, Melissa would still have stood out: with her shoulders, her hips and her calves in heels.

"Oh boy, soldiers know beautiful women," whispered Babacar, who was accompanying Malika. "Only her hair is too festive for mourning. She's blond." He was staring. Malika told him they were at a funeral. Babacar tore his eyes from Melissa, but trampled on the woman in front of him. "Forgive me," he said.

Malika wiped the sweat off her face and blew her nose. For the third time, she asked Babacar for the bottle of water they had brought along. She winked at him as she caught him eyeing Melissa.

"At least that woman knows what happens next in her life," Malika said. "Mine is unclear."

"Why? When I am here..." he said. The statement shook Malika and she fixed her gaze on her handkerchief.

The band rolled out the final goodbye, *Farewell*. The crowd picked it up singing along with the wind instruments that rendered the melody. Force Commander Lieutenant-General Samba Diop stepped forward, bowed silently before Issaitou's remains and mounted the podium. Silence returned.

"We honour Issaitou, an ambassador of our country, who paid for peace in Africa with his life," Diop said. Then he placed a cap of honour on the coffin.

A military parade followed, ending with the laying of a bouquet of flowers on the coffin. Peacekeepers on scooters delivered a last memo. They swung round the coffin, standing on their bikes. "Long live the blue helmets!" they chorused. "Fairness is not naivety! Fairness is not weakness!" They formed the letters UN, ending with a loud shout, "Our heroes, blue helmets!"

Issaitou's final journey began continued in an ambulance from the airport to the cemetery. A long procession of cars and walkers accompanied the casket. Shops were shut and all concerts cancelled. The sun shone on the coffin. Mourners cried and screamed Issaitou's name. At the cemetery, many religious dignitaries made prayers and recitations from the Quran as Issaitou was laid to rest.

"What a pity," one woman said.

"Good night, Issaitou," another said.

"Sleep well."

"May the earth receive him."

The gravediggers trickled sand over Issaitou's coffin.

Malika threw her scarf into the wind and began to wail. She crouched down, too weak to stand. Some men picked her up and bore her away flat on her back. "My husband, ooh! My husband, ooh!" she screamed, as they carried her away. They stretched her out under a nearby tree. Babacar, who followed, fanned her tear-stained face. Her eyes looked as if they would fall out, they were so red, so grief-stricken. He held her hand to take her home. Even then, Malika continued weeping and barely dragging herself, though supported by Babacar and another woman.

"My life oo!" she said in between sobs. "Men. Men. You're the ones who make war. Women do not make war. We do not shoot at children, we do not chop off people's hands."

"Your husband will be fine. He will. Allah is willing," said the woman assisting Babacar.

"Leave Allah alone," Malika refuted, shaking. "I'm not insane, I know I'm not. I'm sound and sensible and willing to look at, no, I mean, to tell the truth. There is no greater pain for a woman than to bury the man she said yes to, or not to know where he is. Is Allah responsible for the evil? Tell me, just tell me. I want you to tell me."

Babacar thought perhaps she would stop crying if he made her speak more. "You know," he said, "I always thought you understood why the people over there are attacking the peacekeepers. They believe their role is to protect them and yet they're attacked. The more they're shown on the news, the more the people believe they're being protected, the more they rely on peacekeepers to protect them."

"The best protection is peace," Malika said. "They should make peace among themselves in their land. I just want my husband back home."

"You don't understand."

"Oh Professor, I do."

"Just understand me. The way we think of the white men here. As rich and powerful, as know-and-do-it-all. That's the way those people there think of peacekeepers."

She winked at him. "Because their blue helmets make them immortal."

"They believe it does."

"My husband is not a magician."

They came to the junction leading to their house. "They're humans, of course, but as we say in Segol, humans are gods to humans," the woman said, letting go of Malika's hand. She wished them goodbye, encouraged Malika to take heart and turned back on her way.

Malika wiped the tears from her clotted eyelashes. She was so angry, she could not see Issa nor talk to him, because it was impossible. Phone calls to Goma were unsuccessful as the phone lines there were reported to have been destroyed by the rebels.

"Issa, Issa," she muttered angrily.

In her vulnerability, she believed that peacekeepers were herculean in carrying out such a task. It frightened her. She felt lost. Even as she reached their compound, she doubted the sense of waiting for a man who might as well be flown back in a coffin.

"If I had known… if I had only known…"

"If you had known what?"

She did not answer. She wiped her face again. Her cheeks were soaked, even reddened. Then her foot hit a stone and she screamed.

"What is wrong?" She said nothing.

"Be careful" Babacar said.

"I am careful."

"Don't lose your feet. You're still a young woman."

"That's the reason for wasting my time?"

"What about those..."

"You men have time! Even at sixty, seventy, eighty. A woman's time is limited. Wait too long and you become something else."

By saying "You men have time", she was referring to the village chief where she had grown up. She had once told Babacar about it. At the age of eighty-two, the chief married a sixteen-year-old girl. A visitor came to see the chief. He met the chief's young wife and asked her, "Is your grandfather in?"

"Ehm," the chief's wife said. "You mean my husband?"

Now at the house-gate, Malika stretched her fingers to check her wedding ring, and wiped away the last drops of tears. Babacar could smell the perfume emanating from her cloth. She opened her bag to take out her keys, closed it, and walked in, at a snail's pace. Her mind vacillated between Segol and Congo. Issa was good, caring and understanding. All he had ever wanted was for her to become the mother of his children.

She tried to pluck up her spirits. It could be no less of a futile hope to see her husband walk in, wave that blue helmet of his, a broad smile on his face, and apologize to her for all the suffering.

The next day, she slept until quarter past eleven. She lay curled on her bed. Each time she rolled over, she opened one eye and closed it again, covering her face with the pillow: the compound was not swept, the refuse truck passed, breakfast was late.

9

Fatimata left early the next day. The Sahelian sky on the Atlantic coast was already roasting and dry, the dusty wind sock whipping against its metal rod. Fatimata reached her farm, bent over the well and peered in. She tied together two pieces of rope and straightened up. The new rope joined a dozen others holding a bucket deep below. The well was now twice as empty. Annual rains were supposed to have come, but still they were delayed. She hauled the bucket from the well and tufts of animal hair fringed the bucket.

Underneath the well, mushrooms grew in twisted clumps, rounded crucibles nipping at the perimeter. Fatimata leaned over in a position that pierced her chest and joints and rekindled her rheumatism. She pushed her forearm deeper into the well, shaking the bucket to slosh water into it. The intensifying sun was burning her skin and making her eyes see shapes and twinkles.

She raised the bucket of the muddy water she had drawn repeatedly until she had filled two separate buckets. A fly tickled at the back of her neck, its perching like the moist brush of a butterfly's wing. She waved it away with her hand. Her reflection wobbled on the surface of the water, her scarf fell over her eyes, and her bangles swung down in a row. Particles of dry leaves had settled in the well, rolling forward and backward. It was almost impossible to avoid them – Fatimata had tried – and she gave up. She lifted the bucket onto her head and trekked the parched land to her vegetable farm. She watered the crops regularly, to save them from drought.

By the time she was done it was already noon, a Friday, and the mosque was starting up on Istanbul Street. The imam's voice mingled with the bells of Our Lady of Fatima Church. Children grabbed their prayer mats, showing off their caftans and boat-shaped shoes, before running and whistling towards the mosque.

The sun suddenly retired. Fatimata suspected it might rain. "Praise be to Allah," she said, washing off the sweat that ran down her body. She put on her slippers and wiped off the mud that gummed them to the grass. She was wearing a brown Cotonou wrapper and Ami Colle's faded T-shirt. She hadn't realized it was her co-wife's when she took it down from the laundry line at dawn. A cousin living in New York had offered them the T-shirts two years ago when he visited. Fatimata packed her now filthy farm tools in her basket and carried them on her head. She hid her well rope in the grass and hastened to reach home before prayer time.

At home, she washed the tools and cleaned them to keep them free from rust. With the last tool lying in her hand and the rest hung up on the nails piercing the wall, she looked up at the sudden dark-blue sky and felt drops of rain on her arms.

The next minute, it began to rain. Fatimata clapped her hands and danced. The heavens had at last smiled on the earth! She stood still, receiving the blessings of the first rains, fumbling with her scarf, her lips pursed in soft noises. Amused, Babacar mimicked the bleating of a sheep. All the sheep ran out on the veranda where the biggest one battled with a dog, raising its horns to the dog's head. The dog ran away. Babacar let the sheep into their pen, lest cold pass through their lungs.

"Rains?" Fatimata commented, gazing at her son. Babacar nodded in a gentlemanly manner and stepped back against the two-piece wooden door, curling his knees above the edge of the bolt in search of the right position as he pushed the yellow knob to lock it, battling with the door's unevenness. The wood had slackened due to moisture. The rains churned up a flood which ran out of the inhabited quarters into the farmlands. It rained the entire afternoon and the flood became like a river.

Fatimata began to farm seriously the year that Seydi, the famous wrestler, died. She was thirty-seven at the time. Fire had broken out at the Thursday Market and burned down all the stalls, including hers. After a year or two of waiting in vain for the support package promised by the government, she started making seed beds and planting vegetables when the rains were generous, spaced out and in good measure with the sun. She loved planting vegetables. Issa divided his time between helping her with the seed beds and preparing for his admission into the military college. Farming with his mother guaranteed him rare privileges: going out to parties with friends and coming back after midnight. His presence made Fatimata feel important, made her farming special. Helping her out was a sure way of winning favours from her. He wondered too if farming wasn't too hard a job for a woman to be doing. Perhaps she could rather just have Dieynaba prepare fruit juice and sell it at home? When, one day, Babacar asked her, his mother replied, "One does not watch the wrestling standing still."

The rains intensified, like a bus changing from second to fourth gear. Fatimata brought out one of her husband's caftans, filled the local iron with charcoal, lit it and waited for the charcoal to glow. White linen covered the rough finishing of the table surface. Fatimata closed the iron, lifted it and rubbed its face over the brittle, white overall, starched to the teeth. The caftan gave a royal impression and as the iron worked on it, a crisp sound was to be heard, just as when Salif wore it, with its thumb-thick embroidery around the cuffs. Different styles of ironing marked the event: a straight line for ordinary days, two double lines for special days and colour-striped runs of the multicolour threads for very special days. Fatimata ensured the lines were perfectly in place, folded it and took it to Salif who dressed, went out and waited for the rains to subside to go to the mosque. Heavy downpours to lighter ones, thick sheets of water to slanting showers alternating all increased Salif's frustration. Once he stood up to dare the rain, but the water had risen thigh-high and he couldn't find a spot to put his foot. Then the heaviest downpours began, pulling out the branch of the mango tree where once Malika sat to eat roasted cashew nuts.

While Salif waited for the rains to abate, Babacar wiped Dieynaba's blackboard clean and mimicked Professor Salim's geography class on climate change. He drew the shifts in weather patterns, the environmental phenomena, the rising water level and its bandwagon of water-borne diseases. He drew the opaque green eyes of children under five, suffering from food shortages leading to malnutrition. He drew women, with silver-bright legs and broken nails, badly doused in pigment. Then Babacar drew the good women of Africa, riding the donkey's back, coming home with lunch in a basket.

"Ah! Chums," Babacar said. He drew girls on braids with well-sharpened tongues, scouting for water, for drinking or cooking, for cleaning or washing, water from the smoked and darkened sky, so angry that men are sloppy. When the rains continued to the third day, Fatimata became worried. She thought about her plants and weighed the cost of the floods. She resigned to Allah to save her from disaster.

Salif's worry was something else. Rather, he brooded about having missed Friday prayers on that first day of the rains. The mosque was half-empty, filled mostly with children. Their caftans were soaked, the covers of their illustrative books showing someone stretching his hand like the Prophet to write down the words of the angel were torn and the girls' burqas billowed like air-ballons. After the prayers, the children sat down on their mats. They imitated their imam, using chalk to draw his hyperbolic moustache on the floor. They argued about whether or not his head was very different from the one on their book covers – depicting a man with grey hair, calloused with dust and creases of sweat on his face. The children's palms became coated with chalk dust and multiple coloured marks from redoing the drawing or wrestling on how best to sketch their imam's moustache. Their voices outdid the drawings, their scintillating voices of innocence rising and falling rhythmically, just like the imam when his neck raised upwards joining sound to meaning.

Fatimata waded through the flood waters to her farm on the fourth day. She ignored Ami Colle's warning that she might be swept away. The tide which has left many families homeless died down shortly after she left the house. She trudged through the slippery mud, juggling her feet above the muck for fear that the mess might throw her. It was eight o'clock, the rains had lightened and she prayed her vegetables would still be there. She crossed over a man pushing his bicycle through flood water. Hard work. Ami Colle's warning returned to her. She held strong on the slippery paths, spread her feet for balance, as her wrapper almost washed away from her waist. She encountered a world of frogs and crickets and the inhabitants of the woods, falling tree branches touching her head. A trunk fell across the narrow pathway right in front of her. She removed her wrapper and tied it firmly around her waist. Her blouse smelled like the plants she had brushed against.

Suddenly, thrown by a mass of mud and water, Fatimata fell. Her legs spread apart and her buttocks hit the ground. She wanted to turn back. But ignoring her farm would disqualify her from Africa Rise Microcredit: her next hope. She mumbled, responding only to the rise and fall of the winds. Her hands were steeped in mud and her courage was stubborn. That, at least, the scorching sun, that could kill her plants, was over. That was what pushed her up from the ground and she battled on. Her feet sank into the mud, deepening into the sludge. Stuck there, she looked up at the horizon where she saw that the flood had engulfed the whole area, washing out all the farms.

"It's not true!" she cried. "It's not true!"

She stretched her hands forward, as if begging her late grandparents to change the picture. Tears trickled from her eyes. She pulled her feet out of the mud, one after the other, with difficulty and set off home. She did not look back. She could not. Like a dog that has detected the smell of death, she remained fixed in her direction.

As she entered the house, she threw away her cutlass and shouted, "Babacar!" He did not reply. "Ka… Bacar!" Still no reply. "Malika-a-a!"

"Yes'm!"

Malika put out her head through the window, adjusting her wedding ring.

"The floods have swallowed up the farms. Full! Full!"

Malika was confused. She bit her finger, ran into the room, dashed out, hurried in again, removed her ring and threw off her gown. She forced on her navy-blue jeans, ran to the tool shed, grabbed the rubber boots and tucked her jeans into the oversized boots. She took a different way to the farm, the longer way, through the woods behind the river, linking up with the expressway, watching crowds of people wading their way through the flooded roads to work. She measured the tide against the height of her boots. The water would nearly cover her waist. She branched off from the site and was soon peering at where Fatimata's farm had once stood, the vegetables swallowed up in the belly of the far-reaching floods, unrestrained, with each drop of the rain rising further still. She observed the movement of the flood, where it came from and where it headed, surrounded by debris.

"Ohoo," she said at last. "I said it, the mad quarrying of sand along the beaches. I said it. The mad quarrying of sand. It has opened the door to the floods." She tightened her scarf over her hair and looked on with astonishment, lost.

At half past one, she was home. Salif sat on the veranda weaving a shawl, a smile of fatigue showing his white and brown teeth listing like misplaced dice. A gust of wind disrupted the lining of his wool, pulled them up. He raised the hinges to push through the set and produce a motif, but failed.

"The farms are gone," Malika said.

Salif looked out at his wives sitting in the parlour. Their faces were solemn. It was a bad day, a really bad day. Malika greeted them too, however they were too subdued to reply. She entered the House of Dudu, changed out of her muddy clothes and came out in a dress. She put on the rubber boots again and departed to the district mayor's house.

Serigne Yero, the district mayor, was sitting on the balcony at the last floor of a three-storey marble building, from where he had an aerial view over Djembe, under water. His area was not like the town he had ruled for five years.

"Djembe's a melting-point," he loved to say. He tipped his lofty cap to the right. How would he save his sector from the floods?

Neighbouring quarters brought in perhaps one or two hundred tourists. However his, in a good season, attracted over five thousand. The floods would change that.

Malika climbed up the spiral staircase to the top floor where she could hear Yero's guttural voice speaking to a visitor, booming though the compound. He was talking about a first-floor veranda that had caved in and crushed a twenty-year-old man.

"I've confiscated the builder's licence," he bragged.

Malika greeted the chief, genuflecting slightly, "Your servant greets you."

"Are you at peace, my daughter?" Serigne Yero said. "You came in the rain." Malika smiled and wiped the raindrops from her cheeks. "Did a baobab tree fall?"

"Worse than a baobab falling, Serigne. The floods have swallowed up the farms," she said.

"Say what?"

"Em, I mean, there will be no cabbage and carrot in our stew this season," she said. "I saw the farms. The vegetables now form a large mat for the floods to lie on."

"Oh come on, my daughter!" said Yero. "Floods can't enter the farms."

"I declare it, Serigne. I have seen it with my stripped eyes."

"How could floods enter the farmlands? That's my confusion."

"I was there, Serigne. I studied how the floods came there. They came from the foolish quarrying of sand along the beaches."

Serigne Yero widened his eyes. He shifted his seat forward and shook his head.

"Serigne, we must do something. Today, the farms; tomorrow, our houses."

Serigne's visitor laughed, amused by Malika's turn of phrase. But Serigne did not. He bit his small finger. His mind turned to the approaching elections, and farmers who make up sixty percent of voters.

"What can I do?" Serigne asked. "Lorry drivers are the most stubborn people I've ever seen." He turned to look at Sambo, his visitor, who lifted the last piece of fried meat and dumped it into his mouth.

"This meat is sweet," Sambo said, munching hurriedly. "I'll send my wife to come and learn from your kitchen."

Sambo was a fisherman, so was indifferent to the issue of floods. He lived from the sea. He swallowed the last chunk of meat and stood up to leave. "Thank you, Serigne," he said.

"You're welcome," he replied. As Sambo turned to go, he gave him a derisive stare.

"I have an idea," Malika said.

"Thank you, my dear. Tell me what you need."

Serigne Yero popped his hand into his caftan, brought out some money and gave it to Malika.

"I'll try, Serigne," she said and departed. She would wage her battle in honour of Issa and other peacekeepers serving at the battlefield.

When she arrived home, Malika put on brightly-coloured carnival gear with a mask and strove to the apartment she and Issa had shared. There, she took out Issa's loudspeaker, a whistle and packets of sweets – *Spider-Man* sweets, which children like – markers, and a dozen of sheets of cardboard. She fought her way to Durban Street, the most populated of their district, but was inhibited at the junction by a giant pool of flood water. She climbed on the highest pavement opposite the bank and a light drizzle fell on her, wetting her gear. Then began her campaign: she blew the whistle repeatedly, shouting, "All the children are expected at the basketball court tomorrow morning for a party. American sweets and other things will be shared."

People soon poked out their heads through the windows to find out who the mad woman was. She ended each announcement by blowing on the whistle. She proceeded down the densely populated Medina Street and into smaller lanes, children running behind her, attracted by her mask. Within hours, her message had spread across the area. She returned home before dawn.

The silence in Salif's house persisted. Fatimata retired before dinner. Ami Colle withdrew quietly to the House of Dudu. Given the lapse of time, she occupied herself, as usual, with her handcraft. Malika briefed her on her plans and prepared for her meeting with the children. She spread the cardboard sheets on the floor and wrote on them in bold writing. She yawned excessively, not from hunger but from exhaustion. She sat before the cardboard sheets and nodded off. With her tongue hanging out slightly, she snored like an old air-conditioner.

The next morning, Malika did not wake to sweep the compound, as usual. As soon as she woke up, she dressed in her garb and headed to the basketball court, carrying Issa's Sony Player. The courts were waterlogged, so she began by sweeping the water away. She put DJ Micky's *Seventy Days on a Picnic* on the CD player, the top of the chart in children's entertainment. The first children arrived in a picnic mood, in sporty clothes. The boys wore caps and made funny sounds with their lips. The girls carried handbags and wore plastic glasses that flopped from their foreheads to the tip of the noses. Their lips were painted red and their eyebrows coloured with eye-pencils. Babacar, now resolute about kissing Malika, watched from a distance, hidden from view. The children's outfits reflected in the windows of the Trust Investment building and the gathering made them jubilant. A hundred and fifty children in all turned up to the lure of American gifts.

Malika switched off the music and the children applauded, "It's cool! It's cool!"

"Now listen children," Malika said, "Floods have destroyed the farms and we have to help our parents."

"I know," said one. "My mother told me about it."

"Thank you," Malika said, "So tell Papa and Mama that the children have decided to do something about the destroyed farms."

"Children, do we agree?"

"Y-e-e-s!"

"Shall we be there?"

"Y-e-e-s!"

"Do we mean it?"

"Y-e-e-s!"

Malika divided them into three batches: small, smaller and smallest. She put the music on again and they danced to its beat. As she shared out the sweets, the children's faces shone with joy. There was nearly a pack for each child. She threw some sweets in the air and the boys scrambled to grab them as they landed on the ground, on top of one another. The girls stood still, their mouths open with astonishment, holding onto their bags with folded hands, afraid of the dirt. They protested in silence against the disorderliness of the boys, all curling and rolling over one another.

"Listen," Malika said. "It's time to go. Tell your parents, we're meeting here at eight o'clock tomorrow, with the approval of the district–" As she was mid-sentence, a boy sped off on his bicycle pursued by the others. The boy slipped in the flood water, his foot scraped the gutters and the bicycle whirled by itself across the court. "Hee oh! Hee oh!" Malika shouted. "These children will kill me."

Babacar ran out from his hideout to help. His hands barely fitted in the bike handles and the hand brake wobbled and coiled in the rolling wheel as he pressed on the pedal. The child lay in the flood water, whipping his knees and ankles with the dirty water. Babacar reached out, tried to pull him up. However the boy's weight was heavier than his outstretched hand and this frightened Babacar momentarily. It was scary to watch a child in a high-speed bicycle accident. He did not want Malika to see he was jittery, so he picked up the bicycle and tried to move each of the child's legs and arms, afraid of causing the boy more pain, afraid that his touch would create an adverse effect. Malika watched them from the court, then closed her eyes, surrounded by all the girls, glued to her waist. Babacar carried the mischievous boy back into the court.

"Where did you come from?" Malika asked him. She shuffled her palms over the boy's head, giving him one, two, three gentle rubs. The boy nodded and stood up, his clothes soaked by the dirty water. He crossed his legs and placed his palms beneath his head in a gesture of wonder. Then when he laughed, the other children laughed too.

"Good for him," the girls said.

"Let's go," Malika said and the boy complied. She wheeled his bicycle home beside him.

10

The rest of the children swarmed in like Migratory Waders, their water bottles slung across their chests. Babacar was at hand, as Malika had asked him to help her guide the children to the beach. He was not concerned about whether Malika would succeed at the fight she had cut out for herself, but rather about how she would manage such a cluster of children altogether. He was a protest die-hard and had supported them all: the university students' protest against delayed scholarships, the fishermen's against the invasion of Chinese trawlers, and the labour union's against the soaring cost of living. Like any university student, protest was etched in his memory and he debated its effectiveness just as others debated the real date of birth of the district mayor.

He lined the children up in two rows and led them along the road leading to Djembe beach. A child raised a hand to ask why they hadn't brought swimming kits. He told the little girl they would find some by the beach. He was afraid that the word "protest" would destabilize her and she looked about the age of a child just about to enter primary one. She watched carefully from her front row position, her eyes black, her hands wet from the mist. He clapped and intoned a well-known song and the children sang along, clapping as they walked. They came across a butcher where, at that very moment, three men were slaughtering a cow. Blood splashed from the cow's neck, staining the clothes of some of the children and the full, glossy billboard across from the slaughterhouse.

The children screamed and scattered from their rows. Frightened, they watched the cow's eyes slowly closing as the butcher sliced with the knife further into its throat. As he hit the eye with the tip of his knife, aqueous and vitreous liquids spurted out, bumping the eyeball and leaving a bank of blood on the eye socket.

"It's dead," Babacar said to the children, wanting to comfort them. He reassembled the group. Within a few steps, they reached the visible stretches of the beach. The children remarked on the magnificent view, the sky and the sea merging in a brilliant blue. The wind swept across their faces, a soul-soothing breeze.

Malika was standing at the beach. Her face was radiant, more radiant than Babacar had seen it since Issa's departure. Looking at the children with fondness, she spread her arms like a hen, gathering her chicks. The children broke from their lines and ran to embrace her. They competed all at once, jostling to hug her, to shake her arms. One of the girls whose dress was soiled by the dying cow's blood showed Malika her blood-speckled dress.

"The cow," she said, pointing towards the road. Malika, without a thought, promised to buy her a new dress. That promise triggered another protest.

"What about me? What about me?" the rest of the children said. Babacar could not grasp how quickly they had bonded with Malika.

"Sit down. Sit down," Malika said. One hundred and ninety-six children and a dog that had followed them obeyed. Malika shared out plastic cups and poured orange juice for them to wash down the throat. While they drank and shook their heads in gladness, she announced their mission: "We are here to protest against lorry drivers quarrying sand from along the beach."

She turned around to serve extra drinks and gestured at Babacar to bring a bag lying on the ground. She pulled out the placards bearing inscriptions of their struggle and handed out one to each child, starting with the smaller ones who spilled their orange juice on the placards, up to the bigger ones. "Hold them up," she said. "With both hands, use both hands."

Written on the placards were, "Risky Environment", "Increased Erosion", "Flooding", "Stop the Quarrying", "Stop the Anarchy" and "The Serigne has spoken".

She went on to explain the meaning of the words. The children looked a bit lost as they fondled their noses and rubbed their eyes. Babacar observed Malika, absorbed in her gesticulations, unaware. The first hour of the protest would be crucial. The children had been on holiday, playing on the streets over the past weeks, enjoying the evenings without homework and waiting to slip into their costumes and compete at the Holiday Awards. Half the protest would be won in the first hour. Lorry drivers would care as little for their protest as they did for the environment, the weather, the season, and whose sheep was bleating. Where to highjack sand from was their worry. They spoke in coded language, revealing secrets within their circle – lift here, dig there, police!

The first lorry arrived. The driver aimed for the closest distance to the stretches in an area of sand, blocking off his rivals. There, the level of sand was not low, but it was interspersed with gravel, cork lines, seaweed and dead leaves floating in on the tide. The sand in a different spot was fine and clear: free of stones, and in large enough quantities to mix with cement. Before digging, the driver and his acolytes crossed over the creeks to see the lines of sand afar. This gave them hope. They smiled, threw off their shirts and lifted their shovels.

"Stop it! Stop it!" Malika and the children shouted, rushing toward them. "Save our farms! Save our farms!" they chanted in chorus.

They held up the placards right close to the drivers' faces. Babacar watched from a distance. If the drivers persisted, the situation would worsen; and if they backed away, they would feel they had lost face. Babacar believed the spirit of the children was fighting in their favour. He swung to the passenger's side of the lorry, a cool breeze making his eyes water. Far beyond, some fishermen were rowing fishing boats against the waves. The children kept on shouting their slogans. Babacar shifted from side to side, vigilant, his toes splayed like a watchdog, the sea breeze whipping across his face.

One of the men lifted his shovel to start digging. Malika whistled and, unexpectedly, some children, led by the boy who had fallen on his bicycle the other day, threw themselves face down where the man was set to dig. Then the rest of the children did the same, throwing themselves flat on the sand, crying, "Dig us instead." Muscles were taut and nerves alert, faces flushed with incisive frowns.

Babacar stared at Malika's expressive face as she stood behind the children, her feet firmly planted, manifesting a lively alertness with which she followed every development.

The driver put down his shovel. He thought about ordering one of the gang to hit a child so the rest would vacate the scene, but he returned the shovels to the lorry. Malika, eyes briefly closed, was singing a song about a badly treated woman. Babacar kept watch for the drivers' next line of action, hoping that the spirit of the children would protect them from the amulets that lorry drivers usually wore hanging from their waists. Suspecting that they might be being watched, the men hopped into their vehicles and drove away. At that, Malika whistled, and the children got up. They applauded excitedly. It was their first victory.

The wind diffused Malika's voice, delicate and soft as she praised the children, saying they were agents of change since time immemorial, since Oumi-Samba, the princess of Kajoor, had presided over the feast of millet, spreading wide the wings of her royal mantle.

The fishermen approached the banks. The children screamed, "Wooooh!" as the waves splashed seawater on them. They watched the sweeping movement toss the boat and engulf it, as if it were empty of the three men in it.

"Look over there, children!" cried Malika, pointing. The green headlight of another lorry was shining toward the beach. The driver, who had been warned by his colleagues, saw the placards. As Malika whistled and the children ran toward the lorry, the driver understood the barrier before him. The children pushed against the lorry driver's door, so that he couldn't get out. They brandished their sign at his window. He smiled as the children's voices rang out like the whine of mosquitoes. He then started the lorry, blew his horn, reversed and drove off. On the way, he encountered another lorry and waved it to a halt.

"Children of Yero," he said.

"What?" asked the driver.

"They are at the beach protesting," he said, then drove away.

The driver entered the beach, but at the sight of the children, reversed immediately.

In a small city like Djembe, every coming and going was a matter of public speculation. The lorries weren't even home by the time the news had spread. A swarm of journalists carrying cameras, recorders and jotters rushed in. Babacar wondered if Malika had anticipated this and he dashed forward to alert her. As he spoke, she rubbed her hands across her face, clearing the sweat from her eyelids. For a moment, she looked older than she was. Her chin was stippled with thick dust, her earlobes were red from the breeze. She pinched the bridge of her nose between her eyes and shook off her tiredness.

"Peace to you, Madam," a female journalist greeted her in Wolof. The journalists held out their recording devices.

"Peace to you," she replied. She laid a hand on a child's head, tousling her hair, and tucking the child against her waist.

"Channel 7. Please can you tell us why you're here?" the interviewer pursued.

"Djembe children are protesting against sand quarrying."

From the rear, they took out their top-notch digital cameras photographed Malika and the children, the flashes popping. It was only a half hour from downtown and Babacar suspected some more reporters might speed along, after the first. He could see from her lips that she had low blood sugar and was feeling limp and tired.

"Tell me," the reporter continued. "Is this a solution for climate change?"

"With these floods, this stupid quarrying of everything must stop."

Babacar shook his head in surprise at her speaking like an environmentalist.

"You campaign with children. Can you tell us why?" one of the reporters asked in an oily baritone.

"I'm a woman," Malika said, "I love children. They're innocent, they're spontaneous, they're creative and generous. Not so with adults. You know what, my husband, a soldier, is serving in the Congo—"

"You mean as a peacekeeper?"

"Right."

"So he—"

"Last year, the Young Soldiers' Wives Association, of which I'm a committee member, organized a campaign for the return of our husbands from a risky mission. Only five women turned up, since we don't have connections with the caftan people, since none of their faces is printed on our wrappers, since we didn't cook them giant pots of jollof rice."

"So you were helpless."

"Surprisingly, some dogs came around and barked for us."

They exploded with laughter. She chuckled at the memory and Babacar laughed too.

"Any word for families who have lost their farms?"

"Oh, those poor souls, mocked by sand lorries, they must adapt. I mean it, they must. These women, the likes of my mother-in-law, are tired. They must move to safer areas, build on higher land, vary their crops and use traditional methods, before help comes from NGOs."

"Thank you, Madam," replied the reporters.

"My pleasure. Have a nice day."

The journalists walked along the banks, observing the placards. The callous marks of shovels and spades lay everywhere.

A flustering, noisy tide came in, meaning it was about midday. From the end of the road some people were approaching, carrying pans on their heads and holding bags in their hands. They were not spies sent from sand lorries, but harmless people. The closer they came, the more Malika recognized them: they were all proud black women, the size of the Millennium Pillars, carrying pans on their heads. She ran along the sandy beach, the children chasing after her. She held her boots in her hand, allowing the sand to weave in between her toes with a dry, grating smack, each leap affording varying degrees of pressure to her feet.

"Wait back there for me!" she told the children, knowing they would not listen. Her foot slipped on rock, she wobbled, then continued. She slid on a rough area, yet she pressed on. The children fell back laughing. There was an irritating ache on her skin, worse on the nose or eye.

"Is the house at peace?" she said to the women at last. They spent the next five minutes greeting. Malika kissed each woman twice on the cheeks and offered to help them with some of their luggage. They were the town chief's wives and their house helps, accompanied by Kristen. They brought fish-pies with a hot brown pie crust over ground fish for the children to enjoy. The fish-pies were barely out of the frying pan and their aroma crept over the nose and larynx, making one's mouth water. The children searched for colours and shapes in its crackly surface.

Aida, the mayor's first wife, greeted the children on behalf of the mayor, praised them for their generosity and told them the mayor had sent her to bring them some refreshments. A splash of a smile crossed the children's faces. The joy in their eyes was evident. One boy was shoved from behind and his pie fell in the sand. He screamed, throwing up his water bottle and fell on his knees, hands up tossing sand and gravel. Tears rushed to his eyes, pushing away the sand that stuck to his face. Malika reached out, wiped his face with her wrapper and shaded him with her body.

"Open your eyes, open your eyes," she instructed him, to blow the sand away, but he would not. She pushed his hands away, clamping them under her arm. The boy yelled even louder. When she released his hands, he rubbed at his eyes again. His face was sweltering and his arms sticky with sweat. Malika pushed his hands away again, lifted up his eyelids and blew into the corner of his eyes whispering, "It's okay." She wiped his face with her handkerchief.

"Take heart. It'll be alright now," the chief's wives assured him.

The boy opened his eyes, in time for the fish-pies and juice being served. It fell quiet and the only noise to be heard was the munching of many mouths. Kristen tuned on her cell phone radio.

Several stations were reporting on the protest right then. She ran to tease Malika, so gallantly cocksure in her costume, the emblem of her lifestyle, her freedom, her femininity. Malika announced the news to the children who shrieked loudly, holding their hands across their mouths like the Mandingue. The atmosphere smelt faintly of garlic. Babacar who was also munching his share of the pie pushed himself upright and requested some more.

The beach grew calm and the water rose and fell in peaceful waves. They turned to look at it. It was delightful to behold. The sky was a graceful blue framed with a thick azure that faded at the far end, where the Americas began.

They sat on the warm sand. Malika removed her wrapper covering her shorts. Underneath, she was wearing a black and white tennis outfit, with an opening at the hem. Babacar shifted up next to her, rolling up the sleeves of his shirt for air. The wind wafted into his nose, and he leaned against her shoulder.

"Are you happy?" Kristen asked.

"Yes!" the children answered. She promised to organize a party for them before she returned to her university. The children applauded. The boy who got sand into his eyes said, "I'm belly, belly full."

"Tic-tac," some called him. Three commuter buses arrived and parked, rear to the beach. They had come to collect the children. Singing and clapping, the children hopped in and the buses drove off, one by one.

At the basketball court, where the bus stopped, a crowd was waiting. As soon as Malika and the children stepped down, the crowd roared for them. The drums were playing and hands were clapping. The women fitted a royal dress on Malika and lifted her up on horseback. She smiled shyly, behind the white apparel, her feet painted black with henna, her hair parted with silver dust, her braids held together by fancy ribbons. She appeared happy, perhaps for the first time since Issa left. She admired the dexterity with which the drummer played the drums, the zest with which the women clapped and the passion with which they sang:

Malika Ndiaye, Malika Ndiaye,
You're beautiful and brave.
Malika Ndiaye, Malika Ndiaye,
You're thoughtful and suave.

"It's a lie," a lorry driver said, shrugging. "This is giving name to a saboteur, it's undeserved." He sneaked out and stood by the children. The crowd moved in the direction of Salif's compound. Malika was waving her scarf cheerfully to the children.

"It's a lie!" the disgruntled lorry driver said again. A short distance on and they were at the House of Dudu. The gate was open, its joists marked in red and white chalks and decorated with palm leaves.

Salif heard the noise and his family name being called. Peeping through the gate, he saw Malika on horseback and his eyes grew wide. He quickly rolled up his weaving threads. He stood there, intrigued, as the crowd entered his compound.

"Welcome, welcome," Salif said jovially, waving. The drummers added a new motif to the drumming and the dancing became frenetic. At the sight of his father, Babacar pulled Malika's arms so forcefully that her dress slipped off her shoulders. He and another man helped Malika down from the horse. The music stopped.

"Return in peace," Salif said. The crowd dispersed, talking about the devastation brought by the floods, Malika's courage and the daring lorry drivers. The white sky faded to a cool blue that harmonized with the quivering of the trees and the furrows of the clouds layered against the horizon.

Malika struggled against a blast of laughter compressed against her ribs which was threatening to erupt. A distance from the stairway, Fatimata ran to her, embraced her and kissed her forehead.

"You're a robust woman, a real jewel," said Fatimata, her eyes filling with tears. The sky was growing dark, as if rains would fall, so Ami Colle ran to close the windows. Salif sat astounded and stared strangely at his daughter-in-law. It was his staring that eventually made Malika's ribs burst with laughter.

"Pa, I can't believe this," she said to Salif. "I wish Issa were here."

That evening, the mood in the House of Dudu changed. The smell of grilled fish wafted over from the backyard where Ami Colle was gearing up to offer her rare delicacies for dinner.

Malika hurried to the bathroom. The water fell on her in slices of clattering noise. She dressed in a light fabric that was slick, dry and glossy. Babacar shook his head, rubbed his feet together and stretched his neck to follow her every move, to observe the lines of her calves. The next morning he dashed out to check the newspapers. "Oh, goodness no," he cried as his eyes met with a photo of Malika on the front page of *The Sun*. He read aloud the heading "Climate Change Ambassador".

Now in the public eye, Malika's status grew to mythic levels. That November day, to mark the fifth anniversary of Issa's departure to the Congo war, she organized a cocktail party for senior army officers. The House of Dudu was so busy that Fatimata opened every window despite the whistling dry wind from the south. There was some discussion amongst Issa's local bosses, led by Commandant Thiam, as to whether Issa's slight fever was reason enough to allow him to return home. But on Issa's end, something else was happening, simultaneously.

11

It was Issa's day off, and he had been feasted on by mosquitoes. His face was pale and his lips, as if an afterthought, were bleeding. He decided to trek to the nearby refugee camp from their base. He was going to visit Mavungu, his refugee friend and Swahili teacher. He would not be able to learn new phrases, he could not even open his mouth or pronounce words correctly due to his fatigue, but he longed to see Mavungu who had packs of stories on how he had escaped recruitment from a rebel group, the Kpanpa Wolves. Mavungu had taught him basic Swahili, which was an important survival tool, because it made him look less a Banyamulenge: an enemy. Issa strolled down the landscape to the camp.

He walked across the dense, garbage-heaped slums that stretched for miles. The acrid smell from mass tombs burned his nose and he stumbled in a pothole in the road. He tried to be careful as he trod. Militias and foreign armies were camping in the bushes. A distance away, peddlers and displaced persons were waving for alms at vehicles slowed down by the potholes.

"Goma should glitter," he whispered, appearing to have lost himself. He kicked a stone and quickly added, "Instead, it rots." He felt exhausted and covered his nose with a tissue. He pressed on. "The bones shall rise someday," he said religiously.

He entered the ravaged camp, home to displaced refugees who had fled the fighting in the mountains of Haute Zaire, home to thousands of the wartorn, surviving on the swampy terrain. The camp, open like a football pitch, was overcrowded and on the verge of collapse, teeming with refugees. Everything was obtained by struggle. There was a struggle for clean water, for food, for even a rag with which to cover the body.

The refugees held onto their mats, having been robbed of everything. Monotony. Squalid. They were wanderers in a foreign country, dependent on sympathy from the UN and NGOs. They had no jobs, no family, no music to dance to, no bed nor seat of their own. But still they smiled, preferring a life in obscurity to death by the M-16s of drugged rebels.

Issa arrived as lunch was being served: chikwangu, Congolese fufu and sauce of cassava leaves. The refugees opened their eyes, their ears rose with the hot wind and their stomachs grew as flat as their chests as they queued for food. Some ate on the spot, while others allowed a slow trip to those thatch-roof boxes in the hills of eastern Congo that made the world weep.

"Come and eat," a woman beckoned to him, tossing her share into her mouth.

"Nice of you," smiled Issa.

Issa was on mufti, armed with his ID and holding a baton. After Mavungu had eaten his share of the food, they meandered through the woods of the war-ravaged villages up into the hills. It took them two hours. The air had turned foul by the time they stood at the edge of the void.

Issa breathed out to escape the fetid air. He smelled the wreckage of a cadaver through the fog of his breath. To their right, some villagers were taking what resembled a bundle of rags out of a thatch-roof hut and laying it in a rut. Issa and his friend looked on. It was a dying woman. She was squashed gaunt like a broomstick. Yet, staring at Issa with her green eyes, she seemed almost conscious. A villager moved her and she screamed, in agony. Her buttocks were covered with ulcerating bedsores. Issa yelled, "You better get her to a hospital or she'll die!"

The man gave him the chills with his eyes. Issa shook his head in disbelief.

Mavungu said, "Just a few faddin' francs and her life would be saved."

"There's a hospital funded by the American people nearby," Issa said. "There's even the Catholic Refugee Service somewhere around."

His words fell into the void. The villagers stood with their arms folded, watching her like a new movie. One rushed forward to cover the woman's legs with a wrapper. There was another cry of anguish. For Issa there was nothing special about the woman's demise except that as she was dying slowly, looking right at him. Since he had arrived in the Congo, people like her had died by the thousands from a lethal combination of conflict and poverty. The woman screamed again, her last breath. It erupted like a volcano and sent Issa staggering a few steps back. He touched his friend and gestured he was leaving.

"See you next," Mavungu said, staying behind.

A crowd of disgruntled Congolese camped on the way. There were hundreds of them; they were coming from the UN mission where they attacked the peacekeepers that came to protect them. Issa advanced, and they looked through the distance to him from the hillside. They sighted him from across the farm that separated the camp from the rest of the village, spotting the blue UN logo on his ID. The previous night a rebel group had stolen crops to eat from the farm, destroying the whole farm.

"He's a peacekeeper," he heard some of the protesters say.

Stones began to rain down on him. They fell on him like the rebels' cartridges when they turn on each other. He dove into a nearby ditch and the stones followed after. There he lay, pretending to be dead. A stone missed his eye by a centimetre. He was laden with wounds, wounds from that spur-of-the-moment dive and wounds inflicted by the stones. Issa lay there till nightfall. When he had failed to return to the base by supper, his colleagues rang his Motorola.

"Save me," he said drowsily.

Sometime before midnight, when power went out and his cell phone was spent, the news spread that a peacekeeper had been stoned to death. The Force Commander ordered a search for Issa's body. The peacekeepers pulled out their weapons and hit the road. A lad pointed them to where the stoning took off. They descended and trailed the signs, the stones and the trampled grass. A Chinese peacekeeper came across a ditch and Issa heard his voice and recognized it. Issa shifted his feet.

"He's here," the peacekeeper cried out in a strange tongue, jumping into the ditch. Three others followed him. The rest stood alert. They raised him and lifted him out of the ditch and into the four-wheel drive. Issa appeared unconscious.

"He is responding to the treatment," the director of the General Hospital in Goma said, some time later. While dressing his wounds, the hospital matron and the nurses called him handsome. They asked him questions, to see if he had suffered a concussion.

He answered them: "I am Issa Ndiaye. Yes, my head feels broken. No, I can't move my arms. I joined the peacekeeping in… oh dear, 2000." They applied bandages to his head and to the rest of his body.

Meanwhile, the cocktail party carried on in the House of Dudu. Two of the chairs were still empty, though it wasn't long before Colonels Samba and Mike arrived and occupied them. While dessert was being served, Malika made a speech for her guests.

"We're gathered here tonight," she said in imitation of a wedding toast, "to celebrate my husband's five years of dedicated service, though difficult for me." At this, Babacar, jealous of the officers present, eyed her necklace. "But I remain hopeful all the same," she raised a glass of drink.

Babacar did not stay till the end of the party. Instead, he was sent to Mansu's house to collect what Mansu had agreed to settle on his debt. He spent the night there and, early the next morning, continued on to the sea. When Mansu's children asked why he was leaving so early, he answered, "I don't want to leave Malika all by herself for too long."

At the water's edge later, Babacar kept an eye out for tilapia, the fish Malika liked to eat with red sauce. He dropped almost a quarter mile of the mesh he had borrowed from Mansu into the water and sat waiting for the fish below to entangle themselves. On the surface bobbed the cork line, hand-tied and thrown into the sea. The net itself dropped sixteen feet to the lead line, a thick rope plaited around floating pellets. Mansu had different kinds of nets, one for each season: a finer mesh from January to March, a looser one in April, May and December, the type suitable for catching mid-sized fish. Different colours striped the net, green next to orange, orange next to grey, grey next to blue. It was quite a variety for a fish's adieu.

A tilapia swam into view, but veered off, sensing danger with its fins and twining the net with its knotted tail. Soon it returned, driven by hunger. Babacar recognized the species as it slapped below the net. It was the ideal size, one of the largest of them. It bore the bronzed scales of the tilapia and its back was finely speckled.

"Super tilapia!" cried Babacar, anticipating its rich, florid and succulent flesh. What a noble fish, with its flat fins, silver-bright eyes, firm lines and glowing scales. Babacar called the scrumptious fish "super", as did Segolians who drove expensive BMWs and whose trendy cell phones rang day and night.

A young wahoo flipped into the net. Although it wasn't to Babacar's taste, he kept it. Young wahoo sold for a few francs per kilo at the market, chicken change compared to the price of king mackerel or barracudas. Since the boom of the groundnut trade had faded, each fish was a treasure, worth a cup of rice, a cylinder of gas, school items. Babacar picked the fish from the net and stored them in a cooler filled with crushed ice. Their slime and bloody gasps smeared the white chips a delicate red.

Driven by lust, he worked the nets and watched the sunrise for a signal. He sat on the sand, sweeping his legs from side to side and rubbing his feet with wet sand. He believed fishermen made good lovers because of their strong sense of faithfulness. He examined his broad fingers calloused with fish gunk, bearing the indents of the fishing net. The back of his hands were reddened, like a love story, with thick blood, and scratched from cutting the fish and wrestling with the net. He rehearsed the lines he wished to whisper to Malika, "Love you", which he would say at the corner with the tree or "I can't live without you."

He wrote Malika's name on the sheet of his mind and imagined roses. "I wonder what Papa is waiting for, to tell me to propose to her," he growled impatiently. A mile from Sangomar, he noticed a man sitting cross-legged on a heap of sand, singing to himself. He was dressed in shorts and a military T-shirt tucked into his trousers at his waist. His hair was blond and he wore an earring, much like the men who enjoy Djembe by night. He looked Babacar straight in the eye.

"That fish for sale?"

"No."

"What for then?"

"For my fiancée."

The man rolled his eyes, stretched his neck left, then right. "For that lady, what's her name again, Malika? By the way, what's she to you… fiancée, sister-in-law or sister?"

Babacar was hesitant to answer. He peered closer and recognized him. He was Bakayoka, a returned peacekeeper. "Hmm, fiancée," he answered.

"I see, former wife to our colleague in the Congo, seventy months unemployed."

Babacar erupted with laughter, "A bunch of unemployed. That's what they've become, unemployed. And soldiers at home were the first to call them that. They left with the eagerness to halt the war, 'using all means deemed necessary'. The spinsters among them sat about plaiting their hair in the laundry room and making semolina in the kitchen. Seventy months later, they have yet to see men bringing them gifts of jewellery or flashing car keys. These bachelors chased after thirteen-year-olds, their blue helmets removed. Some, from countries that sent forces, were rumoured to be sexually ill. They had fooled around with underage girls. The last time the villagers saw them gallivanting with girls in short skirts, they called the *Washington Post* journalist, adding pedal to the noise. As soon as the Force Commander arrived, the unemployed threw their salute, deviated from the subject and hurried to inform him they had caught a rebel."

"You mean peacekeepers included women?" Babacar asked Bakayoka, surprised.

"You know nothing!" he answered.

Babacar's question gave Bakayoka the impetus to speak on. Bakayoka related how they had put the Commander in trouble. While the boss addressed issues of bias and accusations, stressing the mission was not a rogue operation, the peacekeepers thought about their girlfriends outside the tent. They were unworried if the Commander was successful at restoring their lost honour, at first unflagging, before light-skinned babies would be born in Ituri.

Babacar left Bakayoka and branched off into China Street, laughing about the wanderer in his native land. He was in a hurry to tell Malika about having seen him and chuckled about all the stories circulating about Bakayoka.

This was what happened. To everyone's knowledge, Bakayoka had surfaced a few days back in Djembe and was seen fumbling in his pockets for something. It was a Saturday evening. A boy ran into the cultural centre where some people sat with the news that he had seen a wounded soldier, meaning one who returned from one of the wartorn countries. They ran out to see Bakayoka. "He came back from Ivory Coast."

"Actually, he came back from Abidjan," the district pharmacist said. The wounded soldier wore a pair of khaki shorts and a sleeveless shirt. He looked relaxed.

According to tradition, whenever a soldier returned from war, everybody hurried to greet him, to examine his nose to see if it was squashed and to get news of their own relatives from the front. Each new arrival made tongues wag in gossip: "Maybe he fled? Perhaps he was expelled? Possibly he's been suspended..." No one version was held as the truth and such was the case with Bakayoka.

It was rumoured that, like the rest of his family, he had been punished by a divinity. While in class four at De Vaux College, Bakayoka had slapped his English teacher for which he was expelled and banned from all schools in the country, even the private ones. Because he was under-age, the government could not send him to jail, but, as stipulated by law, he was placed in a reformatory. His father, the spokesperson for the urban transport workers' union, opposed the decision and took him out of the reformatory, but later threw him out of his house for rudeness. Bakayoka enrolled into the school of hard knocks, did various jobs, sold recharge cards, repaired cell phones and even became a tourist guide. He was saved by his love of trying out things.

A student from Princeton to whom he was teaching Wolof registered him for the exam to enter military college. After he failed the first trial, the student sent him a second registration fee through Western Union. He passed at the second attempt and was admitted into the military college. Having been through such situations, he had changed a lot, but the lion's claw in him held its trace. He was still garrulous and unpredictable.

In spite of what they knew about his past, the people of Djembe rejoiced over Bakayoka's return and made regular journeys on foot to his father's house. He had pulled out the tree outside the small gate because he feared it would enable people gain easy access to the compound. It was hot for November, and dusty; incomparable with Abidjan, with its mild sun during the day and gentle breeze at night. Still dreaming like an Ivorian, Bakayoka hated it in Djembe, especially how dry it would be till December. He could not wait to see the streets flooded with sheep signalling that the Feast of Sheep was near. Visitors kept coming to see him and soon he became uneasy sitting alone with them, answering their questions, keeping conversation going between cigarettes. He said over and over that he would never forget how people in Bouake had slaughtered one other.

"Though you lived in a blazing bush," his visitors said to him. "You're now back to eat the fish of your native Segol?" He only smiled.

"He speaks Wolof with Ivorian accent," one woman observed. Bakayoka wiped the sweat from his brow.

"Great Baobab!" Mansu called him when he visited, and they greeted by knocking their heads four times. "Only the brave go to war and return with their heads still on their shoulders. And you're one of such. That's why I've come, moved by the force of our legendary *teranga*." Mansu cleared his throat, then continued, "It's a source of pride for our country to help Ivory Coast deal with the threat of segregation. It's Allah's wish. Now that you're back, you can get married and we will come and drink beer and dance in a circle in this very compound!"

"Amen!" the rest of the visitors chorused. They said not much else. They had heard the gossip that Bakayoka was suffering from sleeping sickness, that he would nod off, even while out walking or when he ran out of cigarettes.

As soon as he returned from the backyard where he had gone, Mansu asked to talk to him in private.

"Is your soul at peace?" he asked, removing his cap. His bald head was shining in the blazing sun, though the weather had begun to change.

"It will be one day," Bakayoka said with a smirk. "Allah is great." He meant, "One day we will look upon the face of our Maker."

Mansu placed a hand on his shoulder. "I know the officer in charge of returning soldiers. I drink with his brother at the bistro every evening. You know nowadays, you're who you know. I can arrange something for you." Bakayoka nodded, reaching his pocket for his sixth cigarette. "Why don't you request compensations?" Mansu continued. "Yooou… Aren't you of the Licorne?"

"African Union peacekeepers, rather. White Helmets, anti-smuggling," he said. Hadn't Mansu seen the 'AU Peacekeeping' printed on his shirt? Its lack of tricolour background compared to that of Licorne, was something he had consciously exposed for all to see.

"More importantly," Mansu continued as he led him out of the gate, though Bakayoka wished he didn't have to, "do you have a fiancée? For real? Of any age or nationality?"

"Which soldier doesn't?" Bakayoka laughed, puffing on his cigarette. Mansu promised to visit again, at which Bakayoka returned home.

That night, he woke to find himself sleeping on the floor, on the flat brown tiles where he had spilled liquor many times, along with cigarette ash and vomit. He had difficulty adjusting to the crowded family life back home in Segol. They lived like Europeans in Bouake: one peacekeeper per dorm room, one per shower stall and toilet. In addition to sleeping in a congested room now at home, Bakayoka was sharing a bunk bed with his cousin, Mendy. He was annoyed about sharing the same toilet with ten others, even though it was cleaned everyday by househelps from the south.

Bakayoka knew little about Mendy, except that he had started working in a chemist downtown shortly after his father died of cancer. All night he would leave his radio buzzing, the speakers as big as the ones pilots keep in the cockpit and kept a statue of the Virgin Mary and candles from the Marian Shrine in Abidjan burning.

Bakayoka amused everybody. One night, while the candles were burning, Mendy jumped out of bed only to find Bakayoka restless on the floor. Perhaps he had rolled out of his bed caught up in a nightmare about the civil war. He helped him pull on his trousers. He had been keeping track of how often Bakayoka talked in his sleep: every night about two or three times. He wondered what spirit could be fighting to torment him through the night. Bakayoka smoked more frequently than other people he knew, some of whom, a medical newsletter reported, even had darkened lungs.

Maybe it was just that Bakayoka has lost touch with home or much estranged in his own family. He called his father 'Commando', and called Mendy 'niece' rather than 'cousin'. He confused the rooms and avoided eye contact.

Mendy bent down to wake Bakayoka and helped him back onto his bed. Mendy noticed that he was wearing the same T-shirt he had worn by day with a leather jacket and his hair was ratty and messy. Bakayoka rolled and again fell off the bed onto the floor, so Mendy sat down beside him. There he sat for the rest of the night watching over him, smelling the perfume Bakayoka was wearing. What was it about him, exactly? His eerie silence? His run-away eyes? He must be settling scores with someone, even with a spirit. Others who had returned before him seemed normal and had gotten a wife. "Is it this prolonged silence and ghost sleeping that our family needs from Bakayoka?" wondered Mendy, "when others who have returned are building new houses, setting up businesses, or planning a talk-of-the-town wedding?"

12

When Malika woke up after the cocktail party, Babacar gave her the surprise gift.

"Grand tilapia!" she yelled. "Oh, Smallie. That is really nice of you."

"Know who I saw the other day?" he asked.

"Kristen?"

"No, Ba-ka-yo-ka."

"Rumours aside, I think something is wrong with that one."

The tilapia cooking on the grill, they discussed the return of Bakayoka. For the first time, Babacar heard Malika talking freely about the complications of peacekeeping. According to her, Bakayoka was sick, sick of his disorganized nervous system. His wounded leg was yet to heal, was yet to bend at the knee and he could not join his peer group to search for the fattest ram for the feast.

Malika insisted that women disliked him. They despised his character and felt tense whenever he joined them, especially after he had been drinking and smoking and his mouth emitted a heavy stench of alcohol. He did not talk much, nor did he share stories of how the rebels had taken northern Ivorian villages. He merely nodded dumbly and sang a war song, probably the same as the peacekeepers'. The last time he was seen at the market, he was blinking strangely, as if struggling to focus on people. "You said? You said?" he said suddenly, getting to his feet, looking less pensive and dreamy. "It is only through the Lord thy God that you will reach the kingdom of heaven."

"Welcome," they said, not wishing for any reply lest he knock over the cup of liquor beside him. He stared and folded, almost to his knees. Though he had not eaten from anybody's plate, they were wondering what had happened to him. "Poor guy. The war has taken away his pride and diminished his brain."

"Wait," he cried. "Did you speak to me? What about?"

"Don't worry," they assured him.

Surprisingly, Bakayoka attended well to his needs. He was quick to buy bread and milk for breakfast and ran to the laundry to pick up his clothes. Seeing him in such a hurry, one would think his house was on fire. Travelling had opened his mind. He bought newspapers every morning and used nice cologne. But the lion's claw in him kept its trace. He often seemed to be stretching his ears as if he heard a militia approaching, at which he would halt, as if seeking a cover. Then he would wave, shake his head and laugh with queer enthusiasm, rejoicing over something that he alone knew of. And there were other problems. He picked up every discarded cigarette butt he found. He jumped over walls. If he saw a mango within someone's compound, he cleared the wall to pick it.

Five days after they had been talking about him, Malika was on her way to the market in the hazy light of dawn, when she suddenly bumped into Bakayoka. Frightened, she ran off, scattering her bowl to her right and her scarf to her left. Bakayoka was sitting hidden under the palm tree at an intersection. He was half-naked and holding a long stick. His pubic hair was visible and dripping with sweat.

"It's me! It's Bakayoka!" he shouted to the fleeing Malika. At last, she stopped, her heart pounding.

"What brought him out here so early?" she asked, her hand over her panting chest. "He sleeps under trees now?"

Since Bakayoka was not known to be aggressive, especially towards women, Malika crept back to retrieve her scarf and bowl. Bakayoka was sitting on a rock beside the tree, his hands between his knees. He was gazing curiously up into the air. Malika stood for a while and he ignored her. He tilted his head and closed his eyes, laying the palm of his hand flat on the soil. Something lay heavy on his mind and he made as if he was going to kneel. Still he ignored Malika. He held his breath and did not move, not even to blink. He was frozen, as if in front of an immense creature, as if the creature would devour him should he make a single move. Malika squinted in the same direction, seeing nothing. Bakayoka stooped down, compressed and lethargic, like he was seeking vengeance from the creature or waiting for it to take his life.

A stretch of the beach came into view. The water was peaceful, spread wide, a marvel to behold. Bakayoka gazed in that direction, turning his back to Malika. Perhaps it reminded him of the Ivory Coast. The only time he had been to the beach since he had returned was to fetch a gallon of water that he and Mendy had used to wash their sick dog. Malika imagined Bakayoka discovering peace like the apostles in the Bible did after their master quieted the storms, commanded the sea, dispelled their fears, dispelled the danger, just as he had reassured them the day they stayed all night working the fishing nets on the Sea of Galilee.

An aeroplane flew low over the water. "Psitt!" Malika howled. "Looks as if it would plunge in there?"

The noise from the aircraft forced Bakayoka to turn his rigid head and look at Malika. Afraid he might insult her, but her mouth full of particles of chewing stick, she greeted him mumbling, "Are you at peace?" Bakayoka did not reply. She insisted, "Is your house at peace?"

He turned suddenly, staggering. "My sister," he said, "what is pursuing you so early?"

"Daily bread," Malika said. She was friendly, but firm.

"It does not look like you lack it."

"Amen! Tell me," Malika changed the topic, "when will you be returning to the Ivory Coast? See, in the Congo, they–"

"Forget that nonsense," Bakayoka answered. "Don't you need love?"

Perhaps her mention of the Ivory Coast had annoyed him. Where he just came from – with its mass graves, gunshots and tumbling buildings – was more like Gaza than a little Paris, as some called it.

"Seriously," Malika said. "What brought you home? Fever? My husband will be coming next week. I'm tired of weeping. My eyes are running out of tears."

"Woman, I say, don't you need love?" He pulled out a packet of cigarettes. "Don't you need me?"

Malika drew back, picked up her belongings and left. His question filled her mind, as did hers about the after-war lifestyle. Would she have a husband who slept under trees, who had no friends, who was dependent on nicotine? Of the three soldiers that returned, the first had remained a bachelor at the age of fifty-five. The second, stationed in Central Djembe, told stories of lost love, his last love. The third directed traffic near Renaissance Square, breakdancing in the street.

Malika became afraid of her own husband, of the many uncertainties she had witnessed. Walking or sitting on the sands of Sangomar might be soothing, but sleeping under trees, walking naked around the district, smoking a packet of cigarettes a minute? That all unsettled her. To that, she added the thought of living with a crazy man, the laughing stock of the whole town. Nobody would say it to their faces, but they would still say it. A grey cloud floated over the beach with the appearance of the morning sun and a crowd of women passed. In the crowd was Aisha Mbo, carrying a bucket on her head, whom Ami Colle had spoken about the day her mulatto-lamb had died.

"Did you sleep well, Ndiaye?" Aisha Mbo greeted her.

"Praise be God, Mbo," Malika replied, "and is your family at peace?"

"Allah watched over us," she answered. Then she began to complain about the soaring prices of sheep for the coming feast.

"Is he going to steal one?" Aisha Mbo said when Malika asked her if her husband had bought a sheep.

The last chance came to buy a sheep. Malika and Babacar took the sheep Salif had bought to the river to wash it. The river was full of people who had come to do the same. Unexpectedly, Bakayoka arrived and began to separate sheep that came from Mauritania from those raised in Segol. It was not difficult. The sheep from Mauritania had darker wool and bore curved and menacing horns, not stunted as if still budding. Bakayoka pushed aside the pale-looking animals, a third of which had cavernous teeth, to the edge of the road.

"I know what I'm doing," Bakayoka said, attempting to pull the Mauritanian sheep onto the riverbank. "I've managed refugees before." Before allowing the first batch to drink from the water, he finished a cigarette. "To loosen up and see clearly," he joked.

Malika prevented her sheep from sitting on the sand. Although the poor thing was visibly tired, she would not let it sit, for fear it would pick up an infection from the other animals. Babacar laughed at Bakayoka's demonstrations and approached him.

A cup of coffee and more shots of cigarette passed and Bakayoka was geared up. He started adding to music from the drummers that reverberated. He liked heavy rhythms and was jumping to music, rather than nodding.

"Who's a fool? The dancing floor is sweeter than the battlefield." He pushed himself into the horde to prevent a sheep dealer from interfering. He danced through an entire rhythm, his whole body shaking, all the while watching the people and the sheep. The drumming slowed, for which everyone was pleased. Bakayoka objected with a half-hearted shrug. He moved closer to Malika and put his hands around her waist, his body dripping in sweat. He touched her hair, eyes closed. His hands crept lower. Malika pushed them away. "Don't you need somebody?" Bakayoka said.

Their turn came to wash their sheep. Malika drew a bowl of river water and poured it over the sheep, scrubbing dust and dirt from its skin. The sheep bleated in protest, kicking its hooves. Babacar held its rope firmly with both hands. Bakayoka hung around them. After three rounds of scrubbing, the sheep's white fur, formerly grimy, was shining. It bleated in gratitude and they pulled it away from the beach, heading homeward.

Bakayoka ran after them. The sheep stopped. Babacar yanked at its neck, but it refused to budge. Malika assisted him from the same angle. Bakayoka strayed farther, then approached them and shoved the sheep from behind.

"What a queer couple!" he said, looking at Babacar and Malika. Through the fading sun they caught a sight of Grand Island to the east – far away, but twice as bright as the tiny lamp that had first guided navigators to Segol's shores.

"More force, Babacar. Please, more force!" Malika hollered. "See, the sun is withdrawing." She sensed it might rain soon.

Bakayoka halted. Despite the ravaged cocoa fields, this was by far the driest place he had seen. He complained, "Yet every morning one hears all the talk on irrigation sponsored by Saudi Arabia to save the Sahel from drought. They're packed-full, the Saudis. Petrodollars. They're known for it. I like them."

They placed both hands on the rope around the sheep's neck and pulled it forcefully. It stumbled along begrudgingly. Once, Malika asked Babacar to hold the rope more firmly. She did not talk to Bakayoka, pretending as if he were not with them.

Babacar admired her firmness of spirit. It made him even more zealous of the day when Salif would ask him to propose to her. Bakayoka became hostile towards them and yanked the sheep back by the tail.

"Bakayoka!" Malika cried frantically, wiping the sweat from her face.

He almost knocked her in answering, "Hey, me."

She shifted her hand along the sheep's neck. "What is it?" she had to yell for him to hear her.

"Me?" he said. "I'm cool, fine, happy. And you?" She did not answer, so he sought to annoy her. "If you need love say it," he said. "Why should you die in silence?"

"It takes nothing to find trouble," Malika said.

"What?"

"Stop it! Stop touching this sheep. Leave its tail alone."

"Die!" he blurted out. "I say die. Did I touch your sheep?"

She felt like melting from annoyance, but digested the insult, "Just mind your own business."

"Does any man belong to you?"

"He's–" she wanted to smile, but tried not to, looking at Babacar. "Complete loafer."

Bakayoka did not quite hear that. He was preoccupied with how to talk to her, to conquer her. Perhaps it would be easier if he drove a BMW. "You need to buy something?"

"Hurry up," Malika said to Babacar, who pulled the sheep again, which complied. "I have an appointment, with Kristen." She played with the knotted edge of her wrapper. "She's expecting a visit. She wants me to plait her hair."

Babayoka tried all the more. "You look like one Ivorian girl I once took seriously," he said.

"Oh, God," She looked away, in the opposite direction. He sauntered closer.

"So sorry," she said. "How? How can–" she stopped, then shaking her head added softly, "He's only thirty."

She could see an expression of his manliness from the way he beleaguered her. He went to the Ivory Coast to stop the rebels. The rebels stopped him, however. She looked intently into Babacar's eyes. "It's an unjust world. His fiancée abandoned him. A whisky girl. He did a lot for the girl." She did not mention that the fiancée had gone off with a European tourist in the Small Coast, and of his parents had punished her with a magic charm. "Her name is Coumbo."

"Smallie, life is rude." She shook her head.

Bakayoka couldn't keep quiet anymore. He began to sing. "The road to Central Djembe, is to the left, not to the right." He sang like he was sleepwalking – word by word. He was, in a sense, correct. Due to the new road network around the capital, Malika took the railroad by the right, longer than the one on the left, to avoid the hustle of last hour preparation for the feast. "Where is Bakayoka going?" she whispered.

"Go to hell!" Bakayoka thundered, scooting back. "Why wear clothes? Who came into the world wearing any?" Malika increased her pace. "Go on, woman. Please, go have your bath."

Babacar and Malika still had a long way home, so they quickened their pace. The clouds withdrew and a scorching sun beamed on them, until they reached the bus stop. There were crowds of people everywhere. They could not tell the groups in the crowds apart, in their rush. There was a motley crowd at the garage: the colours of blouses and gowns, traditionally painted woollen hats, the black cap of the Mourides and the red of the Tidjanes.

"Segol is a patchwork, complex in its simplicity," Babacar said amid blazing car horns, cries of bus conductors and the bleating of yet-to-be-sold sheep. A street kid, seemingly from the Guinea, ran across the road and up to Malika, holding out an empty begging tomato can. Malika opened the knotted end of her wrapper, took out a coin and dropped it inside the can.

"Allah lead you, Allah bless you, Allah guide –" the lad sang for Malika, who hurried away.

When they got home, their feet brown with dust, they poured some water in a plastic bowl for the sheep and tied it to a pole close to the tap. When Salif returned from the mosque the following morning, he slashed a sharpened knife across the sheep's throat. He sneezed three times in a row.

"Who's calling you? Somebody is talking about you somewhere," Fatimata said.

"Perhaps Issa," Salif answered, his eyes glowing.

… PART TWO

13

Issa was treated well by the nurses at the General Hospital in Goma. They told him to count himself lucky that the stones the frustrated youth rained on him had not affected his brain. The young nurse assigned to him, about the age of Malika, was the only surviving member of her family. She checked on him twice a day and changed his bandages every morning. Still in pain, Issa rarely left the hospital bed. He only left it to use the bathroom, but those moments became fewer and fewer. He saw no reason to go outside, no need to see the sky. He swapped his peacekeeping attire for the hospital gown.

His ward was opposite the emergency unit. He slept with his windows and doors open. Each day began with gunshots, the shuffle of footsteps, the rustle of the UN helicopter gunship flying overhead, the cries of family members and the groaning of refugees. Watching from his bed, he saw a baby rushed into the unit writhing in pain, bleeding profusely. A nurse worked on resuscitating it. He could not have dreamed of something like this.

"Come and help us," the nurse said to him. Issa, still with his hands and feet in plaster of paris and other bandages, rubbed the weariness from his eyes.

"Help like how?"

The nurse hesitated. "With this child."

A minute later, Issa hopped over to the nurse. "*Naumwa hapa.*" He spoke basic Swahili without a trace of a Wolof accent, but felt more comfortable conversing in French. A string of prayer beads descended from the neck of the woman who had brought the baby in. For a moment, Issa thought she was a nun, then he remembered that most Congolese displayed their rosaries as the Segolians did their amulets.

Deprived of peace and happiness, the war had made the Congolese cheeks and chins appear even more devout.

Kabamba, the nurse, gestured to a small girl, about the age of nine, sitting on the floor beside him. "We need blood to save her life," the nurse said. "Can you donate?"

"Donate? I need blood myself."

"We all do."

The small girl was lucky. She had made it to a hospital. Many others like her had simply died like cockroaches. Medical care was a luxury. Functioning hospitals were rare. Those that existed lacked everything from medicine to food and clean water and they were located far from the villages. The nearest hospital to the small girl's village was several days by dugout canoe. War victims piled up each day, too many to care for.

Issa shook his head. In a paradise heaving with loss, he could not be expected to halt the advancing rebels and give blood to those dying from malnutrition as well.

"The girl's father was caught, tied, grilled and eaten by the rebels on Tuesday. On Wednesday, they raped her mother."

Issa looked at the image of the Virgin Mary on the woman's heart. So much religious fervour, yet so much evil in the hearts of men. "She plays a significant role in Islam as well," he said pointing at the image. The woman frowned. Issa had seen cruel rebels and vicious soldiers, but not such brutal civilians.

"I can't," Issa insisted, but his voice wavered as his excuse faded.

"I have donated blood several times since running this hospital," Kabamba said, switching to Swahili. "The last was a week ago. Eighteen lives would have been lost if I didn't."

Issa gazed out into the corridor to the women who had lost their babies in childbirth due to the lack of doctors. Those who had any clout, specialization or the means of fleeing the Congo River, had long fled.

A heavy rain began to fall, painting the orange dirt road red.

"How can people dying of meningitis and cholera donate blood? No one will be able to help this small girl," said Issa.

"Then she will be added to the roll of skeletons."

"What did you say?" Issa looked at Kabamba. "Who were you talking about?"

"Elima," the nurse answered, saying the name of the bleeding girl.

Elima's father, Kekele, had fled after fighting with the rebels of the Movement for the Liberation of Congo. When Elima had heard the knock and opened the door, despite her mother's warning, she couldn't believe the sight of her father. She had hesitated, then hugged him and teased him about his red eyes and tattered hair. Whatever horrors Kekele had seen near Lake Albert, he kept in his heart.

"Back home, alive," Kekele had said, extending the hug longer than Elima was used to. His body smelled of rifle smoke. They ate dinner by the fireplace, the usual chikwangu: cassava leaves over fufu. Because the rebels had destroyed the electric poles three years earlier, they lived in darkness. Kekele's wife led her husband to the room by candlelight, gestured to the bed. "Be careful Papa. The feet of the bed are unstable."

They passed the week watching. With no excitement, no unwanted questions. The only communication present was body language. Elima observed their queer behaviour, but did not comment.

A jar of marijuana sat above the kitchen wall. Blood had stained Kekele's clothes. A bullet graze was visible on his lower abdomen. Elima had worked at the farm and he on his smoking pipe. Elima had brought cassava home from the farm and he had eaten it raw. Elima had swept the compound in the morning while Kekele snored right through it, like a locomotive engine. There were mornings and there were nights. "He will adjust," Elima had whispered. But Kekele had not had time, for the rebels had soon enough fished him out. They had killed him in the presence of Elima's mother, cut his flesh into pieces, smoked it and eaten it. Then they had raped Elima's mother and bludgeoned the girl on the nose with the butt of a rifle.

Having heard the story, Issa took pity on her. After ten minutes of watching her lying on the floor on the threshold of death, he took himself to the emergency unit, sat down on the only bed left there and stretched out his arm to donate blood. Kabamba came to him with a large needle and collection bag. All but two wings of the hospital were closed following the rebel invasion. She pointed towards the cardiology, internal medicine, and endocrinology units. A layer of dust covered the floors, refugees' footprints leaving a trail. Issa remembered Malika and the turning point their lives had taken.

"Is that all that is left?" Issa asked. Syringes, disposable gloves, beds, sheets, hypodermics, clinical gowns, surgical tape, film dressing, thermometers, intravenous bags and forceps – every item of medical practice had been stolen. Open drawers, empty cabinets, filthy rooms, closed blinds, broken windowpanes, holes in the roof... the battle signs remained.

"Emergency and obstetrics are left. And we're on the brink of shutting them down."

Issa rubbed his palm through his bandages. "Emergency, that I can understand at wartime; one has to create room for critical situations. But childbirth... eh?"

Kabamba's laughter rang down the empty wards. "I know. It's amazing, human existence. In wartime Congo, people either stay in love or die."

"Really?"

"Oh, yes." Kabamba shook her head and wondered if she had offended his good intentions. "Children come into the world and leave it and I witness both."

Issa watched Kabamba boiled and sterilized the needle for reuse, afraid that the equipment was not properly clean. Kabamba saw the concern in his eyes and vowed to him that she had sterilized the material properly. Previously, a peacekeeper had been exposed to HIV from shared equipment. Kabamba pressed the large needle into his vein, recalling a warped joke.

She recalled ten years prior, that morning in mid-May, the day the Allied Democratic Forces for the Liberation of Congo crossed into Kinshasa, when she had woken up in the University of Kinshasa student dormitory. She had eaten a quick breakfast of Bournvita and French toast. Grey clouds had lined the horizon toward Gbadolite as she climbed the stairs of the UNESCO Hall and walked across the Belgian-style Mother of God Chapel to the Faculty of Medicine. She had attended a lecture by a certain Helen Roseveare, and took pride in her ability to dissect the joke her country had become.

Attached to the Faculty of Medicine was a museum dedicated to the history of anatomy and pathology since the reign of Mazabongo. After shaking hands with the lecturer and pausing in the canteen for coffee break, she had walked through the curious exhibits, including one detailing the history of uprisings in the Congo.

A recess was dedicated entirely to the tibia. One room remained etched in her memory or her snapshot of it. The room exhibited a collection of the 1,001 skulls collected by Mazabongo: a fractured skull of a Congolese woman from days of the first Congo Crisis; the skulls of nine children from the province of Katanga, each hanging in a glass case; the skulls of former cabinet ministers publicly executed for coup plotting; victims of the Cold War; Angolans from the oil-producing Cabinda enclave.

But the skull that had struck Kabamba most was that of a Sudanese soldier. Fully intact, the mandible was still hooked to the temporal, the twenty-two bones that comprised the human skull all unbroken. The eight bones forming the neurocranial casing were bathed in halogenated light. From the size of the plates, the prominence of certain supra-orbital ridges and temporal lines, and the overall size and solidity of the skull, Kabamba deduced it was a male. The skull was similar to those of the Ugandan war prisoners, the Sudanese slaves. The nose and eyes, which once gave the male soldier physical distinction, were dark cavities. She read the words addressed by America's special envoy to Mazabongo – by then a tottering leopard – and posted by his opponents: "I said the mess you are in is not our mess."

Kabamba's recollections drew to a close as she finished collecting blood. She kept Issa reclined on the bed for fifteen minutes. She gave him his lunch there and covered the needle puncture covered with a plaster. For the first time, Issa saw from the edge of the maternity ward that it lay in ruins. Kabamba explained that a stray shell from a militia group had levelled it nine months earlier. A doctor and several nurses had been tending to postpartum mothers when the shell struck. All of them had died. One mother had been holding her child, his head a hairless ball protruding from the surgical gown swaddling, when she died. The other mothers were looking on at that time. Their babies lay in an incubator when the shell struck.

"Just like that?" Issa asked.

"Just like that… Just like that."

"Allah-the-Merciful-One!"

"Since the war began, we've had only a few women healthy enough to give birth to healthy children."

"Did their husbands set foot in the hospital?"

Kabamba stored the blood in the old freezer droning by the side. "No bandage," she said. She went out, unlocked her bicycle and peddled off to HEAL Africa, an American-run hospital several hours away by bicycle, at the edge of the mountain. She rode on a rusty three-speed, her blouse whistling in the wind. A kilometre before every checkpoint manned by Government Forces, she stopped and checked her tyres. After the tenth checkpoint, she hoisted the bike frame over her shoulder and walked through the woods, circumnavigating the platoons of the rebels of the FDLR. It was as dark when she arrived at HEAL Africa. The young American doctor, Tom, was inside the hospital with a patient. He had left a comfortable life in California to work in Goma. He was evidently weary as drops of perspiration spotted his forehead despite the cool evening breeze. He stretched his hand out to greet Kabamba. He had seen her many times before.

"Where are you from?" he said to her, checking the pulse of an HIV patient.

"I have no bandages," she said. "My cupboard is empty again."

"Why come at night? It's very risky. Is your skin bulletproof?"

"I have a patient whose head is wet with blood."

Dr. Tom went into the hospital's store and returned carrying some rolls of bandages. He then placed the bandages in the metal basket at the back of the bicycle and helped Kabamba secure them with a rubber band. He arranged them into two uneven heaps, the larger one in front. He checked the band again to ensure it was tight. Kabamba had difficulties sitting upright. Dr Tom took off his shirt and folded it into a cushion for her buttocks.

"Bring it back to me," he said, stepping backwards, wearing a singlet.

"Oh, I will," she said. "Trust me."

"Save the children though."

Dr Tom heard Kabamba's words, "trust me", resounding in his ears. Before coming to the Congo, Dr Tom had heard about the legendary African hospitality. Once in Congo, he had spent evenings playing chess with his neighbours, Ndoki and Mazembo. Ndoki had been a businessman, a middleman smuggling diamonds from Kisangani to Johannesburg. The benefits of the racket provided him and his friend, also a member of the racket, with otherwise unaffordable luxuries. They dined on French cuisine and played chess in their chateau at the edge of a mountain, far from the track of the common people. Then a rebel chief joined them and Dr Tom became wary of his Congolese friends. Mazembo peddled information to a militia group, a far more precious commodity than hawking diamonds to unlicensed dealers.

Kabamba's "trust me" made Dr Tom recall all that as he watched her fade away in the dusty road. His silence became an answer itself. He stood by the pillar beside his patients, biting his tongue. For months they had tried to rescue the health catastrophe, with no success. Dr Tom remembered reading in *A Medical History of Africa in the 1960s* about when patients were referred to the Congo from South Africa. As he supervised the nurse who brushed the crumbs from an old woman's lips, Dr Tom thought of just how crazy human beings could be.

It was midnight, and there was still no sign of Kabamba. Issa rose with difficulty from his bed to sit on a folding chair, slouching against its metal back. Now Elima and the woman who had brought her knew his name. They came to his side. He gave the girl a packet of juice from his small fridge, a property of the UN peacekeeping in Goma.

"What's this?" Elima asked, whose head was outlined in clotted blood.

"Drink some."

Elima turned it over, not knowing what to do with it.

"You've lost a lot of blood. Drink it," Issa said. He helped her open it and showed her how to sip through the straw stuck on the side, one of the items in the overflowing basket from the UN base. She bent the packet, and the liquid trickled out.

"What is it?" Elima said again.

"Put the straw into your mouth." Issa pushed her hand toward her mouth, bending the straw to her lips.

"Is it sweet?" he asked. She nodded with delight.

14

About two weeks after Issa was stoned, Bakayoka turned up for supper at Salif's house. Fatimata was wearing her blue wrapper with a green design, the one she kept deep down in her box. When Bakayoka knocked, she walked to the door slowly, wearily, her hair short and grey and her face sleepy. The ground trembled under Bakayoka's big boots. It was five minutes to seven when Fatimata discovered that Bakayoka was waiting for dinner and went into the kitchen to fry some plantain, to add to the simple couscous and milk they were having. Bakayoka said nothing until he looked up and spotted Malika across the table.

He tried to act friendly by saying hello, casually. Then let the cat out of the bag, saying "So sorry, woman, for what happened to your husband. Thanks be to Allah he did not die on the spot. Those stones were heavy, em. But we're happy he's alive. "

At the mention of stones, Malika froze. Her brain nimbly understood that something was seriously wrong. She waited for Bakayoka to leave, and then she called Commandant Thiam who confirmed that Issa had been hospitalized for serious injuries caused by stoning by the Congolese youth who were angry that the peacekeepers have not protected them from the rebels.

She rejected this news, hoping it was not true. All night, she sat waiting for the dawn, shivering with goose bumps, her jaw aching with the effort of keeping her teeth from chattering. She held her wake, but could hear no birdsong.

Malika did not sweep the compound in the morning. She bit her fingernails and her face was jagged with wrinkles. She was unhappy with herself, with others, with Issa's bosses, with her life. She cursed those who had stoned her husband and moaned that life was full of contradictions, full of lies. She wrung her hands, her teeth rattled and her lips trembled.

When Ami Colle woke up and saw Malika, she feared that Malika might withdraw and become depressed. "You can't go on like this. Speak out if you need help," said Ami, on their way to the market. They had never before discussed the Congo.

"What is there to say? My husband is between life and death, and here am I."

"Pray for him."

"I'm too distracted too."

"Try. Take care of yourself. Other women have their husbands in Iraq, in Afghanistan, yet they haven't lost their minds."

Malika sat bent over at the market that day, her forehead touching the table. She didn't lift it, even when buyers came around. Four customers walked away from her table after waiting in vain for her to react. Although they didn't understand, they didn't ask why she looked so lost while others were selling their fish as usual.

Ami Colle's eyes turned red with fury when she returned to the table. "What are you doing? Sleeping?" she asked. "Our customers are all gone."

"I wasn't sleeping. I only closed my eyes." She rubbed her face.

Ami Colle pushed her chair to the centre of the table. "How could we afford to miss so many sales in this time of steep competition?" Malika stood up, appearing not bothered. They sat in unusual silence.

A person should be used to a situation five years down the line, Ami Colle thought. Issa had sent Malika pocket money as an affirmation of his love. Yet she wanted him back, as if she had won a jackpot for them to survive on. Ami Colle called it chasing the dark, capable of worsening the situation.

"I understand that you want Issa back. That is normal. But given the turn of events, I'd advise you to free your mind, build your reserves and exercise vast amounts of patience," Ami Colle said.

Before they packed up the fish unsold due to Malika's absent-mindedness, Ami Colle joked about how madly in love Issa had been the Christmas that followed their first meeting, how he enjoyed the season in ecstasy, and flashed his joy for everyone to see. Malika smiled gently, but as soon as they got home, before Ami Colle could put down her bowl, she hurried straight into the room and locked herself in. There, she contemplated putting an end to her life. She held herself back from the thought of it. As a young girl she had learnt in Catechism classes that life belonged to God.

She could not imagine Issa dying and him dying without them having had a child together. She remembered the admiration with which he had spoken about her. She loved him because he loved her. She hoped that he had not let that fire die nor let it fade as a result of the distance between them. When he had fallen in love with her, he had taken her as a shelter from the cruelty of the wicked, as a place to feel appreciated and praised. After seeing her the first time, he had run faster than her, jumping from admiration to love, from love to plans for marriage and other arrangements, all in a flash. The wedding gown was hers to choose, yet he chose it. Because it came from his deepest white-hot centre, he had spoken from the heart. His admiration had brought about love, his love joy, and his joy new admiration. They had enjoyed Friday nights together at the cinema or the dance club, when there was no fast. And then came the peacekeeping.

She considered herself without the mirror. *Herself.* The most astounding reminder of Issa's efforts was herself – who she was and who she had become as a result of his influence in her life. She had passion and ambition. People turned to admire her as she walked down the road. She reminded herself of this, using it to dispel the darkness in her thoughts. It would have been a lot better had they been in communication, but phoning was forbidden. "It is forbidden in wartime," Commandant Thiam said categorically. And even if it weren't, shells had severed Kinshasa's central telephone server, making international calls impossible.

Fatimata forcibly opened the door to where Malika lay. "Won't you sweep the compound today? What are you waiting for?" she asked her.

"I'm not myself, Mama," she replied.

Fatimata pursed her lips, surprised at this answer. "An adult like you, instead of going to see the doctor, you lie down and moan." She pulled a plastic bucket from the corner of the house, stopped and surveyed the unswept compound. Then she barked irritably, "Be sure what you're suffering from."

"Don't talk like that, Mama."

"You dare not answer me back! What sort of sickness made you lie down without explaining anything?"

"Oh, Mama! Oh, Mama! I'm against no one. I've... I've... I offended no one. I'm jealous of no one's car…"

Fatimata shook her head. "Then you're really sick."

Malika turned over to her left side. "I feel like departing from this world."

"There is nothing to do. Nowhere to go. Only moths drowned in my drinking glass. It's almost like hell."

"E-e-e-h," Fatimata said, nerves firing off beneath her skin. She paused to fiddle with her wrapper. Malika's words had touched her. "You mean you can't see a better day coming?"

"What is a better day? No, I can't," Malika said, "really, I can't."

Fatimata drew closer. Malika had never before sounded so reckless. "Moths in my drinking glass," Malika answered, turning to her side. Troubles everywhere.

"Then you need to go and see Bintou."

"Leave me alooooone!" Malika screamed, her face puckered up like a one-eyed cow.

Fatimata ran to Salif's workshop to tell him that Malika was losing her mind.

"Which means?" Salif said.

"It means soon she will be bla-bla-blaring all day."

"Take her to the Lebanese doctor."

Fatimata hesitated. "I suggest we take her to Bintou in Cambrina, rather."

Salif turned suddenly to look at Fatimata. It was her mouth twisted, clownish, more than her words, that gave Salif a prickle of suspicion. "Why Bintou? Since when do women become marabouts in Segol? How can they combine having a menstrual cycle and the use of the Quran in a pure manner? Do you take me for a fool?"

"Pa Ndiaye, there is no time to argue about who's a fool and who's not. Something is seriously wrong with Malika and we need to take action."

Salif knew his head wife was talking about Bintou's divination. A group of students that had emigrated to Spain were said to have used it and the newspapers had spent a lot of ink on the story. Even if it were so, Salif thought, then what? Does she think I'll become her client? Islamic esoteric knowledge is the exclusive reserve of men. Full stop.

"Okay," Salif said, "go and try it. Take a taxi to Cambrina. Bring my bag here, so I can give you some money."

A clandestine taxi conveyed Fatimata, Malika and two other women to the Djembe border. From there they crossed the Djembe–Diadia toll highway, arriving at the bus stop twelve kilometres south of Diadia West, just as the fishermen began their work in the morning's breeze. One of the women remained in the taxi. Fatimata, Malika and the other women went on with two Wolof men in a horse-drawn wagon. The rider whipped the horse and it bolted off at a frightening speed. Malika slammed her eyes shut. When she opened them, they were in Cambrina. They spent the first twenty minutes in a small reception room in the front of Bintou's house together with eight other people, half of them young men, all talking about money.

"Where are we?" Malika asked Fatimata. She responded with a sign language. Malika had difficulty understanding why they were there.

"Her amulet is fully cooked," one woman said. Malika didn't understand. What amulet was there to be cooked? She looked down at her now filthy blouse, felt the dust rubbed against her face and palms, and she understood. Fatimata had brought her to see a marabout.

Bintou, the marabout, took a seat in her office. Her aide waved Fatimata and Malika in. It was their turn. Malika took some kava-kava to stave off her fatigue. Seeing a marabout was work. Bintou sat on the floor while they sat on wooden stools.

"What can I do for you?" she asked.

"She's troubled with bad spirits," Fatimata answered, touching Malika. Bintou asked Malika her name and her mother's name. She folded up some pages bearing writing and some green powder into small bundles and wrapped them in white cotton. She closed her eyes for the divination, Arabic geomancy, and then raised her head up for astrology and numerology. She bent down, her forehead touching the ground, sitting cross-legged. Fatimata nodded. Malika's star was exposed.

"You must stay behind for ten days so I can conduct mystical tests to protect you," Bintou addressed Malika. "After that you'll be free of Leviathan's slap and you will blossom."

She examined Malika's ankles, shook powder on her toes and palms and perfumed her hair. "I challenge you, Leviathan," she said.

"You must wear rubber sandals around the compound. You must not wear other people's accessories. If you do, my work will be hampered."

She worked her way back up Malika's body, pausing at the waist to enquire about her weight and diet. She cradled Malika's cheeks between her palms and spoke to her covered chest. "There are no signs to distinguish a possessed person from a mentally ill one," she said. "But from the position of your star, I can ascertain that you have an issue with someone in the netherworld, issues unresolved before the person's death."

Malika gazed at her with an idiotic stare. "Don't worry," Bintou said. Malika's breath was warm against her neck, her flesh a few degrees warmer than the room temperature. "I'll see it yet clearer in visions."

Daba, Bintou's aide, took Malika to one of the living rooms, pushing her into a chair when she resisted.

"You must stay behind," she ordered.

"Don't talk to me like that. I'm not a witch. I'm only suffering from the doubts that cloud my future. Who do you think you are?"

"I'm someone who can help you be free." From a closet nearby, Daba scanned a disordered stack of items from a surviving photo album and picked out a thick portfolio. "Look through this if you need help falling asleep," she said, handing it to Malika. The photo album was one of the few snapshots to survive Bintou's disconnected journeys. She flipped through the photos. They were of the days when Bintou had received her initiation on the mystical secrets of the Quran from her father, a marabout.

Alone in the guest room, Malika lifted the photo album. The spine creaked like rusty hinges as she lifted the cover. By the look of it, the closet was rarely opened and she wondered why Daba had taken the trouble to force it open. She was not interested in looking at a marabout's photo collection, however. Marabouts gathered their clients as a mad person gathered discarded objects. Most marabout clients had proven to be dangerous and the marabout's potions could not erase the evil within them.

Malika was remembering what had happened some months back when a client's charm was exposed in the old neighbouring Guinea. The marabout and his middlemen had fled and the man's magic charms had failed to work. His crime in the "Guinea Annals" burst like an oil pipe, flooding the entire Gulf. After the rattle of guns had drained all the blood, the memory of that blood remained. An expecting mother had slipped, dislocating her shoulder. That had not prevented marabouts from continuing to mix portions and people like Fatimata from soliciting them.

Daba directed Fatimata on what to bring for Malika and the cost of the ten days she would spend at Bintou's house.

"That's all?" Fatimata asked.

"That's all?"

"Superb." Just as Fatimata left, Malika wondered if there was any truth in what Bintou said about her. Had Fatimata acted out of total freedom? She suspected Fatima's decision to bring her there might have been suggested by her conservative friends. "Yes, I'm mad, but my madness now is about how to join my husband."

She was exasperated, but too tired for any real anger. "It's easy to exert your power as a mother-in-law, just packing someone off to a marabout. Wait, doesn't she know she's old enough to become a grandmother?" She called after the aide, "Where is the bathroom?"

"There," Daba said, pointing ahead.

Malika dozed off with the photo album open on her lap. Her sleep wasn't deep, like that of a child, only a fitfulness exacerbated by the descent from kava-kava. Dehydration, exhaustion, poor nutrition, and a depletion of serotonin. She knew the symptoms but couldn't fathom them in her dreams.

She woke to a kava-kava hangover: a headache, a dry mouth and an accelerated heart rate. She went to the bathroom, pulling a bottle of perfumed water from her handbag. She had received two such bottles as gifts from a soldier's wife, whose husband had returned from Kosovo. A few plump drops fell from its mouth, the fragrance soaking into her palms. Flies were not a concern. She walked out a few minutes later, her hands wrapped around her nose.

"I overheard you while you were sleeping," Daba said. "You were speaking Swahili."

"Really? What a coincidence. My husband is in the Congo, in the eastern part, working as a peacekeeper. He once began his letter home with a Swahili word." Malika smiled. "I think it's *habari*. I doubt if I pronounced it well."

"Swahili. It's spoken in Uganda, Rwanda, Burundi and the Eastern Congo. But why did it not prevent them from devouring each other?"

"You mean they speak the same language?" Malika said.

"Of course," Daba said with the authority of a prospective marabout. They are our *brothers*."

Malika nodded. "My husband is there. It's been exactly five years now. We just got married when he left. I spoke to him on the day he entered the country, but have never again reached him since then. I don't know if he's alive or dead. Sometimes, I feel like he's no more. Then that he is. I was about to die. So they brought me here."

"They did well, if not–"

"I just need my chap back."

"Sorry."

"Can Bintou do something about that?"

"Tell her."

"She should tell me," Malika corrected her. She did not want to continue in the mental quagmire.

A Pajero jeep rumbled into the dusty compound, packed with men, all dressed in large, fully-embroidered caftans. Ten minutes later they got out of the car and headed down the street in the opposite direction. They came back and asked if that was the shrine of Bintou. One hurried over a lighted cigarette, pausing every second to massage his wrists. Daba led them into the waiting room. She came out immediately.

"They're her clients," Daba said. "They want a big contract in the government."

"And they came here?"

Daba smiled. "Yes. They… they want some push."

"A *rocket*."

Daba laughed this time. "There's war everywhere."

"It won't end."

"Let me tell you," Daba said, flourishing her prayer beads. "Spiritual warfare is more dangerous than AK-47s. It is more deadly than crossing the border to seize a diamond mine, because you're fighting with spirits."

When Fatimata reached home, Salif and the entire household were waiting. "Welcome," they said as Fatimata rushed to the tap to wash her hands.

"Where is she?" Salif asked. Fatimata merely nodded. "Where is Malika?" Repetition did not change Fatimata's silence, Salif noticed. It merely prolonged it.

"She is at the marabout's house," Fatimata said at last.

"Allah, the Merciful! She imprisoned her?" Salif observed his head wife, as if seeing her for the first time. "Did she misbehave?"

"Calm down, Pa Ndiaye. Bintou said Malika needed intercessions, visions and oracles."

"Ohoo," Salif nodded. "Perhaps Malika saw something, heard something, perceived something. Who knows?"

Salif mused over this. He pulled a fresh bitter cola from his pocket, and threw it into the wind. "For the ancestors."

"I have a list from Bintou."

"I know. It's predictable. I'm not stupid," Salif hurried off, but Fatimata was already walking away. She quickly disappeared from sight, shut the door behind her and went to Malika's room at the House of Dudu. Fatimata looked through the window to see if Salif was following her. She opened Malika's box and began to pick out what she needed for the ten days. Her hand stumbled on packets of kava-kava. She quickly hid them under the bed.

15

Bintou entered the room where Malika was still sleeping and made excessive noise with her divining tools. She banged chains into each other, first dropped one ring, then another. She wanted to make sure Malika was completely alone before she began her work.

"M-a-l-i-i-i-i-i-k-a!" Bintou shrieked, her voice making the wall reverberate. "Wake up!"

Malika's face had swollen over the night. The spot of deep purple that marked the appearance of a stitch on her cheekbone, an effect of the marabout's administrations, had spread. "You must wake up now!" Bintou cried. "Your sky is filled with vultures. There is a dark spot by your eye; a sign of perfidious evil, strong enough to ruin you."

"It cannot ruin me." Fear echoing in her words. She meant the *witch* that had separated her from her husband for so long, the *witch* she smelt soon after her husband's departure.

"Nor do I fear the Beast, which might counter my work," said Bintou.

Malika glared. For a moment, Bintou recited words in Arabic to invoke the past: her life, long before Issa came, sibling rivalry, the beatings she had received from her mother, and memories of her mother instructing her on her last day in the house. How could Bintou have known all that?

Someone knocked at the door. Fatimata entered carrying bags and food. She paid no attention to Bintou's mystical trance and reached for Malika, sitting on the bed. "For you," she whispered, handing her a cell phone and leaving the rest on the floor. Daba had allowed her to take the goods in to Malika. She quickly left the room to return to the waiting room. Wondering if she had missed any calls, Malika flipped open her phone, her eyes gleaming. She went to her inbox and pressed the enter button. "My Malika! How're you? I'm in Goma. I'm doing well… " read a text message from a Congolese number.

Malika read the message again and again, amazed. "I can't believe this," she said. Issa was the only one on earth who addressed her like that. "Could this be my darling?" Her heart was exultant, convinced of it. She read the message yet again. Her heart did a somersault, as if it were jumping out of her chest. She clutched her phone with a survival instinct, as if it were a talisman. Softly, she rubbed it against her chest and across her body, kissing it twice, happily. Like a hot balm. What need was there to wait for divination, what need? She found her deeper self. In the voice of Issa. Her irritability ceased and her sourness disappeared. It was a good feeling.

Malika wished to tell Bintou she was perfectly well and could return home, but Bintou was too busy with her performances. So Malika waited until she had finished trekking through the spirit world, its hallways and deserted paths.

"No language can quite describe my inner feelings, but I think I'm happy now. I can go home," she said.

Bintou's hands roiled down her black prayer beads. "You're far from safe. I say your star is exposed, exposed for Leviathan to shoot at." They paused, avoiding each other's eye.

"My husband just messaged me. He's still alive." When Bintou paid no heed, Malika gave in. A female marabout was not one to argue with, especially if you were in her grips. The likes of Bintou were known to spill venom on those who opposed them, be they clients or relatives. Malika held her phone close to her chest and beamed as Bintou approached her.

"They're here!" Bintou yelled, shaking her head vaguely. She fixed her eyes intently on Malika. "I'll take revenge if you so much as touch Malika."

Malika glared at Bintou. "Who are they?"

"Stop!" Bintou ordered her interlocutor in the spirit world. "She's my daughter."

Malika smiled at Bintou's display of affection and adjusted her phone cover.

"You evil spirits, do you want to kill Malika?" Bintou said.

"Kill who?" Malika asked in a low voice, startled. Bintou was agitated and apparently in trance, ignoring her.

"Nonsense!" she cried to her interlocutor in the spirit world, as if she was challenged. "Of course you know the strength of my teeth!"

"Let me go, let me go," Malika begged as Bintou took the Quran in her arms. "I must wear all my armour to quell this uncommon cold which is testing my power." She began to recite some incantations, displaying a rare mastery of Islamic literature.

After Bintou had finished the warfare against the evil powers, she gave Malika an amulet to wear constantly around her waist and a bottle of potions to wash with. "Using this will make you invisible whenever a wicked spirit is sent to you. Amulet – the hypodermic of defence, aesthetic spit, the client's label. It would lead you to safety, just as it would lead any wicked spirit to doom."

They went through the same process for six days in a row. On the morning of the seventh day, Bintou took Malika with three other clients, two women and one man, south through the scrubland savannah town of Ndinat, then across to Madina-Mer by fishing boat. Malika's amulet and phone travelled with her, but were never actually in her possession. They were held onto by Bintou, who carried it as if she owned her. Although she conducted other new forms of divination there, certain rituals remained constant. Each morning she handed out potions for Malika to bathe with. By afternoon, she was scratching her body and in the evening, she was compelled to wear the amulet to fend off bad spells in the night. She was afraid of Bintou, and aware that she would be knocked down by a car if she fled, that she would put her in-laws in trouble if she went to the police and that she would ruin her marriage if she went home. Bintou was known to possess spells that could create confusion between couples. Malika did not know where she was, what language Bintou spoke, where to hide the pocket money Issa sent her, how to get her phone back, nor how to break these chains.

It was increasingly foggy, although it was only early December. Malika saw ancient mud huts, low brick structures and terracotta roof tiles. Days passed without difference. Time was marked not by minutes, but by divination sessions. Ten took place on one night, twelve the next. At each, it felt like entering into a desolate cave, with the white scarf around one's head, the traditional gowns and the visions; the chants in Arabic, Wolof and Malinke; the powers of sorcery and of magic.

Bintou referred to Malika as "my daughter". Then another woman client told her, "You thought she has been joking all along; meanwhile she has seen *digging* into your life." Bintou had looked through her life, like in a mirror. On an average day, a meal consisted of three pieces of bread, two smoked fish, four glasses of water, and two shots of coffee. They received strips of the chewing stick only, without toothpaste. She spent days sleeping without a pillow. The other woman was right. This was modern-day exploitation.

The days passed, like nights. They spent them on the third floor of an incomplete building, the doors and windows locked. It was dim all the time. Their mattresses were thrown on the floor in the crowded bedroom. Meetings with Bintou took place in a cosy master bedroom, but the clients slept on flattened strips of foam. The room was full of swords, masks, trunks, coins, and other items related to the marabout's practice. One client left. Four more arrived. Of the four, one brought the others plate of rice and fish. They were all in need, driven by one trouble or another that they believed only Bintou, the marabout, could solve.

Three of the women fought over a piece of fishcake found lying on the bench. Before anybody managed to reach it, they were clawing at each other's hair, drawing blood and screaming curses. One of the women pushed through, diving with precision at the cake. She held the bread like food, provoking an omen within it. Her hands began to shake and to swell before Bintou answered the call for rescue. The other women held her to support her.

"This is a poisoned gift," Malika said examining the fish. They stamped on the piece of fish, crushing it.

"That's revenge," Bintou said, rubbing the woman's swollen hands with ointments from herbs. Bintou stroked her beard as she rubbed in the herbal ointment, a nervous quirk that gave her the appearance of a marabout in distress. She did this when something seemed a considerable challenge to her. "How did that thing get here?"

Malika shook her head blankly, as did everyone else.

Bintou's remedy produced confused results and there were no doctor's signposts in this isolated district. Malika examined her fingers with their calluses and bitten nails. She blushed and attempted to hide them, but Bintou caught Malika's hands in her own.

"This ointment relieves the spell of the wizards," she said. "Assassination, failure, you unravel the rest." Bintou's hands were warm. She was yet to conduct a vision to know what the day would bring. Bintou touched her forearms. She had a delicate touch, a female marabout's courage and self-control.

"I keep thinking in Arabic," Bintou said. "*Tariq*. The consequences of forcing nature. Kiss of death. Penknives."

"This is your hair," Bintou said. "This is your life." She touched Malika's chin and her cheeks. "And nails," she said, and leaned on her. "An enemy can harm you if they get clippings of these."

A moment passed and Malika pulled away. She felt something else within. A loving kiss, a falling embrace, sensations that did not come from a magician casting a spell. It was Issa's presence she was yearning for, his presence that would not hurt, never injure.

Later that night when Malika returned to the room, one of the women said, "You vanished."

"How did I vanish?" The others broke into laughter.

They ate three morsels of bread each and drank some hot tea made from leaves of local plants. The woman who said she had vanished had developed a liking for her. Malika wiped the crumbs from her cheeks and chewed on her chewing stick. They threw their mattresses on the floor when they were ready to sleep. All but one florescent tube still held their distressed face in view. Malika pulled the dusty curtain across the window, and the women could see nothing more of the outside world.

"We will sleep on the same mattress tonight, okay?" said one of the women.

Malika nodded, took off her slippers, and slumped onto her mattress. The foam felt like sandpaper against her skin. The woman wrapped her arms around Malika's neck.

"I forgot your name," she said. "I'm sorry about upsetting you."

"I'm Malika."

"Malika. What a nice name." They lay together on the mattress, Malika's breath lighter than the woman's. Malika's mind returned to Issa, as they lay face to face.

"I want to go home."

"Have you found a solution to your problem yet?"

The question worried Malika for a moment. Then she spoke again. "I think I have. Tell me a story."

The woman yawned, tried to summon up a story to give her new friend pleasant dreams.

"An English woman had her husband sent to fight in World War I," she began. And the story unfolded. Malika soon dozed off.

On the ninth day, Bintou conducted the last session as she drew up sixteen signs with red ink on white papers, searching for a vertical line consisting of entirely single marks. Again she questioned Malika about her feelings, and again she replied that she felt nothing.

Bintou shook her head. "You frustrate me, my daughter. Your mind is elsewhere. You're in a marabout's house, so now think with me. You have a problem to solve. Your absent-mindedness is distressing."

"I'm not a witch."

"Nor am I. We're crossing a river together," Bintou said, pointing at the drawn-up papers with her hands, dry as the harmattan.

"Then we are in a wilderness without grasses, without water or calabash to direct us. We are like foam at the edge of the bucket. But you seem to ignore this. You can only see the man you love."

"What's a calabash for," asked Malika, "if not for palm wine tappers in the south?"

Bintou left her to attend to the other clients.

That night, Bintou returned and sat awake beside Malika who slept through her visit as a dry wind carried the murmur of shrivelling plants. She was fully dressed and heavily perfumed, prepared for another trek through the spirit world.

When the bus pulled up to the house, Bintou had already loaded the bags with enough plants and animal skins to grip the hearts of eventual clients in search of lucky charms. Some people are life-takers and some are life-savers, she thought, but all are susceptible to pain. Malika remained asleep, unaware of anything going on around her. Bintou took time to tie an amulet around Malika's waist, before rubbing her skin with ointment. She had blown on Malika's face, exerting mystical power she would sleep through this. When the power Bintou exerted expired, Malika emitted a groan as the marabout's hand hit her abdomen, her eyelids then flashed open and her snoring ceased. She awoke.

The men outside opened the van door, but the sound of footsteps on the floor of the house where Bintou and her clients lodged revealed neither familiarity nor allegiance. Bintou placed a small piece of red cloth on the vein of Malika's right hand, then drew her palm across her face, closing her eyes. The pounding on the floor grew louder as the men outside carried luggage and Bintou's tools. There are innocent people in the world, Malika held, and they are not only the young and naive. Malika was awake now.

When the men walked in through the upper door to say they were done, Bintou covered Malika's head with white apparel. Malika prayed for her mother-in-law, that God may forgive her misjudgement. She prayed for Issa, that she may bury him in their old age, in their land. But when the men started hassling her, when they threw her shoes into the back of the waiting van, Malika prayed only for herself.

Early the next morning, after they returned to Cambrina, Bintou told Malika she had saved her from danger and that she at last could return home. She ordered Daba to accompany her. Malika wondered if this was another poisoned gesture. Daba was to collect the payment from Fatimata. Daba gladly put Malika's bags on her shoulder and they left for Djembe. She negotiated buses and taxis and paid their fares. She cleaned the bags, protecting them from dust with her outer wrapper. When the bush taxi scratched the paintwork of a brand new Peugeot, the passengers all rushed to observe the damage, and Daba alone assisted the driver to negotiate a truce. She slept less and kept track of the bus stops.

At Djembe, Daba held Malika by the hand as if she were a new mother, returning from a maternity ward. When she was asked to sit down at the house, Daba could not sit still, could not stop fidgeting. Once Fatimata had provided the payment requested by Bintou, Daba stood up to leave. Malika wondered if Daba had ever been married, like Bintou. What if she could get the right man to love? But she could, she could, Malika thought, peeking through the door as Fatimata led Daba down to the street junction. With her purse in her arm and a plastic bag in her hand, Daba was returning to Bintou. Malika believed that she could still be a wife, a mother. She shut the door and entered the House of Dudu. She felt happy being home, happy that she had recovered her freedom, but somewhat ashamed that she had been taken to a marabout.

For over a week, neither Salif nor Fatimata, nor anyone in the house, asked Malika what the marabout had done to her. Ten days later, however, when Malika was tying the charms Bintou gave her around her waist, they began to screech insistently, mysteriously. A whistle was heard seemingly from the tiny piece of leather, rotating in a circular movement. Malika ran to call someone. The light in her room went off and the room became dark. A red light flashed from the central surface of the leather-cased object. No relief, only a clatter spurting from the tiny amulet. She ran in a panic, collided with the door and fell. She fled. Fatimata was arranging vegetables into the tool shed, toward the intersection between the House of Dudu and the House of Ndiaye and her wheelbarrow was filled to capacity with some tubers dragging against the ground as she doggedly pushed it along.

A frightened Malika grabbed Fatimata by the waist, almost pushing her to the ground. "Help, Mama, help," she cried. She held tight to Fatimata. She breathed quickly and loudly, hot air coming out of her nostrils against Fatimata's neck.

In the tool shed, she stumbled over the hoes. Tears gathered around her eyes. She started suddenly and crouched down, hugging her knees. Fatimata dropped to her knees too, silently. She took Malika's temperature. She did so with a touch of comfort, nearly a massage. Fatima did everything she could to solve the puzzle, calling those of her friends who consult marabouts frequently. She asked in Wolof, "Do you know what this could be?" and "Have you heard of such a thing?" and "How can she survive it?"

But Malika was suspicious of Fatimata's sincerity. When Salif heard what happened, he recited some verses before the amulet and quenched the screech, commanding the one behind it to quit his house. The amulet was silenced. Salif kept a close eye on Malika for a week.

Most nights when he fought sleep to watch over her, he attempted to find out what had happened that day the amulet had started screeching. The questions he asked were complicated, in spite of their apparent simplicity.

"What really happened? How did the shrieking began? Were you afraid?"

Malika tried to answer, but stumbled over her words.

"I see. I see what you mean," Salif said. "Just start at the beginning."

"The beginning?" Malika inquired. There was no beginning. "My body became like a stone, as huge and odd in the hazy sky."

Salif asked no more as he heard some noise from the bedroom meaning Fatimata was not yet asleep.

Malika continued with Bintou's cure of bathing with her potions. She still wore the amulet at the insistence of Salif, still needed to wear it for another sixty-six weeks as Bintou ruled. She was afraid to open the purse containing the leaves she was supposed to dip in water and drink.

At the market that week, she felt dizzy and fell off her chair. She forgot the charm, but then she remembered it and turned to it. Her arm stretched across to it, her fingers pinching the corner of the charm as customers rallied around her, some touching and turning the fish to see which one to choose. The sight of male customers put her off: wicked creatures incapable of nothing but firing weapons. She had never seen a bullet, never seen a body riddled by it. Only Issa had a heart of gold.

They raised her to a floorboard. A voice came from behind in a language she didn't understand. A customer pushed forward some coins for two smoked fish and the sound of the coins landing on her table made her start. She felt too dizzy to follow what was happening. The customer laughed, then turned away. When she felt better, she searched the ground for the coins. They had fallen against the foot of the stool and she picked them up, rolled two smoked fish in paper and handed them to the customer. She exhaled with relief. She had sold all the fish.

16

Salif finished his prayers, rose and folded his raffia mat. He took his seat quietly and continued working at his weaving. He was listening to *BBC Afrique*. He stopped suddenly and the narrow strips he was weaving loosened and slipped to the floor. A hot wind blowing across the arid landscape blew up fine dust particles. He reached for his radio and turned up the volume. His palms were dry and white so he rubbed them with cocoa butter. Something about UN peacekeepers resonated across his eardrums. He listened more attentively, pushing out his earlobes to hear better. The headlines repeated: "UN peacekeepers in the Congo sexually harassing children."

"Am I losing my hearing?" he said. "No, no, no, no, Salif. Your ears must be deceiving you."

An hour passed and the journalist returned. Salif threw a piece of bitter cola into his mouth. He knew the kola would be dry, but the news had made his mouth doubly sour. He spat out the kola and peeled it back again, yet it remained vinegary. He didn't mind much. "Let the assholes pay the price," he decreed. "Is there no flight to their home countries?"

That night, Malika's phone rang, disturbing her light sleep.

"Sorry to disturb you. Did you hear that?" asked Kristen.

"Oh… hear…?" Malika said drowsily. The line cut out.

"Switch on your TV," Kristen texted her later. Although the message arrived at four o'clock in the morning, Malika hurriedly got up, hastened to the parlour and turned on the TV. Reporters Without Borders had news on peacekeepers, from the Okapi bar, a Belgian-owned nightclub, which was pulsating with Congolese music. Malika bowed her head.

"More rubbish from men," she said, shaking her head balefully from side to side. She positioned herself before the TV, looking carefully each time a peacekeeper appeared in the background to see if he resembled Issa.

"Dirty helmets!" she banged, seeing the image of the base in Ituri. She felt exhausted. Her head was lost in the facts and figures, in the deluge of information. She lowered her head again as more reports emerged. She had not been abandoned like those whose husbands were off harvesting or washing grapes in the fields, mounting guards in restaurants or parking lines, or working underground, like Kristen's fiancé, returning only once in a blue moon. She was not lonely like some of the house helps, so adept at flashing their tanned breasts to ensure they didn't return to their villages without an engagement ring. She felt abandoned in a different way, and she knew it, and this recognition exacerbated her disapproval of the peacekeepers' misconduct. Once again, she held herself back from contemplating putting an end to her life. Ami Colle heard her jabbering as she walked into the sitting room.

"What is it Malika?"

"I don't know, ask the TV."

"Since when did the TV begin speaking?"

"It does, it does."

"Okay, just tell me."

"Dirty helmets."

"Why?"

"Unfit to marry."

"Be serious, Malika."

"Who said I'm not."

"So?"

"They are child abusers."

With Ami Colle – and surely not in Salif's presence – Malika was free with her language, but with not much else. She could only get so close to Ami Colle, and getting close to Salif's second wife relieved her. With Ami Colle, she felt safe in a strange way and somewhat reassured. The TV presenter returned to the topic of the Congo.

"Listen," Malika said, pushing her chair closer to the screen. Reporters Without Borders reran the coverage about the peacekeeping of a *pimp* from the Maghreb, wanted by the villagers of Ituri. He rented a room in a town bordering the Congo River and kept a girl child there, telling her to keep away from the barracks. He had bartered prostitution of the girl in exchange for jam and mayonnaise and was apparently hatching plans to shoot home-made pornographic videos at a wartorn girls' college. He called the Congo "No Man's Land", saying illegal sex was cheaper in Kisangani than in Casablanca. On Christmas Eve, the pimp got his trigger finger shot off by another girl who also gave him a green-purple bruise on his chest, which you could have thought was the shape of a turtle. However it was only a mark of a post-coital fight.

"We're not far from Abu Ghraib," the presenter concluded.

"Do they who did this call themselves UN peacekeepers?" Malika tore her wrapper in anguish. She was appalled. "There is no reason," she wept, trembling, "no excuse, none, really. They have their wives at home. What do they do that for?" She would go to all lengths to find out if Issa had slept with any Congolese girls. Even once. After all, she was staying with his parents and, of all the proposals she had received, his was the only one she accepted.

"UN by day, *nu* by night," she said to Ami Colle who was returning with her prayer beads.

"What an affair," she said. She was wearing her long white gown and a scarf covering her entire head, save for her face.

"What do you mean by *nu*?" She quickly put down her prayer beads on the centre table.

"Look it up in Dieynaba's dictionary. I mean *undressed*."

Malika did not taste any food in her efforts to learn if Issa was *nu* by night. If he had even been, she would take off the wedding ring. Wearing a purple gown and white bonnet, she chewed her chewing stick all day, as another traditional cleansing ritual. Instead of going to the market herself, she asked Babacar to take her bowl of fish to Ami Colle. Babacar liked that she stayed home.

With repeated insomnia, she soon lost track of the days. She fought to keep her mind from its rebellious thoughts, but try as she might, her mind returned to Ituri. Once she sought relief in singing, but it did not last. Her voice was so weak and worn that it did not relieve her and did not allay her fears. Her head was giddy, her nose was blocked, her mouth tasted sour.

Walking casually over to the water tap to wash her dry lips, two nights after the news, she told Dieynaba, "Make me some grapefruit drink."

Dieynaba cut open some grapefruits, extracted the pulp and mixed it the way Malika liked it. "Done," Dieynaba said with pride. "Natural flavour," she added, pouring it into a ceramic cup. "It will pique your appetite."

Malika lifted the cup to her mouth. "She'll grow into a fine-looking woman," she murmured, admiring Dieynaba, standing stylishly in front of her. She sipped the drink to halfway and gave the rest back to Dieynaba. "Bring me my soap case," she said.

Malika walked casually over to the tap to wash her hands and feet and tongue. She hadn't washed off her eye makeup last night so it was smeared down her cheeks. "I have to see into this," she said. "I can't be suffering here, while he's there gallivanting with a girl." She turned back toward Dieynaba. Malika walked past Fatimata's window, grabbed a chair and stood beside the tap. She crossed her leg again, and began to jiggle her foot.

On her way to the market the next morning, she branched off to see Mansu, now a practising prophet-diviner and requested a vision into Issa's life in the Congo. Just then she remembered that Father Du Buit had told her all forms of divination are the works of the devil. "I'll go to confession later," she exempted herself.

Mansu showed Malika how the divination worked, taught her how to throw a stone on the ground face up in a gourd, a curved cup made from cow horn, and how to use the mirror and the photo.

"The white men cannot find this not even with all their technology, but I can," Mansu bragged. He ordered her to think of her husband throughout the search and explained that no matter how attracted she might feel to anybody else, she should visualize Issa coming back to become the father of her children. "You had better die rather than think of a man other than Issa at this time," he warned her.

She fought to heed Mansu's words. At home that day, Babacar walked on water to distract her and she was worried about her in-laws discovering she had gone to see Mansu about Issa. She avoided questions from the members of the family and refrained from sitting on the pavement, no matter how free she was. Outside she appeared happy, yet inside she was perplexed. What if Issa had taken on a child mistress? She pretended she was fine – occasionally she uttered a rhythmless lament, an elegy like the chants of mourners at a funeral home.

As the sun was setting, Malika told Fatimata she would like to pay Kristen a visit. Random changes in the weather had struck the seasons out of forecast. The hot weather lingered and the early December harmattan was tarrying. Malika branched off to Mansu's house again, situated on high ground at the end of an alley, leaning against the rear of a thriving restaurant.

She sat on the tiled floor of his parlour. Occasional winds swelled the crimson batik curtain. The floor was packed with leather cushions that Malika expected had been gifts from people. It was totally dark inside, so Mansu rolled up the edge of the curtain to let in the radiance of the restaurant's security lights. A large stone, which served as the door wedge, lay behind the door.

Mansu threw a stone into a gourd containing a mirror. It was a wonder to Malika how Mansu did that without breaking the mirror. The clap of thunder that followed made Malika dash for cover, crouching on the floor. She adjusted herself in a panic, still lying on the floor. It was a booming noise, with the sounds of brass orchestra, and it shook the walls, as if the roof would fall in on them. Malika moved to a chair where she sat, her eyes darting from corner to corner, holding tightly to her sterling silver earrings (Poppy Jasper Hearts), yet another birthday gift she had received from Issa. Her earrings dangled when Mansu next threw the stone. She observed the gourd and the seven palm nuts from the seaside Mansu had requested from her, a symbol of personal involvement, a sign of completion.

Mansu's white caftan bore stains of onion stew down the front. He stated once again that he was the greatest diviner in Segol and that no bullet could pierce him. Malika calmed down after that and stretched in a yawn, bumping the tapper instrument hanging on the wall behind her. "That's normal," Mansu said. "The tapper instrument plays the role of the guardian of truth." One of the first signals from the stones in the gourd came in, according to Mansu.

Mansu nodded in agreement and put his hands under his caftan to adjust the strings of amulets around his waist. Ritual movements had swung them out of place. He dug through a large basket woven in the shape of a coil, scooping out ribbons, shells and broken pieces of mirror wrapped in red fabric that had first been used by his grandfather.

Mansu waited as he piled up the contents of the basket on his laps and down on the floor. Then he unearthed large needles and strips of plastic used for weaving sleeping mats. The strips would show him where Issa had slept and how.

Mansu smiled at the changes in the gourd and winked at Malika, moving his head up and down, as if bobbing to reggae music. He manoeuvred the strips skilfully, and they swelled with the smell of curative leaves. Malika watched him twist them into the shape of a bottle. Malika's mind filled with images of Issa. Though Mansu still appeared unconvinced of the images even after Malika confirmed them, his hands remained on the objects so that his bronze bracelets did not clatter. When he had seen all he was expecting, he stopped the stones from clinging to the palm nuts, and then tossed them out of the gourd, one after another. The last set of the stones out spun on his palm before soaring up into midair, like a comet. He covered the gourd with his palm, to exert further power. He left his palm on the gourd. He said removing it too soon would defuse the efficacy of the divination. "The last thing is to see what position the picture would take," he commented.

He turned to Malika, pushing the gourd with his foot. "You're welcome, my daughter," he said, as if she had just arrived. "You'll go home contented." Malika turned and nodded with pleasure, though still trembling from fright. Her toes were poking outside the rubber slippers she wore, exposing her traditionally dyed toenails. Her hands had broken free of her earrings. "You're welcome, my daughter," Mansu said again, and began to shuffle his legs communicating the success of the process to her.

Noise from passing cars squeaked outside. Mansu snapped his fingers and went to the backyard. He came in pulling a white ram, with long, curving horns. For a year and half, Mansu, who had killed a sheep every fortnight as sacrifice, had pushed the horns with precision until they became spiral almost like a budding yam tuber. He had hoped to kill this sheep after his fortieth visitor, which happened to be Malika. The sheep licked Malika's feet. "Eeee," she screamed, gesturing to Mansu for help. The sheep kept licking her feet.

"Oh, my daughter, don't bother yourself," Mansu said in a low voice. "It's here for some work." He then pulled the sheep by the red rope around its neck and led it outside. Malika bent down, covering her feet with her scarf. The sheep bleated four times as it went outside, which Malika later understood from Mansu's revelation was sign of good news.

"My daughter, your husband's picture is unruffled. He's blameless, so preserve your love for him," Mansu said.

Malika looked at him. "Thank you, Uncle." She opened her bag, pulled out a stuffed envelope and extended it to him. He pointed to the floor, so Malika placed the money there. Mansu would not receive gifts directly from a client's hands. A coin slid out from the envelope and rolled back to Malika.

Though some visitors were more generous depending on the range of the issues they brought and their financial means, Malika's envelope was not a widow's mite. It could cover livestock, food, a good caftan and a cow's thigh. He led her to the door and stopped there, as he rarely led a visitor beyond the threshold.

"Don't hesitate to come back if any trouble blocks your path," he said, his voice the timbre of a good businessman's. Malika thanked him again, and briskly crossed the road.

"Welcome back. Is Kristen at peace?" said Fatimata to Malika as she returned home. Malice forming under Fatimata's face with a smile.

"She will get married by April. No more meandering through the nightclubs."

"That's good. But was she not married before coming here?" asked Fatima.

"If she did, she wouldn't have stayed so long in Segol."

"I'm surprised."

"Ah! Such is life."

"No wonder she went to a series of marriage ceremonies."

"Goodness! You look too much, Mama. After three years of waiting for the right man, the man said he preferred to live in Italy. Then Kristen agreed to take him to America instead." Malika said she was surprised to hear that and had told Kristen so too loudly, as if commanding a child.

"As long as the man keeps his word. It's a matter of trust, that's the rule. He has been living in Fraaace long enough for her to know how they behave."

Fatimata's way of pronouncing "France" always made Malika explode with laughter. "But not in America," Malika said, still laughing. "Are they not all the same? One foot down and the other yet to come?"

"Ah, they're not, Mama. But the man is ready to adjust. Only that Kristen is worried that his once black face is now becoming white." She smiled.

Salif, accompanied by Babacar and Dieynaba, came in through the entrance. Two seconds later, Salif said, "Hmm, something smells. Does no one else perceive it? Something like smoke – and you sit here gossiping. Malika, go inside and check. Don't you have a nose?"

Malika obeyed and ran inside the house, Fatimata following ten paces behind. She knew Salif's words about gossiping were referring to her. She had become used to Salif's language in her forty-six years of living with him. The older Salif got, the more taciturn he became. She crossed her lips with a finger, lest she be reminded of all her shortcomings.

"Help! Help!" Malika shouted from the interior.

They rushed in the direction of her voice. There was a fire! Fatimata had begun heating oil and had forgotten about it; it had grown hotter and hotter, smoked briefly, and then burst into flames near the gas cylinder.

It was hell let loose. "Allah! The Almighty! Babacar!" Fatimata ran from one side to the other, yelling whatever came into her mind. "Bring some water! Bring buckets! Bring! Hurry!" She peered inside her kitchen as the fire devoured its glossy furniture. "Devil! You're a liar!" she snapped. Babacar ran in with the first full bucket and splashed water through the window. It was like a drop in an ocean. "Please, Papa, call the fa-fa-fa-fire people. Hey! Soon our roof will be destroyed," Fatimata cried.

Before the words were out, Salif had rushed out to call on some neighbours who ran into his compound carrying sand and jerrycans of water to put out the sudden fire. Water, sand, stones, all they could lift up landed into Fatimata's kitchen. But the gas had spread and she had a many wooden fittings and wood is the lure of fire. It was the piece of customized kitchen furniture she had bought with her portion of Issa's remittance. It had taken six months to complete it, during which foot treks of admiring neighbours had been a regular event. Many of the neighbours believed the fire was a curse sent on the family. None of them wondered why it happened to the House of Dudu. It was surely an omen. It only held for Malika suspense and surprise, and her feelings of astonishment grew as the fire consumed the lower furniture and spread out to the wooden window frames.

"Sorry! Help! Who have I offended? Who?" Fatimata cried. Her hands on her head, she gazed helplessly at the raging fire and shook the bucket to see if there were more drops of water to sprinkle on it. She took her cry out to the entrance for the whole street to hear. A woman reached out to grab her by the hands in comfort.

"Shut your dirty mouth!" Salif barked. "You caused the fire."

"That is impossible. Our enemies caused it."

"You had better shut up, before my own madness begins."

"My enemies, oh! My enemies brought fire."

"See, this woman wants me to – "

Soon the horn of the Fire Service sounded and they arrived. Their long red truck pulled into the street, water trickling out behind. But it did not stop at once. Turning around, the driver charged the engine and regulated it. It could not draw water immediately from the tank because it had grown old with age. The firefighters let the engine idle and ran into Salif's compound in the direction of the fire with the fire hose. Clad in their uniform, the head officer let out one long, deafening shout, then raced back to the van. Salif groaned and complained about the time it was taking them to extinguish the fire.

"Do you want my house to fall down before you start?" he asked. "I know the time I called you, the time you arrived, the time you started. I must report all this to your boss."

The water tank now ready, the fire men opened the nozzle. They rolled up their sleeves and began to battle with the fire, their lips moving in a silent search for stamina. Then, to triumph ultimately, they took the mouth of the hose and placed it across the wall, splashing water onto the debris. They pushed the mouth of the hose against the ceiling and the once reddened room became cool.

When they were sure the fire was extinguished, they returned the hose to the van. Since it was the first time they had been to the house, before they left, they issued a form for Salif to fill in and return to their office. The house smelt of smoke or rather like a pot of rice burned black. Inhaling it made one lose saliva, as the smoke numbed the tongue. The resulting heat climbed steadily into the throat, tickling their nostrils like a halted sneeze. An hour later, it cooled off completely and blew away the worst of the smoke.

Fatimata could not believe her kitchen had been reduced to a heap of acrid charcoal. She remembered Salif's words and said, "Papa, how can you accuse me of this?" Salif's mind was elsewhere, and he was too tired to speak. He preferred to remain silent. In addition to the money that he would spend on repairs, Salif had managed to buy two tins of *ataya* tea as a gesture of appreciation for the sympathetic neighbours who gathered to help. He took a taxi to the Fire Service and paid the bill.

"Cursed woman!" Fatimata charged at Malika shortly after Salif returned. "You put oil on the fire and forgot it."

"When, Mama? I had only just come back," Malika countered.

"So who's responsible for it, then? Where is Ami Colle? Were you the one who asked me to boil oil for you in order to fry fish for dinner?" Fatimata rubbed her burning eyes until the brightness of her eyes ebbed and her face acquired a lean, hungry look. Then she continued, "Somebody in this house asked me to put oil on fire. I did so and that person forgot about the oil." She stamped her foot on the floor with a smacking sound. As the red glow in her eyes disappeared, she puffed her chin out, and she sucked at and moved her lips, restlessly. She had never at once charged at Malika and Ami Colle. Malika approached her, and tried to clear her name of the oil issue.

"Can I go and visit Kristen?" she asked. Then "See you later."

"Do you think you can deceive me?" Fatimata barked.

Malika's eyes rolled over Fatimata's face, taking in her grey hair, red eyes, then noting her thin, shaky waist and darkened feet.

She, like most women in Segol under the control of their mothers-in-law, was adept at taking in the whole spectacle of an old woman. Every feature was assessed, categorized and analyzed within the blink of an eye. For the Segolian mother-in-law, it was hard to say whether this method was training or suspicion. Malika was so unhappy with Fatimata's suspicion she would have loved to write ABSURD on a piece of notepaper and flash it for her to see. But instead she held her hands at her side like a good woman and told her mouth not to let out any unwholesome words.

"You see what I mean, Mama?" she asked.

"No, I see what I mean. We were together most of the afternoon. Someone told me to heat up some oil at seven o'clock in the evening."

"But I was not the one. Was I?"

"That's the question."

"God, I did nothing. I said nothing."

"My question is: Who told me to put oil on fire at seven in the evening so she could fry fish?"

"I don't know," Malika said. "Ask the others. Maybe they know."

She looked again at Fatimata, who had an expression on her face that, if examined carefully – even without a lie detector – could be read to be telling lies.

Malika's room was next to the front entrance and she had a lot of trouble sleeping in the days that followed. For the first two weeks of the following month, workers Fatimata hired laboured to renovate her kitchen. They restored it using a new design, a southern exposure that opened into the dining room, installing lights that shone on the white paint on the cupboard and reflected off the wavy glass doors, filling the room with warmth.

Malika walked across the remodelled kitchen with trepidation, still with no assurance or guarantee that the blame for the fire had not been placed on her. The distance between the new kitchen and her room saw her tiptoeing lightly on the floor with a criminal watchfulness, approaching her bed so lightly, her feet barely touching the floor, hovering above the tiles. She carefully measured her steps so she did not make any noise that would rouse Fatimata.

"Ami Colle!" she once heard Fatimata call.

"Horror," she thought. Fatimata's eyes are so vigilant, she must have seen the oil stain on one of the wavy glass doors.

"Were you the one who did this?" Fatimata asked. To avoid a row with her, Malika vowed to cook outside on charcoal fire in future.

"No," Ami Colle replied.

"I can tell it hasn't been there for long," she said, facing the door.

"It's a pity." Ami Colle said.

"Tell me how, in Allah's name, someone dropped oil on the door on which I have spent all of my savings. This is enough! Eh, this is enough."

"I'll clean it," Ami Colle offered.

Though she never revealed it, the splendour of the new kitchen filled Malika with wonder. Blessing is a funny thing. To some, a large win at the international trade fair is blessing or receiving a phone call promoting them to a top job. That surely would be a blessing. But when a fire burns down one's kitchen, blessing takes another turn. The surge of flame that misses your eye is a blessing. Only your kitchen burning and not the whole house is a blessing. And having the money to rebuild and modernize your kitchen? Hurrah, count your blessings.

Malika thought of these blessings each time she looked at the new kitchen, how it stood radiant on a place where ashes once lay; she marvelled at what a blessing it was. She had always hated comparisons, but the unpredicted fire was making her aware that another story, if seen a certain way, could make you feel as though it were your own.

"The Lord surely moves in mysterious ways," she exclaimed. Assured of that, she savoured the certainty that things might get a little better for her, just as Fatimata's kitchen had improved after the fire.

17

Babacar found a piece of paper and pencil and drew a sketch of Malika with the long braids she had fixed for Kristen's wedding. Then he drew her again without them. He drew both while standing for an hour outside the House of Dudu, looking at her. Babacar had been drawing since his childhood. As a pupil, he had drawn numerous figures in his drawing book and his schoolmates haled them as pro. His teachers had encouraged him and sent samples of his drawings to *Songbird*, the premier children's magazine.

Babacar showed Malika his drawings. He was expecting her to clap her hands and squeal with amusement, but she was preoccupied with updating her life's story on how to find blessings. After looking at his work, she looked away unresponsively. Nothing remained of her cheerful face. When she finished her reflection on her life, she brought out her swimming kits to wash them.

In her mind, she skipped ahead to how it would all end, if Issa would finally return from the Congo, in good health, perfect and rich. They would build a beautiful house – like a mansion, to them anyway – so they could live a normal family life, surrounded by beautiful children. That would be their blessing. Her mind went back to the early chapters of her personal agony.

As she raised her swimming costume to spread it on the line, she heard Fatimata screaming, her voice overbearing and provoking: "If you hang that dirty thing there, I will throw it away."

Malika clipped her kits on the line, and stayed by them as they dried. She got up several times to touch them, to check if they were dry. That day, the sun was generous. She shook her head sadly, in silence, wondering how best to resolve her conflict-ridden relationship with her mother-in-law. Fatimata peeked through the window at the yellow kits, but did not emerge.

Malika eventually took them down when they were dry. She paid what she considered an intolerable situation no mind, trusting that soon she would be counting her blessings and would be able to rise above in-law quarrels, to a level higher than disdain could take her. In the evening, her head began to throb.

"Come out with me and lighten up," Babacar told her and offered to take her to Youssou's concert at The Thiossane. She smiled and started talking about all the men wishing to marry her. She joked about what it would be like to say yes to them all and live like those women who say "yes" to everyone who flirts with them. Babacar left to purchase entry tickets.

"Hey, beautiful!" one white man said to Malika as she entered The Thiossane. This white man thought he knew her from somewhere. The place was booming with mbalax music and bustling with eclectic fans.

"Ah, thanks." Malika laughed, straightening out her high-waist velour miniskirt.

"Will you give me a kiss on the cheek?"

"Well," she laughed nervously. "My husband is around."

"That doesn't matter."

"Oh," she said looking towards Babacar, her hand over her mouth. "Oh, oh, oh." In a blink of the eye, three other men, her childhood friends, surrounded Malika. Each tried to hold her, to pull her closer.

"You're here," one of them said, grabbing her hand. "It's been a long time. A welcome kiss or no access."

Malika jumped and pulled away from him, laughing and swinging her head. She called Babacar who was returning with entry tickets. The men pressed after her as Babacar left her to search for seats, accompanied by the shouting and laughter of the pre-concert comedy act. When she tried to balance her head from one angle to another, one of the men held her.

"A kiss on the cheek," he said, the others watching.

Malika kissed them playfully on the cheek. "You are happy now?" she asked.

"She's married, guys," Babacar said loudly.

Malika curtailed her excitement. She observed Babacar as he stood still, alone toward the air-conditioning, his feet spaced apart. He appeared struck with jealousy and was gazing at her with mixed feelings. When the men grabbed her as she tried to leave, Babacar lowered his head. He made as if he wanted too to leave, but could not step an inch away.

Malika suppressed her laughter and lowered her eyes. "Have fun," she said, waving at the men. One of them tried yet again to block her.

"I have to go now!" She slithered out of their presence, raised her head and hastened toward Babacar, pulling her skirt straight.

It was unclear to the men who Babacar was and Malika had skipped the topic. Giggling, her eyes followed the comedians as they lit up the hall with laughter. They gave her uncontrollable belly chuckles that she wished would last for ages. Their comic antics were so unpredictable that even jealous Babacar could not stop laughing, especially when a comedian mimicked Youssou's soprano voice. Malika clutched her stomach, tears streaming down her face. Babacar rubbed her back with the palm of his hand.

Youssou walked onto the stage, wearing his stunning sunglasses. Some fans shrieked as he started up with a Grammy title. Others stood up to dance. Some saved energy for the intricate rhythms and percussion to come. A few sat quietly, sipping their drinks amidst the cigarette smoke filling the air. Malika was transfixed by Dewel, Youssou's lead dancer, who was moving to the sound of the talking drum, sporting a clump of dreadlocks and a wide belt over his multicoloured gown.

Malika checked the button of her skirt to make sure it was done up, thinking of when best to climb up onto the stage. She was not afraid. All she wanted to do was laugh and dance.

"You like Youssou, Smallie?"

"Youssou's the best." He held her hand. Malika smiled. He was leaning an arm on her, they were holding a glass of cocktail each and giggling like schoolchildren.

"Malika, you know nothing about mbalax music, do you?" said Babacar.

"Well I know how to dance it." Then as they toasted each other, she leaned against him and said, "And let me tell you something – I want to dance. But, hush, do not tell Mama."

"You so like to dance, yet you married a man who has two left legs."

Malika stood up to dance and with everyone watching her, Babacar was not as happy as he might have been. Not even when she winked at him, slapped his back and said, "Of course, Smallie. I've proved to you that I can dance."

"Yes," he answered, clapping and nodding to confirm her pace.

Babacar then left to buy some more drinks. When he came back carrying two bottles of beer, he seemed in a hurry. "We must go now, woman. It will soon be dawn."

He tried to pull out the cork from the bottles, but they were tightly wedged in. Malika shook with laughter. A waiter had to be called. He came along, grabbed the bottles and tucking one under each arm, yanked out the cork.

"Come, we must leave," Babacar told her.

"It's been a wonderful night," she smiled. Then, with a rush, they downed their last bottle. They stood drowsily on the now quiet Greater Djembe Road and soon climbed into a taxi. Babacar held Malika firmly. His breath smelt of beer, but his chin was warm and soft against hers, his neck and palms freckled with goose bumps from the cold.

When they got home, Fatimata was lying in wait in front of the house. She bounded over in two steps towards Malika, and, even in the obscurity, discerned the expression on her face and eyes. Had she been drinking alcohol, smoking cigarettes, forgetting she's my son's wife? Malika looked groggy, but she stood still for Fatimata to examine her.

Babacar watched terrified as Malika slowly stretched out her hand before her mother-in-law. He wondered why his mother had asked this gesture of her. Fatimata looked at her daughter-in-law from head to toe and saw how she was struggling with her wrapper, from one side to another. Malika winced, withdrew her hand and stood in the middle of the door, tired and quiet. For a long, long time, Fatimata examined her. Then, without pronouncing a verdict, she walked pass them into the house.

That day, Malika felt giddy. When she returned from the market, scared of what might have transpired in her absence, she called Babacar. "Let's try something," she said. He waited for her to tell him what he wanted to hear, something about what she was experiencing. She said nothing. In silence, she simply placed her head on his laps and gazed into the distance. He swept his hand down her hair and tenderly caressed her earlobes. He looked at her, from down to up. He looked at her countenance which was full of sadness and confused emotions and he saw himself in her. She was lost in thought, worried and pensive.

Malika closed her eyes and took a deep breath.

He whispered into her ear, "He's been without you for five years."

She held her breath for so long that he feared for her health. Then she recovered enough to say, "He's married to the Congo."

"You know some of those Congolese women like to bleach off their skin. And, Maa-lii, their young women have courage," he added. She smiled at this judgement. He held his chin and asked himself: Is love an inspiration? Like the inspiration of a poet, a sculptor?

He wished he could fly high above to ask the Maker or sink down below to question the void: how could he overcome this incomprehensible trepidation, this unfathomable excitement?

Malika rose to prepare dinner. She seared the meat on the grill – the last chunk of leftovers from the Feast of the Sheep – before placing it on the firewood to finish cooking it. Her movements revealed her anxiety. "Could he have forgotten his marriage vows to me and the Lord's Commandments as well?"

Night began to fall. The stars budded like grains in the sky and the clouds gathered toward the south, ready for slumber. Babacar cleared his throat, and from out of the shadows he began to sing a crisp song, alone, breaking the silence. He moved up and down as he sang with a supple tenderness, so penetrating, so soul-searching that tears streaked down his cheeks. He sat down, bending his head towards the window. When his voice rose, Malika shook her head in surprise and came out from the kitchen to join him. She sat in consternation, laying a hand on his shoulder.

Engrossed in his song, he was unaware of her presence. His jeans, polo shirt and rubber sandals dribbled with water from the bottle he was carrying and his big eyes were red with tears. In a fraction of time, the volume of his voice decreased, then rose again in crescendo.

Desire.

Malika felt like falling at his feet. The night breeze blustered, alternating short gusts of wind and a heavy flurry that blew dry leaves to the wall. The swirling air separated the leaves from sand, and in its wake of freshness, blew over Babacar's lips. She looked at him in his vagueness. Yet, he was the same Babacar, his clothes clean and ironed. His eyes shone, despite the darkness. She nodded with approval and held him close to her, grateful and silent. The atmosphere was ebullient and seemed to last forever.

Together, they looked so new, so marvellously complementary. They were aligned in the joy of discovery, the discovery of love. In the love of nature and the nature of inspiration. In the inspiration of art and the art of friendship.

18

When the lecturers suspended their strike, Babacar got ready to return to class. The morning that lectures were to resume, Malika prepared French toast for him to eat at break. He bounced off to the bus stop, in a shirt and a tie. Amid the cry of conductors, he squeezed himself into a commuter bus heading to the university. The bus was loaded to the gunnels, the passengers packed in like sardines. Babacar hid his phone in his bag, afraid it would be stolen, as had happened once. The other passengers were pushing and squashing, holding tight to their purses. As the bus moved faster, their faces became brighter.

At the open windows, allowing the air to circulate, Babacar dried the sweat from his face. Under the cracks and patches of the burgeoning flyover, he saw the professor of Climatology searching for a way out of the heavy traffic on the boulevard. Babacar lowered his head, a bit lopsided as the woman in front of him was plump, nodding as the bus lurched and braked suddenly. One pace forward, then another, and he raised his head to see the university gate. "Chauffeur, let me drop!" he yelled, heading for the exit.

"Allah, bless me," he muttered as he approached the lecture hall. He perched on a step in front of the hall, pulled out his jotter, and read his notes. But then, thoughts of Malika invaded his mind and he forgot all about his lessons. He felt as if she was standing in front of him and was spellbound. A strange warmth ran across his skin. He spoke as if she was right there with him.

He turned to a clean page and began to sketch her. He drew her with such folly, wearing jeans, that he forgot what he had come for. Then he heard a voice.

"Smallie?" said the voice. It was Malika. He listened as the rhythms of her voice mingled with the strokes of his pencil. This unworldly ritual stirred his heart.

"I came late, so I couldn't get a seat in the hall," he told her. "Behold an hour and the professor is yet to arrive. More French toast for me? And this, what is it?" he asked, pointing at what she was holding.

"Hmm!" Malika shrugged.

Babacar felt the urge to skip his lectures to be with her, to hold her against him for a long time.

"What brought you here?" he asked. He felt her eyes lingering on the drawing. She examined it at length, and gave him a gloomy, restrained look.

"Give it to me," the voice sounded within him. "I'll keep it for you." He closed his jotter, obeying decisively. It was if she folded the drawing into a tiny square and slipped it into her bra.

Babacar shook his head and returned to himself. He looked out behind the lecture hall into the dim grove, and there was nothing. Dry leaves fluttered and fell. He was astonished to see that he had drawn a figure that resembled Malika so much, so rapidly. He felt ashamed about his dreams, yet somewhere deep within his imaginative spirit lurked a feeling of triumph about the drawing.

Five minutes later, the lecturer, Dr Camara came rushing in, his French suit flapping. His fingers were rolling down his prayer beads and his lips moved with whispered prayers. He moved as if he wished to elbow or jostle someone out of the way. When he reached his table, he dropped his briefcase and leaped to the blackboard. He chalked up the words *Global Warming: Do You Care?* and turned to face the students with a practised smile, guessing that they understood why he had arrived so late. The noise in the hall stopped, but ongoing whispers boiled in the students' ears.

He began the day's lecture, watching his class attentively. He explained that over one hundred years ago, long before the students were born, their ancestors burned coal and oil for their homes, factories and transportation. The burning of fossil fuels released carbon dioxide and other greenhouse gases into the atmosphere, causing the climate to warm more quickly than ever before.

The professor continued on the plague of global warming, saying that the earth's crust would swell and burst, if nations tarried to stop the ravages. He drew the makeshift tables of hope and despair that stuffed the Kyoto report. He regretted that it was all about talking, drinking and eating.

He asked the students a question about the lecture he had just given. Waiting for an answer, he tossed the stub of chalk he was holding into the chalk box and sat down. He frightened them with his warning eye.

Dr Camara spoke to no one outside the classroom, not even offering a nod of the head. Rumours circulated about him. On this morning, he had begun without preliminaries. Ordinarily, he would begin by warning the students of things: bad weather for the weekend, the approaching river blindness, of policemen who would arrest them for speaking to the press and for all this, he expected thanks.

The professor was still waiting for an answer when a student got up to leave without permission. He leaped from his chair, flung open the back door and ran after the student, terrible and menacing, too fast for his ageing legs. "Don't ever enter my class *again*," they heard him shout. The last word was the most important. They wondered what Dr Camara would do if the student defied his order.

Dr Camara returned to grab his briefcase, indicating that the lecture was over.

Babacar withdrew to a corner to eat his French toast. With the last crumbs in his mouth, he boarded a white bus, one of those the government had imported from India. The bus could not start. The driver and the conductor got out and knelt to adjust the wheel with some tools. The driver dashed across the road to fetch a last cigarette before returning to his seat behind the steering wheel. A female passenger heaved a sigh so loud and full of frustration that it seemed to cover the screams of five conductors fighting for one passenger. Then she got off the bus. Babacar, who was leaning against the bus, exhausted, hurried to take over the seat abandoned by the disenchanted woman.

A man tapped him from behind and told him to be careful of the seat. "So where is the foolish driver? Does he take us for jobless?" the man continued, peering through the window.

"Aie! Djembe guy," cried the man, suddenly recognising Babacar. "Since when?"

Babacar turned around and looked at him thoughtfully. "Which wind brought you here?"

"So, what are you up to?" replied Bakayoka. Beaming with an intriguing smile, Babacar shook his hands respectfully, in both his hands.

"What a fitting chance. I was just looking for somebody going in the direction of your house, like I knew and got on this bus," said Bakayoka, bending to reach for his briefcase.

There wasn't much room for him to stretch his legs. His uniform was crumpled over his thighs and back. From his briefcase, he struggled to pull out a document, pushing aside his smoking pipe in the process. His beret fell from his head, revealing his Bronx-style haircut, sharp, clean and finished with a good clipper. Unable to retrieve the document, he stood up, further revealing his rumpled uniform, stained at the buttocks. It would be hard to tell him apart from the city's vigilantes. To avoid exposing the contents of his briefcase to other passengers, he asked Babacar to stand up, so he could use his seat to unpack his possessions. Bakayoka's eyelids fluttered in approval as he pulled out an envelope from a bundle of assorted mail, upon which they both sat down again. His fatigue seeped through the joints, releasing a crack.

Having failed to start the bus, the driver summoned a team of other drivers to assist him. A push, a kick, a jerk on the clutch, and the engine roared to life.

Happily, Bakayoka straightened out the envelope. "The president has written to all the peacekeepers' wives, sending them a cheque."

The driver turned the volume of the stereo down, worried that the passengers would complain.

"They're lucky he remembered… Lucky they're not treated like breeze, lucky just one died. So here comes a proof of receipt. Sign here, please." Bakayoka, now a member of the presidential guard, gave the letter to Babacar. Babacar took it carefully and slid it into his jotter.

When the bus reached the flyover, Bakayoka said, "Okay, man. I'm dropping here. Don't forget to deliver the letter at your girlfriend's house. Go straight home. I'll take care of your fare." Babacar laughed.

Two stops later, Babacar alighted too. He adjusted the strap of his bag over his shoulder, and strolled along the road. His shirt smelled slightly of grease. Then he broke into a run, to catch Malika before she left for Kristen's house to help with her wedding preparations. He rushed into the House of Dudu, shouting, "Surprise! Surprise!"

"Who's that?" Malika said, knowing full well it was him. It was the first of April and she thought he had returned to play a trick on her.

"It's no April fool. I've got an important letter for you. Guess who from?"

Malika put down the basin of corn she was holding on her head. She craned her neck to examine the envelope before taking it from him. She was surprised, so surprised, she didn't ask him how he had gotten the letter. Quietly, she left the house with it.

A sweltering sun fell across every face. It made the sand hot and burned the soles of the feet. Babacar had his lunch on the veranda, watching the fleeting clouds. There was a blue sky. A sky blue with hope. Soon the day began to cool and was gradually wrapped in darkness. Babacar pulled off his sandals. But when his feet caught the lingering heat, he put his shoes on again, checking his feet for injury. He removed his bracelet marked with his name, then his shirt, and was engulfed by the sudden night.

Calling to mind the number of times the weather had changed over the course of the day, Babacar wagged his index finger at the darkening clouds. He searched for his wallet and went to his room, scouring the cooling ground. He dabbed the sweat running from his armpits.

"Don't you think it'll rain?" he asked Dieynaba, who was coming in, in a baritone voice.

"Oh, come on. I understand nothing of this weather, fickle and changing like Djembe's housemaids." Dieynaba was not paying attention to him; her mind was elsewhere. She had come to collect her beads. She dashed into her room and finding the bag that held them, grabbed it and ran off again.

Babacar was unhappy about Malika receiving a letter from the president. "It will swell her her head with pride," he thought. He scratched his head until white particles fell to the ground. He needed to cure his dandruff. His face, the shape of an avocado pear, now resembled a sour soup. He returned to his room and watched the darkening sky through the window, observing the raging wind. "Through the night," he mumbled. "Through the night." He brooded over there being no one to speak to and rubbed his eyes with trembling hands. The heat had sent every family member outside to chat. He felt like drinking *ataya*, Segolian tea. As soon as he had lit the fire to boil water, Malika walked in slowly, holding up her gown. He was happy to have her back. Admiring her Gucci handbag, he said, "You're everything to me, Malika."

She took a breath before answering. "Do you mean it? Do you mean you won't forget about me after you get a government job? That you won't run after younger women?"

He put his hands on her shoulders. "Of course not. We can move forward. I'm ready to marry you."

"Eh! Not until Issa is declared dead."

"Maa-lii," he called her, in that quirky way of his, holding her firmer. "Let's move forward. I give you my word to propose to marry you."

He kissed her gently on the mouth. His breath smelt of beer, but his lips were warm and soft. Malika stood still and closed her eyes. When she opened them again he kissed her once more and pushed his wet slippery tongue into her mouth. There was a flash of lightning. She could not breathe and, choking, pulled back from him. She pushed him away, gasping to catch her breath.

"Are you annoyed, baby?" he said. "Baby, come to me," he stretched his arms out to her. She turned away, silent. "Okay, okay. It's over now," he said. "Or should I…?"

Malika stepped outside. He stood by the wall, at a distance. He wanted to see where she was going to. When she turned back, he stood before her.

A sudden, forceful thunderstorm exploded. The atmosphere was filled with sound and fury. The sky thrilled, the wind exhilarated, the trees roused, the rooftops spoke, and the cool breeze gave way to a heavy rain. In confusion, Babacar and Malika ran back into the house, their bodies pounded by the shower of rain falling thickly on Djembe. It fell with frightening, chilling, stinging drops. They fell on the ceiling and on the soil intensely, forming a torrent corseted with bubbles that swept the litter away.

When the rest of the family returned, Malika and Babacar had gone to bed.

Ami Colle was the first to wake up the next morning. Her eyes were red and dull from the mist. She stood outside the house, examining the effect of the all-night rains: the flooded streets, the power cuts, and a large eucalyptus tree that had fallen on the roof of their neighbours, the Diops.

The city began to wake. It was drizzling. The children were impeded by the floods on their way to school. Some caught the droplets in their hands and jumped to catch butterflies, enjoying the unofficial holiday. Some ran into the flood, chasing each other, gesticulating with humour. Others stood aside, their eyes crusted, their uniforms wet.

Facing a carpentry workshop now under water, Ami Colle yelled at two children playing football in a pool of water. They had missing teeth and their school uniforms were splattered with mud. They pulled out their shirts, as if to drive out the worry of dirtying them and ran after the ball, a happy smile punctuating their faces. Then remembering the old Wolof saying – that there's no such thing as bad weather, only bad clothes – she turned her attention away.

Ami Colle entered the house to find Babacar ready for university. He had exams that morning. He had tried to revise, despite his mind wandering to dwell on the kiss of the preceding day. He folded his jeans, grabbed his bag, and braced himself for the day.

"You look sad, Smallie," Malika said, handing him a piece of pancake.

"Thank you so much. I'll only eat it if I do well at the exam."

"Give me back the pancake then."

"I was joking. You know I've always been on my faculty's Honours List."

"Better be!"

Malika was in a slightly better mood that morning. She had fallen asleep after rereading the president's letter and had slept off yesterday's news of the militia raping women before turning to their children in the Congo. Now she was almost herself again, teasing and chatty, her dimples deep and perfect. "Good luck," she said.

"Thank you. Have a nice day."

"Thank you. Nice day too!"

She kissed her palm and waved at him. His knees sunk deep into the orange-coloured flood. In the distance, there were flies, traffic and buses.

"Courage," she said.

Her voice reached Fatimata who shouted from across the room: "Malika!"

"Maam," she replied in a tiny voice.

"Malika!" Fatimata called again, raising her voice to cover the noise of the neighbour's plumber. Malika blinked resentfully.

"Is Papa going out today?"

"Yes," she answered. "He has appointment with Uncle Mansu."

19

Salif and Mansu sat at the bar over a bottle of rum. Mansu yawned as the technician from Canal fixed new appliances on the bar's TV. This would give the customers access to over four hundred channels.

"Congo's been at war for a long time. Everyone's tired out," Salif said. "Another bottle," he ordered the bartender, "for the road."

The technician flipped through channels with the remote control. As he zapped past CNN, Salif said, "Stop, stop, stop, please. I've seen that man before."

The man he recognised, who was shouting to awaken the Belgians that morning, was N'dombolo. He was a fat, baby-faced rebel chief with a bold gaze and a nose as big as a horse's. He was being tried in Brussels for war crimes, "crimes against humanity," the CNN reporter said. The reportage turned to the Congo. In retaliation, N'dombolo's rebels had unleashed an awful battle through the mountainous Congolese village of Walungu.

From the TV, the clatter of machine-gun fire and the thump of shells growled in the village and throughout a thirty-mile region, stretching from Kuba in the north to the mountain district of Haut-Zaire. "Genocide! Genocide!" the village children shouted, recalling the previous killing chant, "Erase the board!" At the roar of guns, the children took to their heels in droves.

Running into the verdant bush and fields of Walungu, they beheld MONUC clashing with MLC rebels. In the frontline, near Kibati, north of Goma, government soldiers fought General Kpankpa's squad. At the southern tip of Nyiragongo, Mai-Mai militia and CNDP turned on each other in a grisly battle. The fleeing children turned back and redirected their search for safety to the Rift Valley waterway, Lake Kivu, which was used for smuggling arms and said to be spared of direct attacks. The children trembled at every sound. They feared the stray bullets, they feared rape.

Their eyes rose to the skies, as UN peacekeepers flew over Goma in a helicopter. The peacekeepers were channelling food to a refugee camp, but later landed in a jungle, away from the airport.

A woman, who was lying on the grass, raised her hands up, crying, "Help! Help! Oh, help!" She spoke a mixture of Swahili and hesitant French. The peacekeepers landed nearby and hurried to her aid. She felt too ashamed for them to touch her, as her injuries had left her incontinent. "Get up, woman, get up," one peacekeeper said, trying to help her up. "You're human, like us all."

"My son," the woman began pathetically, "are the jungle creatures gone? Are they gone?"

"What happened, Mama?" another asked.

"Should I really tell you?"

"Yeah! Tell us."

"What if they capture me again?" She muttered briefly and then continued, "They were the militia of General Kpankpa, those ones supported by Uganda."

"Yeah..."

"They came to our house. They came to kill my husband. They caught him like a day-time thief and tied him up, like a goat about to be slaughtered. They sliced open his body with sharp knives. He was still alive then. I could see his eyeballs. Then they cut off his fingers. And... and... and... chopped off his m-a-n-h-o-o-d." She shook and wept uncontrollably at the final word. The peacekeepers wiped her tears. Between sobs, she added, "They punched his heart, he died... his heart... the punch." She keeled over.

"Sorry Mama, sorry," the peacekeepers said, each in their own language. They retrieved out a container of water from the helicopter and poured it out, washing her bruised face. That seemed to help. When she regained her calm, she told them more, between sobs, her voice wavering.

"They turned to me. I begged them to spare my life. One hit me on the skull with the butt of head of his gun and I fell and blacked out, losing consciousness. You see the wound on my forehead," she indicated. "They forced me to gather all the parts of my husband's body and to lay face-up on top of them. They tore off my dress. One by one, they jumped–" She stopped, unable to continue. Tears dripped down her cheeks and into her slightly open mouth.

"What, Mama?" the peacekeepers insisted. "What did they do, at last?"

"My life-e-e… e-e, my life… my life in Congo," she cried.

"If we know what happened at last, it will help," they said.

"They ra-ra-ra-ped me."

She stopped and fell back, her wide, worn face crinkled into bitter wails of mourning.

They waited for her to mourn. Lying down on the floor, she whispered: "They raped my two daughters and carried them away." The woman breathed her last.

The peacekeepers lifted her slumping body into the helicopter and took her to the mortuary of a hospital run by a group of religious nuns.

When the peacekeepers arrived, the nuns were attending to a woman kidnapped and held for two months as a sex slave by the FDLR. "Victims number in the hundreds of thousands," a nun said sorrowfully, grasping the crucifix hanging from her neck.

The news report from the Congo ended there.

"Aw," Salif said sorrowfully, lifting the glass of rum to his lips. "This is an abomination, child soldiers raping old women. It can never happen here." He placed his now empty glass quietly on the table.

Mansu asked, "Why do they rape women? What have women...?"

"What are your grey hairs for?" Salif interjected.

"I'm not omniscient, my friend."

"You don't need to be. When there is war, there is rape. Rape is a weapon of war! War is a cover-up for rape!"

"You don't mean it," Mansu said, nodding in agreement.

Salif looked carefully into the bowl of soup they had ordered, plucked a piece of meat from it, waved it around, politely inviting other people in the room, and tossed it into his mouth.

"We saw the crimes of World War II," he said, munching. "When we were young, living under the French colonial masters. But I've seen nothing like the Congo war."

"Who is to blame?" Mansu asked. "Rwanda? Uganda? France? The United States of America? The United Nations?"

Salif adjusted his black caftan. He licked his fingers and added, "When those boys on drugs rape women in public," he paused to recover from the heat of the pepper in the soup, then continued, "when they humiliate them, destroy their sexual organs before their children, they disgrace and destroy the women themselves. That's the first weapon."

"Purr!" Mansu said and got up.

Salif stretched and scratched his ankle where a mosquito had bitten him.

"It's not new. Let me tell you, the second weapon is to traumatize the whole clan and the entire village who witness the rape scene. You see, when a man witnesses the rape of his wife, or children of their mother, the sense of family and community is destroyed."

"You mean they stand there and watch it like a movie?" Mansu said, sitting back down to his plate of soup. "Why would they just watch, when they should be wielding clubs of wood to break the head of the rapists?"

"You talk like a child," Salif said.

"I'm confused. I'm really confused," he answered, spilling on his clothes.

"I said families are broken; social ties are dislocated; the whole village plunged into disarray. But what I'm seeing in the Congo beats my imagination. The regular soldiers rape also."

Light from the three lanterns that lit up the room faded out, due to power cuts. Their heads darkened, producing a shadowed drawing covering most of the wall. It was like the plain dark shade of Goree Island by night, but it was a kind of flowchart, with ovals and rectangles with a nose in them. Some of the noses looked squeezed. Salif and his friend hurried over their plates of soup and rose to leave.

After the parting of the two friends, Salif did not linger. He walked straight home and arrived before Babacar. Malika was at the back of the compound.

Babacar returned and walked up close to her. He lifted her head gently and brought his mouth close to her neck. He sank his teeth into her lips, and from there moved his mouth onto hers.

It was the night children sang *Tajabon,* the sacred night spirits visited the living to inspect their lives. That night, Babacar noticed a change in his body. When signals of passion were transmitted from his brain to the nerves in his pelvis, he could not achieve an erection. Even when close to Malika, he noticed no change. Everything in him seemed dead.

"Could it be that the spirits are penalizing me?" Babacar said in a low tone, looking puzzled. "Something is wrong."

He observed himself continually and touched his manhood. But it remained deflated. The next day, he confided in Malika. She panicked and judged what she heard too serious to reveal to others.

"What happened to it?" she asked him in a whisper. Babacar sat on the ground, his eyes filled with tears he was too embarrassed to shed.

Malika battled secretly to help him heal his impotency. She took him to traditional healers, marabouts, fortune-tellers, clairvoyants, bonesetters and disguised cheats. Each of the healers left a signature on the healing journey. Soon the secret leaked. The more healers she took him to, the worse the ailment became.

Two of Malika's friends brought him purifying water or potions from Nkisi River. When they saw him convulsing on the floor, or heard him in throes of anguish that he would never impregnate a woman, when his waist was laden with amulets and mystical powders rubbed into his chest, they called upon Allah to save him.

Mansu, who assured Malika he could cure Babacar, gave him Fava beans and Fava bean sprouts. Mansu massaged Yohimbe balm into the thing between his legs, steamed his feet with herbal infusions, named him in visions for forty days, and applied other techniques and secrets unknown to many forest masters.

At the suggestion of a griot, Malika arranged for Babacar to be taken to Koubi to touch the tomb of Serigne Koubi, believed to exert mystical powers. She lit incense in his room to ward off the evil eye and before he went to sleep, weaved scarves like a turban around his head.

When Malika became doubtful of the efficiency of the traditional healers they had consulted, she suggested they turn to modern medicine. She mentioned the names of doctors people said were reputed for bringing a speedy remedy to a patient. Together, they knocked at the doors of clinics and sought the help of one doctor after another. Some said they would cure Babacar in a month, others in less than a day. And Malika continued to throw around her savings of peacekeeping dollars.

The turnaround story delayed in coming. Treatments from certain doctors even added water to kerosene. They recommended Sildenafil, Veldenafil, and Tadalafil.

In four months, Babacar and Malika had consulted every doctor of influence in Djembe. The list of medical do's and don'ts was long and confusing: Get a clean bill of health, treat your body better, do regular exercise, adopt a healthy diet, desist from indulging in nicotine and alcohol, and boost your self-confidence.

With blood tests, queries, consultations, massages and injections, some doctors told Babacar to fatten up; others advised him to get married. While Dr Kane forbade him to sleep face down, Dr Soussou insisted that he do so. Where one doctor suggested he exercised more than Kenyan Olympic gold medallists, another proposed a good workout on the weight machine at intervals.

"Try the American hospital in Banjul," some nurses suggested. As he lurched from one hospital to another, Babacar was also advised to give up drinking the local tea, reduce the quantity of rice and fish he ate, sing love songs, listen to hip hop, drink brown ginger juice, and sleep with twelve tropical pastilles in his mouth. Babacar's ailment became a therapeutic roller coaster.

Struck by the heaviest form of impotency, the dysfunction led to changes in Babacar's social behaviour. At dinner one Friday, as Fatimata was ladling out her special soup made of an Ivorian recipe, he complained that the soup was not tasty enough.

"Tasteless, tasteless," he moaned. Babacar's complaining began to annoy Fatimata. In Segol, a child may not call his or her mother's soup "tasteless". Instead of apologizing for his gaffe, he reached for the Maggi container and sprinkled some seasoning on his soup. When Fatimata brought out the main dish, Babacar pushed his chair back from the table and fanned his nose, as if the food were emitting an unpleasant odour.

"I cannot eat food meant for pregnant women," he said.

Fatimata jumped out of her seat, grabbed his plate and poured back the soup she had served him. Salif squinted at Babacar. "You can only give such orders when you run your own home."

"No, I wasn't…"

"I said not in my house!" Salif barked. He dropped his spoon and joined his head wife at the open window. They stood side by side, their heads thrust towards the wind. Malika winked at Babacar. She alone knew why he was behaving in such a way. Dieynaba gazed on. Fearing he would let loose further insults and irritating words, she hurried to his side to prevent him from speaking further and indeed from continuing that dinner with his parents. She softly asked him to go and get an extra bottle of water. Then she followed him into the kitchen and told him to stay clear of Salif until the next day. Hesitantly, he nodded.

From that time on, Babacar refrained from having dinner with his parents. He spent his time on the floor, at the extreme right of the House of Ndiaye. He would sit there on a slab at the end of the wall next to the tool shed, a space in which he could not comfortably stretch his legs. He would gaze at the adjoining latrine, the encircled space for the water tap, the section of the wall without barbed wire, and at the flower pots. Sometimes he would apply his balms and liquids, his legs splayed in a triangle.

Fatimata did not hold his criticism of her soup against him. Rather, she served him chops, fruit and the lion's share of whatever she cooked. Some nights, she even sat beside him on a folding mat on the veranda, telling him stories about how to run a home.

One evening, sitting on his slab, Babacar begged the spirits to help him. "Take away this curse! Send it to a pig," he prayed.

Soon thereafter, he observed something about himself. His beard grew quickly and his muscles seemed doubly firm, and his milky teeth shone when he smiled. "Please tell me," he said looking at himself in a mirror, "is it right for a man to waste his years, slouching beside his wife, incapable of making her pregnant?" He extended his idiosyncrasies to issues beyond those of food and drink. He began to consider himself the only normal person in the family.

Gradually Fatimata, who could tell if a dog was pregnant before its belly budged, sensed that something was wrong with her son. She noticed that Babacar, who had rarely spoken, was now given to undue arguments and she noted him frequently checking something below his abdomen.

On a walk together one day, Babacar began, "I'm jealous of you, grandfathers and fathers, drinking soup and reading newspapers." He looked at a man on the other side of the avenue and said, "Me, too! I want to visit my wife at the hospital the day she delivers, wearing a glossy caftan." After a brief pause, he added, "I want to be called 'Papa' and to raise a child and preserve my name."

But his moaning did not prevent him from sharing jokes too. During the mango season, Babacar jumped over the wall and stole mangoes from the neighbour. Had he been caught, he would have spent the night in a police cell. He took the risk for the mangoes which were as sweet as honey. Malika could not understand why he ignored the mangoes in their compound, preferring to steal the neighbour's. He stayed up all night and dropped into bed in like a bag of rice after the expedition.

"Got what you want?" she asked, as he crept in.

He laughed at the question. "I've got to act desperately, lest the spirits forget about me in this prison of ailment."

"Oh, no," Malika shook her head.

"Oh, yes," he insisted, laying his palm against the lower part of his abdomen. "I'll offer them a good chunk of the mangoes to eat."

"Doctors will cure you. The next appointment is just a week away and we need to invent a reason to go out. We need to figure out what to say."

"Forget the doctors. This ailment was brought upon me by the spirits. And when the spirits tie a knot, only they can untie it."

At this, Babacar smiled and his milk-white teeth gleamed in the dark.

20

Many months into treatment, Babacar still could not get an erection. Exasperated, he projected his chagrin upon every member of the family. He said that he wanted a wife to test his manhood. He wanted to be touched, cared for, and guarded from reckless habits. He wanted a loving wife who would keep a permanent eye on him, improve his nutrition, and reduce his stress. He wanted to prove that *he could*. Like Salif and Issa, he wanted to be served dinners, give orders occasionally, and keep a sacred box that would accompany his daughter to her husband's home.

He bothered Malika for the details of her traditional marriage. He wanted to know the meaning of the blessing song sung by the clan's women, of the traditional fabric that protected one against the jealous eye, and of the scent of incense discharged by the nuptial scarf. At his insistence, she brought out her wedding fabric, embossed with designs of two opposite docks and Portuguese crosses. Babacar studied in detail the weaving that bore the meaning of the ceremony: the two opposed docks that stood for two lovers, the herbs tied with strings that symbolised fertility, the Portuguese crosses that fended off hidden adversities and the motif of shells and silver coins expressing prosperity.

"I'll buy one like this for my wife," Babacar said, stroking one of the twenty-five amulets fencing his waist. "It will be a great day."

"Oh, my love!" he cried. Expectation seemed to prolong his days and he sang for a wife. He sang for the one on whom his hopes lay, who would prove him *capable*. His waist was still bordered by lucky charms of four-leaf clover and boxes of perfume and fragrance he sprayed at his neckline and on the veins of his wrist. He mumbled some words with his tongue out and massaged his feet and waist randomly. "I must conquer this," he said. "My manhood will rise again. Whose manhood died under the age of thirty? Get up, man!"

Babacar's mournful chants became habitual, his monologues endless and his sleepless nights frequent. His arms pulsed with rebuff and his eyes were dull from unshed tears. His face stiffened with disapproval and disgust as he walked alone in the painful room of sickness. Yet he walked all the same.

In his most painful moments, Malika would put her hands around his neck to comfort him. She would praise his courage, his hope, and resilience. She would give him the lion share of the food she cooked.

Once as she sat beside him, he whispered, "Only death would make me abandon you to suffer alone. Only death."

Malika would insist that he persevere, her voice gracious and at those moments, Babacar would brighten up somewhat. "Thank you, Maa-lii," he would say. That was all he could say and it gave him further courage to fight on. At times, he would sing as a response and there was something in the singing that gave Malika hope.

Once when she failed to cheer him up, she encouraged him to accompany her to pick up her blouses and jewellery. She believed that going on a promenade, as they call it in Djembe, would afford him a change of atmosphere and perhaps increase his chances of finding a wife.

"Anyhow, no prospective wife wants a husband who cannot do anything," she pointed out. "Even if you lie your way through to the wedding day, your truth will soon be known." When Babacar heard that, he brooded, moped, growled and exhaled.

"But how can I know if I'm capable or not, when I'm not married?" he asked. "Who makes me dream, who rubs my feet, walks beside me to a function? Let's face it: no woman can say 'Babacar can't' until she has tried, after marriage."

His next medical appointment came. Dr Latif of See-You-Soon Clinic prescribed a new treatment, the most demanding Babacar had received yet. When he began the treatment, he grew warm to the touch and complained of headaches and dizziness. On his way to lectures, the morning after he began Dr Latif's new treatment, he fainted under the flyover. He fell, his feet in the gutter, his arms flung wide and saliva dripping from his mouth, resembling an alien in the prime of his life.

Witnesses said he staggered before he fell. His groans echoed through the vast intersection and pedestrians rushed to stop him from slipping entirely into the drains. They made him sit up. Then they removed his shirt, fanned him with it and brought table water to pour on him. Passing spinsters jostled around, sighing in lament as they witnessed his anguish.

A man pulled Babacar's wallet from his pocket and found his ID, with his home phone number on it. The man dialled it from his own phone. Malika, who answered, rushed to the scene in a taxi. She told the crowd gathered around that she knew why he had fainted. She thanked them for their kindness and asked the men to help lift him into the back of the taxi. Malika and Babacar were bound for See-You-Soon Clinic. There, Dr Latif examined his mental stimulation and, nodding worriedly, advised that marriage would be inevitable.

Malika and Babacar were not yet back from the hospital when Mansu, wondering why Malika had not kept her appointment, breezed into Salif's workshop. At first, Salif pretended to be too busy for a long chat. But Mansu told one story after another and it became clear that he wasn't going to leave before noon. So Salif smiled and motioned to his friend to take a seat.

"So," said Mansu, changing topic, "I'm so sorry about what happened."

"Come again?" Salif asked, engrossed in his weaving, searching for the best fabric lining. He had to finish the work before noon and was uncertain he would meet the deadline.

"I mean your son's fainting this morning."

Salif suspected his friend had been drinking before visiting. His hands swung at his weaving strands, unrestrained.

"It was pathetic," said Mansu, lifting his pipe to his mouth.

"I beg your pardon? Don't grasp what you're saying."

"Your youngest son, the one at university. Didn't he collapse under the bridge, sending his school notes flying abroad like birds?" His voice resounded mournfully.

"Oh, that happens to some people during the month of Ramadan," Salif said quietly. Ignoring the look Mansu shot him, he slipped out through the back door to find out what had really happened. He found Dieynaba, hurrying out. Deciding not to bother her, instead he returned to his workshop.

"What story have you come to my house with?" he asked. With sobriety, Salif listened doubtfully to the details of what had happened. Even though Mansu was known to be generous with his time, visiting people when they were mourning, he had been known to spread false stories. And he was known for having spread the story that a Djemberian immigrant was jailed for a terrorist bombing in Spain when the man was seen, at that very time, walking quietly in his district.

"Not at all," Salif said. "My son does not sniff drugs." He meant to state his dislike for drugs, which young and disoriented men about Babacar's age sometimes smoked.

Out of sheer curiosity, Salif kept listening. No one had rung Salif's home to commiserate. Mansu, who had less alcohol in his veins, was a shadow of himself. The soles of his feet were as brown and cracked as that of early Fulani nomads. His skin was the colour of dried hibiscus leaves. What could have made his friend like that? Mansu's last topic was politics and he expressed his robust suspicion for the political class: "They are at the root of all our troubles."

By evening, news of Babacar had begun to spread. Before the next morning, three different marabouts had come to examine his forehead and declared there was clear evidence of the evil eye. Gossipers used Babacar as their street-side subject. Salif, now fully informed of his son's condition, consulted with the elders to determine if the family of the girl Babacar said he liked was one their family could marry into.

For days, be it when they were returning from the Central Market, picking up baguettes from the baker's or queuing to purchase cooking gas, people whispered at the sight of a member of Salif's family. They were puzzled to hear that Babacar was getting ready to get married so soon after his collapse.

Malika, who did not bother about the gossips, imagined Babacar as a husband, assessed the beard below his chin and appraised the protection he would offer a woman. She admired the hair on his chest, the length of his eyelids and the elegance of his posture.

"What would happen to him that has not happened to every man who got married? They say..." and she paused, thinking, "he'll survive it if there is love."

Babacar was delighted by Salif's agreement and began at once to see himself through the lens of a father. With support from Malika and money from the sale of the ten sheep he had raised, he made arrangements to purchase a beautiful suit. He removed Fatimata's farming tools from the storage room and cleared up the room to make it more spacious. He gave money to Fatimata for bags of rice and onions and jotted down ideas about his wedding in his memo pad. He drew up the guest lists, sauce lists, and even a list of top tourist sites in Segol for his honeymoon. He applied Vaseline to smoothen his hardened palms and he ate less sugar to reduce his risk of diabetes. Ahead of time, he went to Best Tailors where they made him a new caftan in brocade with embroidery, depicting the thumb over clenched fist, meaning "Up You", a gesture of congratulation.

On one of those preparatory evenings, Malika sat in the corner of the kitchen, crushing tomatoes, while Fatimata bustled to and fro between the kitchen and the storage room. And there, at the new dining table, so comfortable with a leg propped up on a chair, sat Babacar. Beside him sat a young woman.

At the sight of his mother, Babacar greeted her, "Salut, Mama." He went over to her.

"Babacar," Fatimata nodded. She looked at the pepper dispenser and redirected him to the sitting room. "Did you offer her something to eat?"

"Mama, this is Aminata, my wife's friend."

"Future wife," Fatimata corrected him and with that, it became clear whom Babacar had really decided on, Penda.

Aminata's teeth were jagged. They showed each time she smiled, but she did not care and tossed her hair about. Aminata sat like a proper Djemberian woman, her sharp eyes flashing and her feet crossed at the ankles. When she excused herself to go to the toilet (again, like a true Djemberian, saying "I'd like to use the white room"), Babacar reminded Malika that Aminata had won first place in the Miss Segol beauty contest and had the crown to prove it. Yes, she was refined, just like her friend, Penda. And perfect on account of her thin calves, which, though a bit slim (Malika whispered to Babacar), were attractive.

"Congrats," Malika smiled. She did not believe in flashing out signals of attraction. She believed rather that personality was worth more than appearance. While attraction could be based on one's appearance and attitude, a woman's true beauty carried that to a deeper level.

"Thank you," said Babacar. "My wife is a woman with meat on her bones; she has class."

In Penda's case, there were elements of flair Babacar loved to boast about. Though petite, she was chesty, which could not escape the attention of a bachelor. Malika, sitting across from Aminata at the dining table, developed a sudden stammer.

How Babacar had broken into the circle of such sophisticated Djemberian women was no surprise to Malika. He could dare, she thought, and young women are looking for husbands. The last issue of *Women's Magazine,* which Malika had just bought, revealed that most men placed good health and beauty at the top of their "must have" list, while others did it in the reverse order.

Still, the sight of this young woman at her dining table and with such a sharp stare, was too much for Fatimata. She finally asked her son's visitor, "Whose daughter are you?"

Aminata put a finger at the side of her nose. "Niang's," she answered.

"Which Niang?"

"Niang, the journalist," she said, pulling from her bag the day's issue of *The Sun.* Malika nodded. She had seen Niang's editorial.

Noticing that Fatimata was lost, Babacar said, "Mama, don't you know Niang, formerly with the radio station, who was once decorated as a news veteran by the president? He has gone on to establish his own newspaper." On the front page of the day's tabloid was a photo of Segol's first female presidential candidate. Pointing at the politician, he said, "What does she want?"

"You grew up here? Your *Fraaaçais* sounds different," Fatimata said, making Aminata laugh.

"Really, Mama? People always tell me that. I'm a third-year law student at the American university, Djembe Campus. I grew up in Paris VI. That's why. I spent my childhood learning the right accent."

The Parisian street she mentioned was populated by African immigrants, on the menu of French politicians. When a new immigration law was adopted, these French-speaking African immigrants protested. They refused to be treated as second-class citizens in their "new country". With so much "typical" French being spoken, parents became afraid their own children would suffer discrimination if they spoke French like francophone Africans. Therefore they raised money, hired tutors and funded pronunciation classes so that some of the time, sixty percent to be exact, their children could pass as "typically French".

That night as Babacar waited for sleep to come to him, he listened to Salif and Fatimata conversing in the sitting room. Penda's name was mentioned repeatedly. Despite his university-level lectures and bulky ecology books, Babacar did not know exactly what it meant to be a husband, and he was eager to fill this gap before he would stand in front of the mayor.

Penda's family officially received Babacar's relatives in their home. After that first step, Penda rolled out her own wedding folly. She took her friends to the counters of every reputable jewellery designer and, peering into the glass cases, asked them for their opinions, especially on the celebrated John Petit & Mary. Looking through the main showcase of a particular shop, she pointed to a bronze bracelet, to a necklace of superimposed shells, and then to a bracelet glittering with bright pearl. "I will wear this one," indicating the latter, "on the day Babacar's family comes to pay the bride price. Then the bronze bracelet for the civil wedding and the shell one for the religious ceremony."

At the House of Ndiaye, Salif and Fatimata kept to the wedding schedule. Unmoved by Babacar's ailment and indifferent to Ami Colle's withdrawal, they spread the word about their son's wedding. Fatimata stuffed a giant bed in her son's tiny room, its walls covered with posters, art prints, serigraphs, and wall tapestries.

"It's up to the bride to decide," Salif said to Ami Colle who reiterated the subject of Babacar's health.

"If a woman decides to marry a man, it means she wants him," Salif told his second wife.

Sitting beside Salif on the wooden stool and waving the raffia-plaited traditional fan, Fatimata nodded in support. She had a heat rash on her neck and the mentholated powder she had applied was caked into the wrinkles of her neck.

Fatimata said, "That girl is lucky to find a man like Babacar as a husband. She knows it. Babacar can do any work, he speaks softly, he's practically self-made, he cooks and cleans up. He raises sheep, plants vegetables. Which young man in Djembe is as enterprising as he is?"

Salif and Fatimata understood the implication of her words. "With full knowledge," Salif said repeatedly.

Ami Colle was convinced that before long, Penda would discover what lurked behind the wedding and she insisted that they postpone it. Babacar still wore amulets around his waist and thighs. Ami Colle wondered what explanation he could give as to why he wore them, other than because of grave sickness. He was not allowed to consume nicotine (having just begun before he became impotent) and, in the event that Penda offered him a cigarette, he would not be able to accept.

Salif and Fatimata kept arguing in favour of their son, resolute about carrying through with the marriage. "It's for his good," they said.

But Ami Colle felt it was doing an injustice. "Babacar merits a better wife than Penda," she said. But Fatimata defended her son with these words, "The best thing is to find someone who motivates him, who encourages him. And he will perform. I know my son."

"What if the family is accused of gambling? What if the marriage lasts only for two weeks? " Ami Colle asked.

"Is there any reason a man with impotency shouldn't get married?" Malika asked, on one occasion. Then she added, "Babacar is one of the most attentive, patient and loving young men around."

Babacar did not take part in the debate, but kept Ami Colle off his tracks. "None of her rubbish," he said. The day after he graduated from the university, Fatimata cooked a delicious meal for him.

"You look like a billionaire," Malika said, bringing him the pepper he had requested. Babacar rejoiced over these words and shook his head, looking at Fatimata sitting beside him. "When I become a billionaire," he said, downing the last glass of water on the table, "Ami Colle will send Dieynaba to collect some money."

Babacar addressed a monologue to himself.

"Uh, I'll confess, though, Babacar, there are times I feel this wedding will blow off your peace. A bouquet of troubles, whispering so quiet you never heard it."

Then he felt as if he heard Allah's words saying, "Babacar, take your time. Why gamble? It may well end in fight or fury. Oh, laugh while you have teeth, Babacar. Laugh while you have teeth."

Babacar startled as if he had been struck with a cane. It began to drizzle. Malika brought her own bowl of rice and groundnut sauce to eat. Minutes later, she said, "There are chances a baby would call you 'Papa' very, very s-o-o-n. Oh, keep your feelers out. Good things are coming."

"You seem to love complicated situations," Babacar said, before adding, "and you have a way of getting out of them." He meant that, by nature, she was opposed to the easy, the straightforward.

"Peace to you," Salif interrupted. He put down a piece of paper in front of Babacar and asked him to write down what he wished to have printed on his wedding invitation. Babacar stole a glance at Malika and smiled. After reflecting for a moment, he scribbled in capital letters: "BABACAR, THE MOST AMAZING BOY IN THE CITY, WEDS PENDA, CHARMING AND CLASSY."

They erupted with the laughter of happy women. The words Babacar used for himself made them believe he had regained self-confidence. But it was a worry to Salif and Fatimata, as no such thing had ever been written on a wedding card and no bridegroom in his right senses would appear so ignorant.

"The ugly are ugly, so the beautiful will look as they do," Salif said.

"Why call people ugly?" Fatimata added.

The rumour was circulating that Babacar was being given a wife because he was unstable, talked to himself in the street and argued with invisible people. A marital advisor in the district, who peered at the fourth finger of every young man she met, described Babacar as "a risky boat". But Penda did not buy into that viewpoint.

To tune down Babacar's ego, Salif now criticized any unfatherly behaviour his son exhibited. "Commenting on every detail will blow up your relationship," he advised Babacar, in his mother's presence. "If you want Penda to respect you, listen to her more than you talk to her."

Fatimata joined her husband to curb Babacar's excesses. She teased him about how he would react should Penda wake up on her left side, meaning if she awoke in a bad mood. Fatimata talked to him about how to live under the same roof with a woman.

A relative of Penda's came one morning to visit in connection with the wedding. Fatimata hurried to call Babacar and whispered to him, "Ask our visitor, 'Is my joy at peace?'" (By "my joy", she meant Penda.)

When another relative unloaded bags of rice before their gate, she told Babacar to smile and say, "My joy and I are grateful."

In the period leading up to the wedding, Fatimata taught her son two methods with which to calm one's wife. The first was saying "I'm in control." The second was "You shouldn't worry about that."

Knowing that rumour-mongers would come to look around in their house, Fatimata prepared him on how to react to provocative questions. "They will stare and ask stupid questions," she said. "Does he own a brand new car? What is the range of his salary? Does their parlor have a leather sofa? Is their compound newly painted? Where does he work? Will it be a big wedding?"

The mid-July day scheduled for Babacar's traditional wedding arrived. For the occasion, he was dressed in white and wore a long scarf around his neck. He was accompanied by the elders, as Issa and Malika had been. They arrived before noon at Penda's family home. There they waited till four-thirty in the afternoon, but there was no sign of Penda. Even her parents did not know where to find her. The elders of Babacar's family exercised further patience until dusk, but still, the bride-to-be did not turn up. Babacar tried to call her, but her phone rang dead. At last, the leader of the delegation from Babacar's family announced their departure.

Babacar's condition then went from bad to worse. He became something of a misogynist. He did not want to see any women at all and cast his face aside when one passed by. In his humiliation, he still dreamed of becoming a billionaire. He secured a job as an Agricultural Science teacher in a private school and started a new life. Frequently he recalled Penda's sweet words to him. He could not have imagined that she had been planning to vanish.

"Allah is there for all," he replied when his relatives sympathized with him. He assured his father that his bones would grow strong one day. His resilience impressed every member of the family.

Babacar attempted to reconcile himself with what happened one morning. Words came to him like in a vision: *It's like those times when your glass of ataya forms one smooth greyish dome and you're not aware of it being spoilt, until the foam glides off from the glass and draws the map of an unknown mountain on the floor. It's like that. A kind of fluttering cancer of the soul? You would not even be fully aware of the darkish dome until it spilled over.*

Thereafter he rarely spoke of the incident, but only to Salif. He would not speak of it to Fatimata, Malika or Dieynaba, relatives, or friends. He did not want to make his troubles the subject of conversation, even within the family. At his graduation, he had received the prize of the most productive student and he counted on his capacity to work hard to survive. From all his personal inquiry, he concluded that money, not impotency, had caused Penda to vanish on their wedding day.

Other than watching over him and helping to pay for his prescriptions, Malika could do little to improve his situation. She had her own troubles, seemingly forgotten with Babacar's ailment. Fortnightly, when he had finished correcting his students' homework, Malika would cut his toenails. At his request, she massaged his back, lit a fire for him to brew tea and she jogged by his side from the House of Dudu to the seashore.

Throughout, Babacar remained resolute that Penda loved him. "She could not escape," he told himself. "I cannot have lost her. What happened? She had gone to prepare for our wedding."

21

After the announcement that the Muslim brotherhood would start the Ramadan fast that day, Malika heard from one of her customers that Penda was two months pregnant. Nobody could have known it better than that customer, as she was nicknamed RFI, from Radio France Internationale. That evening in the tool shed, Malika broke the news to Babacar, who jittered and wept. It rained in his heart as it rained in southern Segol.

"She made me believe I was the only one, meanwhile she was cheating on me." His breath came in chortling, gasping sounds and his forehead was fixed against a snaking crack in the unpainted wall. "But I will not curse her," he said. She should have told him she was unwilling to continue with the wedding, rather than bring shame on him before the elders. He banged his hand against wall. The news fuelled the dissident within him.

Malika rubbed her palm against his shoulder and wiped away his tears with a white handkerchief. She took him by the hand to the bathroom and handed him soap and a towel. According to the RFI customer, Penda had had several boyfriends before meeting Babacar, whom she merely added to the list.

Babacar decided to give himself a holiday. While on a promenade on the beaches of Cap Skirring one afternoon, he ran into Penda, fully pregnant. She tried to take off, but stumbled in the sand and fell heavily. Some English tourists rushed eagerly to assist her. Her feet were trapped in the sand and the tourist guide attempted to free her. One of the female tourists doused her with seawater from a bottle. Another woman cleaned her hands with a handkerchief. A hawker of traditional hats picked up Penda's fallen sunglasses and extended them to her. An elderly tourist cooled her with his raffia fan, agitating the air from every possible angle.

"So this is what you have turned into?" Babacar said aloud.

"Who's that man?" one of the tourists asked.

"She's a dupe," Babacar said. "Look at how swollen her stomach is, like she'll deliver a goat."

"Why is his mouth hotter than the sun?" the guide asked.

"It looks like they have had something together!" the female tourist suggested.

Despite the tourists, Babacar could not keep quiet. He gnashed his teeth and swung his arms, gesticulating at Penda. The tourists wondered what had transpired between them. Why would he be talking and pointing so furiously at a pregnant woman who had fallen?

"That's enough!" one of them said finally. Then Babacar remembered the first time they had quarrelled, how she sunk to her knees, saying it would be the last time. The memory freed his heart from the grips of inertia. Penda began to weep.

"*Monsieur*, why are you so annoyed?" a tourist asked.

"She's a witch! She disappeared on our wedding day and brought shame and humiliation on me, before the entire town." His eyes were wide as he spoke.

The tourists remained silent. Some of the women accompanied Penda home. As she walked, she muttered as if cursing someone, but otherwise appeared to be recovering. Her palms were bruised and nicked, her hair was tousled, her gown caked with dirt. Babacar followed from behind, at a safe distance, his jeans rolled up at the bottom.

"She needs to see a doctor."

"An x-ray would be necessary."

"Some tablets would do."

"Let's wait until after a doctor's supervision." Suggestions from the female tourists echoed while they were boarding their bus. But when they reached the bungalow in which Penda lived with her toubab partner, he refused to let anyone in. Babacar gazed spitefully at him.

"The medical risks are too high for an expectant mother to be jogging alone on the beach," one woman advised.

"Is it because of this queer white man that she ran away?" Babacar mused. He left the premises sorrowfully and that night, he suffered terrible insomnia.

After supervising the School Certificate Exams in the southern part of the country, Babacar returned to Djembe. His mind could not leave the corridors of his journey in which he had encountered Penda.

At the House of Dudu, he climbed the stairs to the roof to recall the first time he had texted "I love you" to her with his new cellphone. He recalled the instant reply she sent and how, from that moment on, she had lavished gifts upon him: swimming kits and the best ice cream in the town. It had begun so well. Dreams, surged upon him, uninvited.

Babacar turned to marijuana as a palliative, affording himself evasion. Over time, the quantity of marijuana on top of his shelves grew. Its odour filled his room and the corridor leading to it. His lips darkened from smoking so much.

While she was cooking outdoors one evening, Ami Colle noticed Babacar sitting alone, smoking a long rolled joint. Then she watched him prepare another to smoke. Ami Colle ran outside to the shopkeeper and asked him where Babacar got the weeds from.

She needed to know, should the police come to arrest him. Ami Colle feared that the police might smell the smoke coming from their compound. The shopkeeper told her that Babacar had bought a great quantity of it.

Ramadan passed and Christmas came, with its promise of end-of-year holidays. Even though Djembe is a predominantly Muslim country, Djembe Muslims join Christians to celebrate Christmas, for fun. Djemberians were shopping and planning for the holiday. Mbalax music blared from speakers mounted on pillars and from car stereos. Street shops and markets stayed open till midnight. Parents bought their children balloons and inflatable Father Christmas figures and families purchased goats, cows, or frozen chicken and recharge cards to call their relatives abroad. The days grew hotter and the evenings cooler. Many Djemberians dressed in buttoned-up long sleeves shirts. An arid wind from the south made their throats dry. Children, munching candy and wearing rubber sunglasses, went to tailors to collect their suits.

On New Year's Day, predawn, Babacar made a New Year's Resolution. He packed all the weeds from the shelves of his room into a box, took it up to the roof and burned it. Before the next big Eid feast, he left the House of Dudu, leaving an envelope containing a cheque of 25000 francs on the dining table.

No one heard news of him thereafter.

One day a friend of Babacar's wrote to his parents, explaining his situation. The letter arrived a month after it was posted, as the address was inexact. Three months later, Malika asked Dieynaba to clean out his room, have a carpenter repair the wardrobe and have the mosquito net fixed.

"Should Babacar return for the Easter break, he will at least find his room in a good condition," she said.

Fatimata nodded in support and placed a new pot for burning incense in Babacar's room. Malika decorated the room with paintings and sculptures and hung a new pair of running shoes she had bought for him on the wall, should Babacar choose to jog.

On Salif's instructions, she replied the letter on behalf of the family. She reminded Babacar that they understood about his condition, that they loved him, and she urged him to visit home soon. Babacar received the letter, but refrained from writing or calling. He retreated into a deep silence, so prolonged that Salif began to doubt – after his brother, Issa – whether his son was alive or dead.

Malika took turns phoning everyone she knew who had relatives around the area where Babacar was said to be living, to inquire about him. She was fond of him and could not understand his weird isolation with respect to the family.

Babacar's isolation rekindled Malika's inner affliction. She drank and ate little and began to dress like an old woman. She prayed fervently that he would return home soon, but she was never the first to talk about him.

"Why is life full of challenges?" she pondered. It has been one trouble after another since she had married into the family. When she added Babacar's long isolation to the uncertainty of Issa's return, she wondered if she was normal. Perhaps Anta was right in calling her "Lady Misfortune".

One morning, Fatimata found a stapled note by the gate. She waited until the four women in the house were at home to show it to them. Dieynaba opened it and read it. The news was that Babacar had found new love and the hopeful Mrs Ndiaye was pregnant. Babacar reported that he was doing very well, but would not go into details as to how he met his fiancée. He gave his whereabouts.

Fatimata was glad to receive the news. The four women quickly prepared a cereal meal with yoghurt and raisins and departed for South Keba. When they arrived, Babacar was glad to see them, but would not reveal his fiancée's identity. In vain, the women searched for traces of the union, some clue as to their relationship, but their room was appallingly bare. Fatimata suggested that they return to Djembe and Babacar agreed.

Babacar later invited Mame Hady, his fiancée, to the House of Dudu. The day Mame Hady arrived, already three months pregnant, Fatimata was stunned, but accommodating. She forced herself to treat her new daughter-in-law to a warm welcome. Seeing Mame Hady's visible pregnancy, she understood why her son had been so secretive about the love affair.

Mame Hady carried the baby to full term, and on the third day of September, she delivered a baby son at the General Hospital. Fatimata showed her how to nurse him, bathe him, and lull him to sleep. Dieynaba sang him *berceuses* she had learned at kindergarten. Malika bought him assorted baby kits and loved to help the new mother dress the baby in caps and socks made from the fabric she had saved over the years.

Malika assisted Mame Hady during her pregnancy and Babacar loved Malika even more for that. But this time, he loved her differently. Not as a boyfriend, but as a steadfast friend, one that has taken her over mountains and valleys, through the oceans and seas of life. Babacar told Mame Hady marvellous stories about Malika, even to the point of igniting the fire of jealous feelings in Mame Hady.

With time, Salif forgave Babacar. Gradually, he came to terms with the idea of his son leaving home and returning with a pregnant woman. He had been worried by Babacar's style of marriage, since his son had failed to inform him and the elders and they had not followed the marriage customs required in their land.

Salif tried to forget about all that, however. He had the house painted, the windows and doors varnished, he replaced the cushion covers and the broken tiles in the parlour. He spread word within the extended family of Babacar's marriage who then purchased caftans, suits and gowns and everything else needed for a wedding. They held a simple ceremony in Mame Hady's compound, and did what they could to recover from the stigma. Mansu visited him regularly during those days and Salif leaned heavily on him for advice. At each visit, he served Mansu a glass from the remnant of the wedding. Salif said he would like to see the gossip about his son stop.

"Life is full of ups and downs," Mansu began philosophically. "Babacar has a child now, so be grateful that you're a grandfather. Many wanted to be grandparents, but are not. Tomorrow, Babacar will become one too. Such is the song of life."

"What about the disgrace?" Salif asked.

"Forgive your son now. Is Allah not there for all? Your son has found healing and Mame Hady had a baby. What else could you wish for?"

22

It was very early in the morning when Malika crossed to her in-law's living room, greeted them politely and told them solemnly what was on her mind: "I must go to the Congo."

She had been waiting for Issa for six years. As she spoke, her jaw slackened like a grandmother's.

Salif saw no reason for her to risk her life going to a war zone. He urged her to think of the gunmen, the rapist soldiers, the drugs, and the hard conditions. "You're going to the largest peacekeeping mission in the world," he said. He encouraged Dieynaba to talk to her auntie about the idea.

"Why do you want to leave us?" Dieynaba asked. "It's so dangerous there." They were taking a walk after dinner. Malika did not answer. "You can still wait. You've been waiting all along," the girl reasoned.

"That's the problem: *just* waiting. And do you know that Mama wants me to convert to Islam?"

"Was she not joking? Mama talks like that."

"That is even worse than that, worse than the use of force, worse than separation, than not having a child. I have to go now, Dieynaba. I have to."

Malika had taken time to reach her decision. She checked her deposit slips daily and read the Bible passage that advised one to prepare fully before embarking on an important journey. She felt bound for the Congo, like a calling, a mission, a plan.

Her world now was reduced to seeing Issa, nothing less. A passport, an air ticket Djembe-Kinshasa-Djembe, a vaccination card and 1,500 dollars of pocket money. A travel agent warned her to be ready to battle her way through the airport and the roadblocks to North Kivu. She had withdrawn some of her savings and hidden it in the north-west corner of the compound, away from prying eyes. Time after time, away from the tool shed where Fatimata or another family member was likely to wander, she shed her tears.

When she had first joined the family six years back, the remote spot seemed promising. The half acre of land covered in manure had seemed an ideal spot to develop into flowerbeds. It was large enough to grow flowers with which to decorate their home and bring up happy children, but peacekeeping had halted her dreams.

Malika counted the days. Each morning, she checked her passport to see if all thirty-six pages were there. Her vigilance did not stop there. She felt each dollar note with the tips of her two fingers before returning them to her hiding place. She enquired as to whether the vaccination she had received at the Health Centre was still valid and wondered if she was simply anxious about entering the dangerous region of North Kivu.

On the twenty-sixth morning, ten days before she was set to board a South African Airways flight to Kinshasa, Malika washed some select clothing. She was torn in her emotions and her humming became more frequent, more sober.

Dieynaba lay face-down on the mat, reading *Le monde s'effondre*. The novel, set in pre-independent eastern Nigeria, was on her school curriculum for the year. Lifting her eyes from the book, she told Malika to peg her clothes lest they be blown away with the wind. She asked if she remembered where the clothing pegs were kept and offered to collect them.

"Auntie, why are you washing all your pretty clothes?" she asked.

Without replying, Malika pushed the soap suds from her clothes. It took some effort to get upright, after having been bowed over for almost an hour. She huffed out a breath and pushed aside the bag of Omo detergent lying on the side.

She flipped her head away from Dieynaba to avoid looking at the girl's eyes.

She stole a glance at Dieynaba. "Wonderful girl," she whispered. She remembered suggesting to Issa that they take her to live with them until she finished college. Then, having finished the laundry, she went to her travel agent and returned cradling a small folder in her arms.

"What is that under your arm?" Dieynaba asked.

"Air ticket."

"For whom?"

"For me."

She entered the House of Dudu and carefully dropped the ticket on her make-up table, shifting fast to prevent her arsenal of make-up gear from rolling onto the floor. "If I lose these... I'm not sure I will get any there to paint my face."

Instead of letting sleeping dogs lie, Dieynaba thought at length about Malika's words. Dieynaba pressed her palm to her opened mouth and her lipstick stained her palm with the redness of it. The redness of it confused her.

The girl rose to welcome Fatimata, her step-mother. "Peace to you, Mama. Is it true my auntie will be leaving us?"

Fatimata hesitated. Whatever she said would worsen the situation. It wouldn't render any service to the family, which was so heavily burdened already. There would be the crashing sound of arguments and slaps of disharmony that would attract the attention of neighbours and shake the family's unity.

Fatimata eyed Malika's clothes on the line suspiciously. The sight peeved her and she hurried into the House of Dudu to speak her mind.

"Why are you washing all your clothes? Tell me, are you going crazy again?"

"I'm not mad, Ma."

"I heard you bought a ticket to the Congo."

"But I told you and Papa about it, Ma."

"So," Fatimata said, holding firmly to her wrappers, conveying her willpower.

"I'm getting ready, Ma."

"Ready to go where? Into your nose?"

"I'm going in search of Issa, Ma."

"You're mad! You must be mad!"

"I just want to see my husband, Ma."

"Which husband? My son?"

"But Papa said it's up to me, Ma."

"Papa said so, because he is tired of arguing with the mad daughter-in-law that you've turned into."

"I'm not mad, Ma. I've never been mad, in all my life."

"When death lures a dog, it hinders it from perceiving the smell of shit."

Fatimata stood still, observing Malika and after a while, she left the room. Malika went outside to gather her clothes.

The day ended without further incident. Malika was resolute on her decision to go to the Congo and Fatimata remained watchful over her movements. Salif played the role of mediator. One night, he took Malika outside the compound and tried to dissuade her, but failed to convince her that it would be best to cancel her travel plans.

The conversation only strengthened her will to persevere with her plans. Salif chose to be diplomatic. When he understood how resolute she was, in that she did not yield to the suggestion of paying her parents a visit instead, he told her to do what she thought best. He did not want to be tyrannical. In the past, he had used his authority to bend Malika's will, but feared it would be to the detriment of her husband's authority. Issa had once cautioned his father, "I'm her husband, not you."

Fatimata provided no room for negotiation. From her point of view, Malika enjoyed great freedom in their house. She received her visitors, visited her friends and went to the Catholic Church. Fatimata thought it was time to put an end to this freedom.

"It's time to convert to Islam. If you marry a man, you marry his religion." So she called the imam who would convert her. Fatimata curtailed her daughter-in-law's movements, flashed a stern look at her when she went out to answer phone calls or when she came home later than usual. Fatimata blamed Issa for sending his remittances directly to his wife. She said Malika dared to argue with her because she had so much money to manage. "He gave her too much money," she complained.

People! What people would say about such nonsense? These thoughts disturbed Fatimata. The tongues would wag, the endless questions, the curiosity and the rushed conclusions… "She wouldn't try such nonsense if she were Muslim, if Issa had a second or third wife."

Fatimata was bewildered, because she had thought Malika was not adventurous by nature. Surely she would prefer a cosy, quiet life of knitting and cooking and raising her children? The last thing Malika should do was wander off into a wartorn country, where she knew no one and would hear only hear gunshots. Her internal conflict in getting there would cause greater suffering than the war itself. And if Malika were to be killed, it would be sorrowful, a fateful stab to Issa's heart.

The next morning Fatimata observed her folding something, her air ticket, into her passport. The very sight of her daughter-in-law irritated her. Fatimata saw the determination in her eyes as if it were boiling water. It ignited a fire in Fatimata's eyes.

"The imam is coming tomorrow evening for your Quranic class," she said.

"Which Quranic class, Ma?"

"Am I a machine that repeats things?"

"But Issa and I agreed I would remain a Catholic."

"You see that devil in you, that devil in you? I'm going to drive it away!" Fatimata retorted. Malika kept quiet.

"You know," Fatimata said, firmly, walking away, "I try to be nice to her. I try to be nice to her. She doesn't deserve it, because she's a hopelessly ungrateful woman, the coldest, most wicked woman I've ever seen. I try to be nice to her, because I consider her my daughter."

Malika began to cry. "What have I done wrong? Who have I hurt?" she sobbed. She wailed such that their neighbours heard her. She wept all night, as if this was her final expression of sorrow, saying goodbye with tears, before going in search of the man she had said yes to.

Salif refrained from interfering further. He was torn, not knowing with whom to side. Fatimata expended more energy trying to convince her husband to wield his ruling power and to use his authority to impose the conversion to Islam upon Malika.

When she stopped weeping, Malika ate some nuts and spent time familiarizing herself with the map of the Congo. She recited the names of large Congolese cities, afraid she would mix them up at the airport, before soldiers or at checkpoints manned by rebel groups. She recited the names while doing the dishes, while walking to the market. She recited them even while drinking her last bottle of the bissap juice. Throughout, she avoided Fatimata like the plague. If her mother-in-law walked in through the left, she took the right door and did everything in her power to ensure their paths did not cross. Most of the time, as a woman, but sometimes as a lover, she anticipated her meeting with Issa. She did so with her whole heart.

Fatimata returned home after wrapping up plans with the district imam regarding Malika's conversion.

"Malika! Malik-a-a-a!" she screamed. "Get ready, for tomorrow you shall embrace the Islamic religion." She said it with authority, to make sure that when her daughter-in-law crawled into bed she would mutter "Fatimata", instead of thinking about her travelling plans. Fatimata wanted her name to ring repeatedly in Malika's ears, to ring so terribly that the young woman would sleep as still as a roasted yam.

Fatimata developed a hatred for her daughter-in-law. She could not stomach her language anymore. Getting the imam to accept to convert her required money and she did not wish to be disgraced before the imam. The neighbours had said that Malika was the cause of all the troubles that had come upon the family. Malika had heard those words, but all she had strength for was going to the Congo to find Issa, alive or dead, much as she dreaded the latter.

Fatimata curtailed her words. When she addressed Malika, it was only to give instructions. Eating together made no more sense and rarely occurred. They both preferred it that way. The very idea annoyed Malika. Every time their paths crossed, their flesh sponged up in pain and their blood thickened. The mere sound of the other's voice turned their mouths sour.

"Has she returned the ticket?" Fatimata asked her co-wife.

"I don't know," Ami Colle replied.

"How can Malika be so recalcitrant, so stubborn?" Fatimata wondered. The tension worsened her rheumatism. She took pills for everything she was feeling: pain and nausea, loss of appetite and insomnia, even irritability. She sent Dieynaba to buy her soda water and tossed her pills into the back of her throat and swallowed them.

Salif brought home a copy of *The Sun*. "LRA leader to kill African UN peacekeepers in the Congo" the headline read. When she was alone, Malika read it.

The Sun reported that since it had been forced out of Uganda, the Lord's Resistance Army – there had to be some evil name for it – had spilled into previously peaceful parts of the Congo. The LRA's crossing over onto Dungu Ridge led to beating, killing, looting and abduction. People and their homes were burned. People seeking refuge in a church were massacred. The LRA starved women into prostitution. The Congolese people witnessed new sights: children's corpses, necklaces strung with teeth, bodies hanging from trees, and human blood staining walls.

The shock of reading the report robbed Malika of her voice. She wondered if Issa was still alive and she shook her head. There was a great wound in her soul, in the soul of the world. She asked God the whereabouts of the LRA leader, Joseph Kony.

Reading about the LRA gave her cold shivers. It was as if she had read about a devouring lion let loose. She looked at the photographs depicting how the LRA raids spilled across the Sudan and the Central African Republic, how they kidnapped children, killed and buried them. There were mass graves everywhere. Mass graves. "Why would God permit all that on *his people*?" she asked.

Malika pricked and scratched herself, creating pain as a distraction.

Dieynaba returned home and found Malika sitting, desolate, in front of burning white candles. The newspaper lay folded on the floor.

Dieynaba went to call her mother. Ami Colle came quickly, straight to where Malika sat and blew each of the candles out. She was afraid they would cause another fire. Instead of retaliating, Malika continued her prayers for guidance to Goma. Ami Colle's blowing out the candles did not upset her. Rather it made her believe her prayers had been answered.

"So be it," she said. Ami Colle's action was providential, and the fragrance of incense in the room seemed to give her strength.

"Why did you light those white candles?" Malika said nothing. "Have you forgotten about the fire incident?"

It was a sign. Usually Ami Colle did not touch her belongings, and Malika suspected she might now even be helping Fatimata search through her possessions. She got up and crosschecked her box, to see if anything was out of place. Going through her travel bag was like connecting with an inner part of her life, one from which she had been alienated.

Malika's next destination was the bathroom. Upon coming out, she encountered Fatimata unzipping her bags in the dark and so she stood watching, unnoticed. Fatimata was looking for Malika's travel documents, but could not find them, as they were hidden in a different place every day. She peered at Fatimata who was muttering to herself as she rifled through her belongings.

"Excuse me, Ma," she said, innocently.

Fatimata startled and trembled with embarrassment.

23

They had less than a week left together. After six years, they were ready to part company. It was her decision to move on, but still, breakups hurt.

Malika was breaking up with the house in the courtyard of the House of Dudu. Like all her relationships, it had started with admiration. With its paned windows and carved wooden doors, the rooms had taken her fancy. Moving there with Issa was a dream come true. There were peculiar little rooms with unexpected connections to secret spaces and doors that opened onto tiny porches, gorgeously decorated with raffia and cowry shells.

Malika and Issa were the second couple to live in the old bungalow. Salif's sister, a childless woman, had left it to her niece and nephew who, at that time, were living in Europe. Malika had hoped the buzz of her children's laughter would ring out from the front stairs. She had hoped that their noise would join the birds chirping in the coconut tree in the front. She had hoped that their noise would mingle with the soft murmurs of tenderness that characterize family life. She remembered how she first thought that the house in the courtyard would afford them a space to live in a loving embrace.

"I'll miss you," she said tenderly. In the good old days, Malika began her day in the southern kitchen, preparing breakfast. The orange light that shone on the polished wooden fittings, reflecting off the Moroccan utensils, felt like the rays of the morning sun. It wasn't a big house by any measure, but every room was joined with crown mouldings and 20 cm baseboards. It was perfect for a couple starting out. Well, almost perfect. Malika changed a few things, touching up here and there and the home sparkled. She helped to make it so. And everybody acknowledged her work.

It was not only the kitchen that touched her memory. The sturdy foundation, like the floor of the House of Slaves, bore the weight of her failures and shortcomings. When Issa had suffered a loss, the apartment seemed to take it with a smile. Even when they thought they would run into financial difficulties, the apartment made them not feel for every spending. That was why Malika was quick to do an after-rain supervision and purposely passed by the curved brick path (the bricks and the curve which she had designed), looking upon the place as a bosom friend.

Thinking of how she would break up with all that, in addition to her pals, the family and neighbourhood, all of pulsing Djembe, she almost changed her mind.

Then a voice within her said, "Change is good!" Yes, the saying is as old as the hills – and she believed a fresh start would be energising. A fresh start would mean she had overcome the worst and was upon the threshold of change. Though change felt strange, it would prove worthwhile.

She kept to her decision to take the unpredictable journey that would be her first out of the country. She would have no farewell party, just endurance. She might have no living room and pictures to hang on her wall in Goma or no kitchen to cook in. But she was ready to sort herself out. She was moving forward from the passive Malika of the early days to the proactive Malika now. She was convinced that to clear the rubbish that cluttered her life, she would have to move.

"It will open up other possibilities for me," she urged herself. "One way or another."

For days before her departure, she tried to be quiet, to hear the voice within and purge her mind of vengeful thoughts. She wrapped a white scarf around her head, made devout movements and whispered prayers. Prayer infused her with hope, chewed up her fears and kept her focused on meeting her husband. In perfect order, she confirmed her flight, controlled her diet and practiced self-defence moves, twists and drills.

The second last night, she woke from a deep sleep, from a crooked rape dream, her hand clenched in resistance. She memorized the moves, the tips regarding self-defence, and rehearsed what to do if she were to hear gunshots.

On the day before departure, she asked Salif for his blessing. "May Allah give you what you want. May he guide you," he extended his hands into hers. But he was shrewd, not saying it in front of his head wife.

A gentle wind blustered, wrapping itself around Malika's throat as Salif concluded his blessing. She exhaled at the end of the blessing and felt a reassuring sense of freedom. She wished that the blessing would sweep evil from the hearts of all she was going to meet: the airport authorities, soldiers and all the agents of destruction. Her heart beat faster and faster, her stomach flattened and the wind tugged the scarf from her neck. The wind enfolded her, the trajectory of what life brings, the journey of an unpredictable existence.

She lay on her bed for what would be her last nap before the plane lifted her up into space, to the upper room of the universe. Her blood cooled as her flesh spread on the wooden bed. "God is my strength," she said with trepidation.

In the evening, she woke and swept the compound. She made herself a cup of tea and put her travel documents alongside it. After the first sip, she said quietly, "the flight is at ten o'clock."

At that, a voice suddenly bellowed: "If you step out of this house with your luggage, don't ever come back to it." Malika kept her lips sealed, turned her head and sipped her tea. Then she heard whispers in the new kitchen.

She tiptoed to the kitchen window, nervously, imagining what was going on in her mother-in-law's mind.

"If she leaves she will never step into this house again," Fatimata would be heard saying.

"We'll all go home one day," Malika retorted, to herself. "Somehow. Should I wait for a hundred years?"

"I told them I was not in support of this marriage, early enough," Fatimata would add.

"It was between Issa and me."

"I was still sleepy when she said that rubbish. If I had been properly awake, she could not have said it," Fatimata would say.

"What then shall I do? Put yourself in my shoes, Mrs Lawyer," Malika would say.

"She'll die on the way," Fatimata would think. "She will die."

"You're not the Maker of the world," Malika thought. "You're not the Maker, who gives or takes life."

"We'll see," her mother-in-law would snort.

"Yes, we'll see in the Congo," Malika thought.

After a long silence, Fatimata would reflect, "I like you, Malika. Don't do this," speaking in a soft, inner voice. It was so soft, Malika wondered if she had mistaken her for somebody else. She was not looking at her. She stared straight ahead, avoiding any eye contact.

"You dare not," Fatimata would say, as if to have the final word. "I can see it."

"I mean it, Mama."

"I've always liked you," Fatimata would say. "You know it's true. I heard that you fought once and I defended you then. I made enemies because of you. I fought a woman for it, though I never told you. I punched her in the face. All this because of you."

Malika tiptoed down the stairs so Fatimata would not know she had been up there. She felt the unbearable urge to grab her luggage and head off to the airport. Of all the things she desired, she longed to see an end to her trauma. She walked around her chair, over to the sink, into the kitchen to wash her cup. She saw the look that Fatimata had been giving her since she had decided to leave the House of Dudu, a rugged stare, as if God should never have created her.

"I heard the Kinshasa airport is closed," Dieynaba said.

"Are the roads leading to it also closed?" Malika asked.

"You mean to travel to the Congo by road? Congo is not an enclave of Segol, like the Gambia."

"Small lady, keep quiet if you don't know. People can travel from here to the Congo in a Pajero. This is how it works: a four-wheel drive takes passengers from Segol to Ivory Coast, and then on to Kinshasa through the West African coast and inland to the shores of the Congo River. You understand me?" Dieynaba gazed at her in astonishment. Malika walked out of the kitchen, with a gait Dieynaba had never before witnessed.

In the evening, Dieynaba watched her auntie sitting before the mirror, arranging her hair. How she would miss her! And the questions her school friends would ask, the thousand questions. Watching Malika combing her hair made Dieynaba feel tangled in anxiety.

Ami Colle turned down the volume of the TV. Malika came out from the room, but Ami Colle wasn't sure if she wanted to talk. Ami Colle noticed she was wearing her jogging shoes.

Malika hurried back to her room and brought out some belongings she wished to leave behind, including her old make-up case. She turned off the lights and returned to the bedroom. She pulled the sheets and folded them and, as she inspected her section of the room, she patted her foot, signifying she would not take what did not belong to her.

The old grandfather's clock on the wall was ticking away. She was seized by the magnitude of the voyage ahead. There was so much to consider, bits of hope and bits of doubt. Panic dragged through her veins and a sudden fever melted her lipstick. Sharp droplets of sweat trickled over her eyes. Her mind had decided one thing and yet her body wanted another. And in this restless state, she lay awake till dawn.

24

Salif's compound was unusually quiet. The sun had been rising earlier and earlier every morning and this day, it rose before the first city bus passed. Malika pulled out her luggage, set to leave.

Ami Colle and Dieynaba were sitting on a mat in the parlour. They had refused to eat breakfast and the kettle of hot water, tin of milk, and jar of honey sat unused in front of them. A car horn sounded twice. Malika started towards the sound. She peered through the window to check if it was from the taxi she had arranged. Her teary eyes were too troubled to focus on Ami Colle and Dieynaba.

"Auntie, please don't go," Dieynaba sobbed, but Malika would not meet her eyes.

A taxi parked in front of the gate. "See you," Malika said hastily, bending to pick up her luggage. She walked quickly to the door, but when she opened it, someone was briskly entering. She turned to look at him.

Their eyes met. Her luggage fell from her hands and she drew a shuddering breath. Malika fainted.

"My honey! My sweetie! My darling!" Issa yelled, spreading his arms wide.

Malika staggered to the floor. She fainted, not from shame or rage, nor from the wish to die, but from sheer shock.

"Honey! Honey!" Issa called, bending over her. "What is wrong?" His face stiffened with confusion, even with a trace of disgust. Malika gasped for air.

"Immortal, invisible Allah!" Issa yelled and he applied the rescue skills he had learned in Goma. He opened the door, ran to open the windows and yanked off his jacket to fan his wife.

Aware that Malika was suffering from shock, Ami Colle broke the news to Issa, as gently as possible, of his wife's attempted departure to the Congo. She spoke in broken sentences, disguising clues that revealed things slowly but surely, as in the telling of a parable. Fatimata and Dieynaba were there, too, looking on. Issa did not ask questions, but began to weep with sudden compassion, laying his head next to his wife's. He was inconsolable.

Eventually, Malika opened an eye. Facing the peacekeeper there was a spent, exhausted, worn-out, small face. Slowly, she opened the other eye. Issa lifted her from the ground and placed her on the sofa. He laid her down, with loving tenderness.

Looking at her, he found her still young. But the façade of her dark, calm face revealed her fatigue and exhaustion. Her eyes were dull and she gazed as if from another world, with a look of exhaustion, suggesting a lack of mental energy. Her look of disorientation began to dissipate, with Issa calm by her side. Her pulse was rapid and her body temperature had risen. She had no memory of how she had ended up on the sofa.

Issa was too spent for conversation. He found the feverish surrender in her eyes surprising. She looked defeated. He clasped her tightly around the waist and they sat like that, silently, for a long moment.

"Well," said Issa, in a soft, even voice, "the battle is over."

He then talked at length about the end of the war. He told her how much he had suffered to return home, because he cherished her so dearly. The long separation had devastated him. He wanted to be a present husband and father, to wake up with his family every morning and go to bed with them at night.

"My Malika," he reminded her of his pet name for her, "I have been so lucky. I escaped death a million times. I thought I would never see you again in my life."

Issa burst into tears as he spoke of fellow peacekeepers who had passed away in North Kivu. "I tried to be there, tried desperately to save their lives, at the risk of my own..." He paused to swallow a thick lump of saliva, looking as if he would weep again.

"Honey, I did my best. I finished my assignment close to the border with Rwanda. Then I went to the capital, Kinshasa, and had one long, painful, emotional conversation with the Force Commander about the mass atrocities and crimes."

Then Issa remembered his visits to that Congolese girlfriend. A tear escaped from his lashes and slipped down his cheek. "I'm sorry," he said, suddenly.

Malika wondered what he meant. She gazed at him for another long moment, at the scars, the wounds, and her lips parted and trembled. She lay still, blinking. Issa leaned closer to kiss her, intending to lift her up by the arm. Malika resisted. He tried again and she consented, accepting the sincerity of his love. She smelled his cologne.

Issa then took her in his arms to their small house in the compound and laid her once again down on the sofa.

Epilogue

Malika shivered. Issa pulled her wrapper properly around her and handed her soap and a towel to take her bath. He made her a nice cup of English tea, the type they drank at the UN base. He then went across the road to buy the ingredients for okra soup and then into the kitchen to prepare it. It was his best dish, people agreed.

She sat a quiet vigil as he ate, watching him. She observed him spoon rice into his mouth. She watched as the soup plopped softly and silently onto his puffed out chest. His feet spread under the wooden table. He plunged his hands into the dish in search of *escargots* and served himself a second helping.

She folded her arms, changed her position and averted her eyes. Returning from the kitchen, he stopped in front of her and his arms slowly fell to his sides.

"You're happy to see me, my Malika?"

He looked bedraggled. His uniform was not buttoned properly and the collar was up on one side and down on the other. There were two buttonholes with no buttons to fit them. The khaki uniform was only tucked into his trousers at the front and behind, it hung out like a playful schoolboy's. One of his bootlaces was undone.

"You're happy to see me, my Malika?" he repeated, this time singing it.

From the inner pocket of his jacket, he retrieved a bottle of perfumed water to clean the smell of *escargot* from his hands.

"We're here at last, my Malika," he sighed, rubbing his hands

He pushed his peacekeeping cap aside and carried the empty plates to the basin to wash them.

Then he leaped behind Malika, whispering, "I'm here, honey, I'm here at last." His hands circled her neck and the warmth of his touch tugging at the bangles on her wrist. Devotion lit in her eyes as she gazed in astonishment at him.

He went to his parents to express his gratitude for taking care of his wife all the time he was on mission, while Malika went to their bedroom. She lit the incense and let its perfume pervade the room. It was their wedding anniversary, she realised, by a wonderful coincidence. He had returned on that very day.

"Should we go out for the anniversary, perhaps to the coast? We could spend the night in a hotel with an ocean view," she wondered. But imagining how Fatimata would react, she made of their bedroom a makeshift hotel room instead.

Issa found her in the bedroom, smiling and curled up into her pillow. Her feet dangled from beneath the covers. He slipped into bed and drew her to him, so that her warm back rested against his chest. They held each other, feeling once again, safe and secure.

Acknowledgement

I would like to thank Sulaiman Adebowale and his team at Amalion Publishing for the brilliant idea of a fiction series in contemporary African writing and for giving this novel a smile; Karima Grant for being my first reader and for the insightful comments; Estelle Jobson for the editorial assistance and challenging questions; Juliet Ibekaku for believing in me; Ndidi Nwuneli for the friendship; Jean-Maurice Hétuin for the Latin and Greek classes, and for the bundle of novels and the weekly discussions around them in Dakar. And special thanks to everybody for reading and for their support.